ALGERNON'S

ANOMALY

Valentyne

Dedications:

My Love

My Walking Tour Family

My Online Family

My amazing helpers, Connor, Alastair, and Alicia

And my friends on the other side.

1

LADIES' NIGHT OUT

Once upon a time, I knew everything.

"Hello and welcome," the young man standing before my mother, her friends, and myself said as he extended his arms, "my name is Algernon and I'll be your tour guide tonight."

I was done and we hadn't even started yet as I rolled my eyes away from him. Sliding down in my leather build-a-chair, I kept my arms tightly crossed over my chest, closing me off from the rest of the world. The historic building we were in creaked around us, musty air hung under the vaulted ceilings and black-and-white photos lined the walls.

"Thank you for joining me on this ghost tour. Tonight we're going to go investigate a few peculator sites in downtown Evanesce then return here to hang out in a creepy dark basement. Sound fun?" The tour guide said with abundant enthusiasm though I'm sure he had said the same damn thing a million other times.

My mother and her friends cheered, making fools of themselves.

This was stupid.

I spared him a glance as he rambled on about paranormal classifications and other nonsense. He couldn't have been much older than me, but he was certainly much stupider. He walked around and told ghost stories with a straight face, how did anyone take him seriously? Average in build, his hipster-like glasses didn't help him appear credible as he ran his fingers through his brown disconnected, clean yet voluminous, undercut. I snickered a little, looking away from him and his dumb name tag again; maybe he actually was old- he was going gray. How lame.

Suddenly everyone was looking at me. I hadn't been paying attention, why were they looking at me? Eyes wide, a bit of surprise jumping in my blood, I looked around at the others sitting about as they smiled at me.

"Did you hear my question?" Algernon said, approaching me some with a stupid smile.

I shook my head with the least amount of effort possible. I was too cool for this shit.

"On a scale of one to ten, one being 'I don't believe in any of this', and ten being 'I literally see the dead', how do you feel about the paranormal?"

I don't think I could have rolled my eyes any harder, "Negative ten-thousand."

The way Algernon blinked at me suggested he hadn't ever received that reply before.

Turning from me, he returned to where he had been standing before us next to a large stone fireplace, "How old are you kiddo?"

"Sixteen," I said proudly, as if I knew everything, because back then I did.

He chuckled and made my blood boil as he turned around to face us again, "You don't seem pleased to be here, now do you?"

"It wasn't his choice," my mother said from the seat to my left, earning a glare from me as her irritation surfaced more with each word, "his sitter called in sick at the last minute so he has to tag along on ladies' night out."

"Can't be trusted to be home alone?" I hated his mocking tone, laced with a smile so it would be considered in good taste, "What's your name, Mr. Skeptic?"

I had to try to not bark at him, "Thaddeus."

"He has an attitude problem," my mother said flatly, obviously already done with my shit and we hadn't even started yet. "don't mind him, he's just a pain."

She glared at me as I glared at her and the tension rose until Algernon laughed and took a large black lock-box up into his hands from the floor. "Well Thaddeus, I hope you find some enjoyment in tonight's adventure."

Jaw clenched as my mother and her friends laughed, I locked my eyes on the ground. I hated the way he spoke, it felt like he was patronizing me. Everything about this was dumb, fake, rehearsed forced. He walked around with the open case, handing out little gray devices with a line of lights at the top. It was some probably-rigged ghost hunting device, I wouldn't know though. When he got to me, I did not uncross my arms, keeping my eyes averted from him. He softly laughed as he moved on from me. I was too cool to walk around in public holding one of those dumb things.

There's no way he could really believe in all this.

"What about you?" I said, begrudging the curiosity that willed me to speak to the dumb tour guide.

"Pardon?"

I looked away from him as he handed the last device out, "On your scale, what number are you?"

Setting down the box, he closed it as he hummed quietly to himself in thought, "I haven't been asked that before." straightening, he looked at me, I could just feel it. "I would consider myself a six, perhaps. I'm not sure what's out there, and I'm not one for blind-faith either. But I'm a bit too sensible to have the audacity to claim that I know it all."

What a decidedly undecided answer.

His tour guide tone took over again as he looked around, "One last thing before we head out. It is believed that high levels of paranormal activity are known to cause those sensitive to it to feel unwell. If you start to feel unwell at any point in my tour, do let me know and we'll move away from the problem. I won't be offended, I promise. I'm horribly sensitive myself, so I understand."

He motioned for us to stand as he took one of the devices in his hand and we followed him to the door. He demonstrated the way the little device picked up electricity from an electrical panel but I could not have possibly cared any less. Standing in the back, I was a shadow to the group with my black skinny jeans, black band-merch t-shirt, back shoes, and bad attitude. I fussed with my black hair that all but obstructed my vision it was so messy and long as we followed him out onto the sketchy streets of downtown Evanesce.

Eyes down on the nasty ground as we walked along, my gaze caught on a scene painted on the street in vibrant colors. It was summary, beautiful, masterful, but I was too much of a brat back then to really appreciate it. But even with that said, it stuck with me.

As I followed, my mother yanking me forward with the group on occasion, I couldn't help but be audibly unimpressed. Ghosts didn't exist and my mother and her friends were just paying to be lied to, how did they not realize this? Groaning, sighing, in the back, I didn't even try to hide it. Satisfaction shot through me when I'd earn Algernon's glance. He must have been doing everything in his power to not snap at me as he flawlessly continued along his monologue. Life was worth nothing, the only joy to be found it in was in generating issues for others.

He said he wanted me to have fun so I would, just not how he intended.

Stories of dead firemen, of a corrupt past, of shootings and drunken spirits, Algernon couldn't have looked any dumber as he told them with a raised voice and bright smile. What enjoyment anyone got out of walking around in sketch-ville, attracting attention of all the wrong sorts as the sun went down, was beyond me. We started to approach a parking lot and Algernon spouted some shit about it being a burial ground or something and I groaned so loud the entire group turned to glare at me. Well, everyone except Algernon, he just raised his brows, his dumb smile almost challenging me to flatten it.

"As I was saying," he stopped in the center of it, taking out his stupid ghost-hunting device from his back pocket, "since this is a particularly haunted site, I'm going to send you on a mission, should you chose to accept it, and you don't have a choice," his bouncy tone made the others laugh but I wasn't fooled, "Whoever finds a reading of red or higher on their EMF detectors wins. But please do pay attention to your surroundings, this is a parking lot after all and death is bad."

I stood, staring at them as they all scattered into the dark parking lot like a bunch of idiots, looking down to their devices and getting excited every few steps. The sun had set, the lot floodlight lighting up the far corner. I didn't move, huffing to myself about how stupid this all was, like I had been the entire time. My eyes locked on Algernon's back as he stood, leisurely in the cast of the flood light, watching my mother and her friends wander about. What sort of sick satisfaction did he get out of watching people act so ridiculous. Hands in my pockets, sharp gaze ahead, I bemoaned the bullshit under my breath.

There's something magical about youth, an invincibility, a truth. I was above everyone but above nothing at the same time. I thought I commanded respect when really I garnered mockery. I was a walking disaster, my music was rough and my ego large enough to eclipse the goddamn sun. I knew everything, I truly did believe that back then. And perhaps that would have never changed, had that floodlight not flickered and changed everything.

It's only when you know everything, do you realize that you actually know nothing.

Algernon stumbled to the side, bringing his hand up to his face when he nearly lost his footing. A bright white light bleached my world when it flashed, blinding me as I stumbled back. Scattered gasps and voices echoed around me as I opened my eyes again, no longer dizzy. I could see Algernon standing on the other side of the lot, bracing himself against the light post. Between us my mother and her friends gravitated to a specific spot in the parking lot, but I didn't see anything else out of the ordinary.

Starting to approach, I looked around. Did a light bulb blow up or something? When my wandering eyes met something, I stopped walking. Algernon stood, still bracing himself, eyes wide in utter horror. It was only for a moment, but in that moment I saw through the tour guide persona and into his eyes.

I had never felt my heart beat like that before.

Pushing himself away from the pole, he walked up to us, too. My mother and her friends all looked at him, great wonder painting their features for no particular reason. As if the air had been taken away from their lungs, the group of ladies just stared.

Algernon was about to say something, his guide smile nervously back on his face, when he was cut off by my mother's friend, "Do you see it?"

"See..." Algernon looked down to the parking lot below us where she was pointing, "what, exactly?"

"The sky beam," my mother said, looking down to the ground.

Algernon's nervousness was becoming apparent again as he fiddled with the knot of his tie, "Sky beam?"

"Yeah," my mother's other friend said, "there is a bright white light, emanating from the ground, into the sky-"

"How do you not see the sky beam?"

"It's right here."

Algernon's eyes drifted to me but I just stared back, equally at a loss. Were they messing with him? There was nothing there, nothing but a dirty parking lot littered with puddles in the middle of that miserably moist city.

"No, I don't see anything," he said, taking his smart phone out, "but I'm not surprised, I'm not sensitive enough to see anything. I'm what they call a 'psychic block'." It almost sounded like he was simply humoring them, as if he had caught onto the same thought I had. "If you could all step away from the area, I'll take a picture and see if it shows up."

We did as told, our shadows still long across the lot and probably caught in the image. I watched Algernon as his expression went from controlled to absolutely horrified as he stared at his screen. Looking back up then down to his phone again, he didn't say anything as the ladies rushed him. They blew up in excitement, talking of the supposed sky beam like it was actually there. Algernon appeared dumbfounded as he looked down at his phone so I decided to approach. Looking over his shoulder, because I was already almost taller than him, I saw the image.

The parking lot before us was captured in it, our shadows stretching over the puddles, that was all the same. But sitting there in the middle of it was exactly as they had described, a bright white funnel-like light bursting from a circular point on the parking lot and up into the sky indefinitely. Looking back up to the lot, I rolled my eyes.

"Your photo editing skills are bad."

The way Algernon looked at me, I don't think I'll ever forget the way Algernon looked at me.

"What?" My mother said, actually upset with me for some reason.

I walked toward where the picture had been taken, "I get it, you guys are just trying to make a fool of me. You didn't want me to have to come so you figured you'd pull something. I'd apologize for crashing but you guys forced me to come. I catch something on fire one time and you never let me stay home alone again."

"Can you not see it?" My mother's friend asked.

"Of course not because there's nothing there and ghosts aren't real." My anger, my insecurity, frustration, youth, whatever it was, it was a pressurized bomb waiting to blow and I was getting dangerously close to detonation, "Do you really think I'm that stupid? That picture is obviously edited, and he's in on it." My voice raising, my core bubbling, I should have been able to control myself but in that moment that embarrassment felt like the biggest disrespect. I started toward Algernon as he stood there, frozen, "Do you enjoy getting paid to lie to everyone? You don't even believe what you're saying," shoving him, he didn't resist as he was sent stumbling backward, "You're the worst kind of person," I shoved him again as my mother and her friends called at me to stop, "Stop taking advantage of people's stupidity and go do something productive with your life." taking his tie in my fist, I was about ready to knock him on his ass when I suddenly felt dizzy.

"You're standing in it," my mother called, her friends all staring in horror, "get out of the sky beam,"

Looking down at our shoes, my vision was jarred by white. The flashing was like a strobe in my mind, disorienting me as my ears rang. Pain shot through me, locking my legs and not allowing me to run. The device in his hand was entirely lit up, brighter than it had been before the red light the brightest as if the bulbs were about to explode. My grip tight on his tie, Algernon appeared to be taken by it too as his hand flew to his face and a muffled sound of pain escaped his clenched teeth. My hand holding his tie burned but I couldn't let go. Vision barely able to focus, I could see a light reflecting off of Algernon's glasses, a white somewhat transparent wall surrounding us. Looking down it was like we were standing on a spotlight our shadows cast into the heavens and for a moment, just a moment, I saw the sky beam.

My world spiraled as pain took over again, the light getting brighter. Everything flipped back and forth, between light and night, like I was being violently thrown between two slides on a View-Master. Then, as quickly as it had started, it stopped. Letting go of him, I dropped to knees as the blood fell from my head. He landed on his knees before me, hand to his face, and all was silent. As if we were the only two people in the whole world, the cars, the wind, the people, the sirens, trains, the city, ceased to exist.

All was still.

Something didn't feel right.

My mother's yells faded back into the world, drawing me out of that secluded space. The feeling of her hand on my back blinked her into existence, her friends stood around Algernon. Helping us up, questions were throws our way but I couldn't catch any of them. Looking around, I felt removed from it all still, despite the world being there.

Like the View-Master stopped, trapped between slides, I felt out of place all of the sudden.

"I'm alright," I finally said, able to drag my eyes to my mother's.

The street light flickered.

An awkward pause took the air as Algernon straightened his glasses.

"Well, that was certainly something." he said, turning from us, "Let's move away from this parking lot, shall we?"

Following behind as the world around me slide wayward, I zoned out. Not listening to Algernon, I hadn't any idea what he was going on about. All I knew was that I wasn't okay. Barely able to bring my eyes up from the ground, I was just focusing on not falling over. Rounding a corner into an alley as we continued onto another stop, a person brushed into me. Stumbling to the side, I looked up and my blood stopped. A large looming man dressed in ragged layers glared down at me, his long beard and piercing eyes making him beyond intimidating. He grumbled something at me, slurred and drunkenly, before hobbling off. He left a puddle behind him as he walked, as if he had crawled out of a river somewhere.

Now that my eyes were up, my breath was stolen. People of all walks surrounded us, heading every which way. Some were alone, others mingling, they stood out against the background as if they didn't belong. As we waked along the roads of the night cub district of Evanesce, I couldn't help but be amazed. Was there some form of historical convention going on for all the nerds that wished they were born in the past, despite the plague being a thing?

I ran into my mother when the group stopped and I hadn't noticed. She scolded me and I jumped back, looking away. But my breath was stolen wen I realized all of the people I had just been observing were gone. As if they had disappeared into thin air, we were just left in the company of Evanesce's finest, harassing and pan-handling the tourists as they waited in line at one of Evanesce's most famous novelty doughnut shop.

Don't collapse.

A soft voice, one that wasn't mine, echoed through my world. Jumping as I looked around, I had no idea where it came from.

You have a job to do, do not collapse.

Bringing my hand up to my ears, it didn't stop the echoing of the voice. It was in my head?

Keep smiling.

My heart started to race as terror deposited in my blood, where was that voice coming from? Tears threatened to glass over my vision but I fought them off. What was going on?

Too terrified to bring my eyes up, they stayed, unfocused, on the grimy ground below my black shoes as I followed the group. Arriving back at the historical building we started in, I walked in after everyone else except Algernon as he held the door open for us. When I took my first step in I stopped. It was so loud, rowdy, like the background sounds from a bar scene in a movie. Algernon almost walked right into me, but managed to graceful maneuver around me before he did. Standing before me, he asked me a question I couldn't hear. Looking around, there was no one other than the group, nothing that could be making all those sounds.

"Thaddeus?"

My world zeroed in on Algernon, my glare tightening on him as the other sounds stopped. "Don't talk to me."

Eyes maintaining intense contact for a moment, the world paused.

His eyes are gorgeous.

He snickered a little with a raised brow as he started away from me, saying things about flashlights and a basement.

What even is this kid?

The hushed voice grew louder and made me jump again, looking around. Before I realized it, I was about to be left alone. And I totally wasn't scared, nope, no way, as I rushed toward the others as they waited to enter the basement in the back of the business. Algernon warned of low pipes and darkness, old stairs and small spaces, as he and the rest of us picked out flashlights from a table siting next to the railed off stairs that led into a dark abyss.

He handed me an EMF meter.

Our eye contact held for a moment until my gaze dropped to the device and I felt the rock in the pit of my stomach sink further.

Because going down into a dark old basement was definitely a good idea.

For sure.

Algernon kept having to switch out his flash lights because every time he turned one on, it started flickering incessantly. Taking out his phone, he turned on the flashlight but it did the same thing. Staring at it, he put his pone away and smiled.

What the fuck.

The voice intruded upon me again, making me look around once more to try to locate its source. Algernon started down the stairs first, laughing about how he needed to change the batteries on some of the flashlights. Staring at him, I suddenly saw something on his left shoulder. Small, black, like a scribbled over doodle, I only saw it for a moment before he descended into dark obscurity. I was the last to walk down into the basement. Darkness, damp dreary air, it was a dismal space but far larger than I had expected. That was worse, though, because the darkness had space to expand and hide all under its sheet.

As I stepped off the last stair, I felt a shiver take me. Turning around, I saw a young lady standing there, looking at me. Long dated dress, the layers and lace made it look straight out of a western movie. My mother snapped at me for hanging by the stairs, ordering me to join them over there. When I looked back, the young woman was gone.

I stood closer to my mother than I had been before.

Algernon talked of old-time prostitution, of myths and racism, maintaining a professional tone to it all. The space we were standing in had a tainted past and I could feel it as if it were digging into my skin. Taking us further into the basement space, he talked about ghost-hunting shows, their misinformation, and that ended us up in a smaller dark room down there. Standing around in a circle, he asked that we put our devices out before us and I watched as six green lights made an attempt at a circle.

"And, for dramatic effect," Algernon said, holding his detector out like the others, "let's turn off our lights."

A wake of whining later, all lights were out and we were left standing there in a dark crowded basement, staring at stupid ghost hunting equipment in silence.

This was stupid.

"Is anyone down here with us tonight?" Algernon's tone was clear, the only thing in the darkness as we stood, staring at the green lights just waiting for them to fluctuate up into the yellow, orange, or red levels.

"I know we have a lot of people down here and that makes you nervous, but they seem pretty nice."

Well, most of them anyway.

The EMF detectors lit up into the red levels when I heard the voice again.

"Huxley?" Algernon asked gingerly, as if he truly believed he was talking to someone, "are you doing well tonight, Huxley?"

The lights went up into the orange then back down to the green levels. He must have been rigging this somehow. It was so, conveniently dark, though, there was no way for me to tell.

My mother cleared her throat, "Is anyone else down here with you tonight, Huxley?"

"Yes, you guys." I heard the voice of a young boy come from behind me, making me fly out of my skin. No one else apparently noticed it as they asked if I was okay. Staring into the darkness, I could feel my eyes struggling to focus on something.

The lights on the devices held in the red ranges as I heard footsteps approach from the darkness that I was staring into but saw nothing in. "I'm always down here, I can't leave. None of us can."

"Do you guys hear that?" My voice shook, I was barely able to speak.

"Hear what?" Algernon asked from across the way in the abyss.

"That voice," I said, unable to pry my eyes away from the darkness.

"There is no voice," my mother said, "stop trying to mess with us. I know you don't want to be here, but don't ruin it for everyone else; otherwise you're grounded."

I didn't have the thought left to debate the absurdity of her hypocritical statement because when I blinked, a young boy appeared before me. Surrounded by the darkness, his specific features were unobtainable to my eye but he was short, young, scruffy, and most importantly: smiling. Nothing about him was inherently scary, but my heart raced out of my chest as the sharp sting of toxic adrenaline tore through me.

"There's a-" my voice was merely above a shaking whisper, "do you see-"

"That's it," my mother said with all the artificial self righteous authority in the whole goddamn world, "you're grounded."

Algernon snorted.

The room plummeted in temperature.

The darkness behind the boy started to fester, morphing around itself to create a demented human-like shadow. As it sculpted itself from the shadows, I felt my heart slow to a stop. Red pinhole glowing eyes appeared on its head and a smile ripped across its face, showcasing sharp irregular teeth.

Dropping my EMF that was holding in the red, I shoved through the circle of people and ran out of that part of the basement, stumbling along in the darkness as my flashlight's beam erratic in my abysmal surroundings. I ran right into a low hanging pole, sending a hollow thud reverberating through the basement. It was covered in bubble wrap but it still hurt like hell. I dropped to my knees, groaning through grit teeth for a moment but then I hard footsteps behind me.

The monster was coming for me.

Eyes open, I saw darker shades of darkness crawl around me, like claws seizing every inch of the basement. My heart completely stopped when I heard muddled whispers, a light breeze blowing behind my neck making me shiver. Like I was falling into a spiraling abyss, the noxious darkness dug into my skin, leaving some of its feelers in my core as I struggled to stand. If I didn't get away, it was going to eat me up, swallow me and I'd never see light again. It was the darkest, most tainted feeling I had ever encountered, something so innately evil and wayward about it that it made even my royal edge-lord soul squirm.

White eyes appeared out of the cloud of darkness forming around me, two blinding beams blinking. As if the light piercing through the darkness was even more poisonous than the shadows, my mind screamed out in agony as a physical pain shot through my head. Closing my eyes, I shook my head, dizziness taking me over again. I had to get away, I had to run far away from that place and never come back. I had been dropped in hell, there was absolutely no other explanation.

Standing, I ducked under the pipe and ran through the cloud of darkness, making it and its white eyes disperse into nothing. Fleeing from the basement, nearly tripping up every step before I was out. I ran toward the door but on the way there, my foot caught on my other and I wiped out, absolutely ate it on the old original wooden floor. Tears took me over as I brought my hand to my mouth, I felt like I was going to be sick. When a hand landed on my back, I flew away and ended up crashing into the wall and facing whoever it was.

Algernon knelt there, hand extended, eyes wide, concern painting him.

It was then that I realized his eyes were an otherworldly breed of hazel.

Sitting on his left shoulder was a smudge, the black thing that looked like it was a layer on top of the world, out of place, jarring.

My world fell from focus as another pang of panic took me over.

"I didn't mean to scare you," I heard the little boy's voice but I refused to take my hands from my face to see if he was there too, "I'm sorry."

The sounds of the bar flooded my ears again, yells and full bodied laughs, glasses clinking and things slamming. It took over my mind, numbing me as I tumbled further into inconsolable internal ruin. Algernon's piercing eyes stayed with me, prying their way into my mind as everything else shut down. Unable to breathe, my world started to spiral into darkness. The last thing that crossed through my mind as weakness flooded my body was a voice, soft, scared, it became apart of me in that moment.

There's no way.

For a moment I felt suspended, free of gravity and outside of the pull of everything else.

I wondered what that voice was talking about, who it belonged to, why it was in my head. But most of all, I wondered why it sounded so very sad.

When I woke, I was surrounded by unfamiliar walls, a set of hazel eyes trapped in my mind, and a psychiatric doctor at my bedside. Maybe it was something in the way he looked at me that day, but I knew before they said anything. Something was very wrong with me and if he had it his way, I'd never see the outside of those walls ever again.

I should have done something productive with my time when I knew everything because it wasn't long after that that I realized that I knew absolutely nothing.

2

PERSONABLE BLUE

"It's time for your medication,"

I looked up from my desk to see my nurse entering my room, "Already?" Leaning back in my chair like my doctors always told me not to, I watched the nurse as he nodded and set down a trey on the counter top of my hospital room, "I feel like I just took a dose."

"This is the new one," he said as he shook some pills from the bottle, "you take it four times a day instead of two."

Sighing, I looked down to my drawing, "What's the point if they never work?"

"They do work," he approached me, his tone soft and melodic like it had been since the day I met him, "you don't see things anymore,"

"No," I brought my hands up and laced my fingers through my hair, "i just never stop hearing things."

Handing me the tray with some pills in a small cup and a bottle of water, he smiled, "We'll find the right combination someday, I promise."

I opened the bottle then took the pills in hand and looked down at them somberly, "It has been five years, I'm tired of waiting for someday."

A beat passed as I took the pills.

"I know..."

Staring down at my drawing, I felt my heart sink as the nurse quietly left. Five years ago I was introduced to this room and I never left. Schizophrenia wasn't something people liked to mess with and since they had the money, my family kept me here.

Finishing up my drawing of a scribble that never left my mind, though I could never remember where I had seen it, I stood and walked over to the wall next to my bed. Pinning up the paper where there was space, I stepped back and admired the ever growing collection of demented pieces that decorated my walls. What looked like demons, monsters, corpses, they were echoes of the things I used to see when I left that room. For some reason I had never visually hallucinated in that room, only outside of it.

A yell laced with agony ripped through my mind, threatening to take me to my knees as I stumbled into my bed. It passed as quickly as it took over and I was left there, hissing through my teeth. That never stopped, it didn't matter where I was. Screams, phrases, things that made no sense to me, a voice that wasn't my own was trapped inside my head with me. No amount of medication could silence it.

Laying on my bed, I stared up at the ceiling. I had finally run out of space on my walls. I pondered how long it would take a nurse to notice if I put my chair on my bed and stood on it to start pinning things to the ceiling next? Would they stop me or would they help? The psychiatric wing had became my home and the people inside were more of a family than mine would ever be. Not that they were much of one anyway, at the end of the day I was just another patient, another number, another set of instructions. I was no one's child.

What kind of mother would just leave her son here?

One who never wanted him in the first place.

She did say I was grounded, I just didn't realize she meant for the rest of my life.

Running my hand over my face, I groaned.

Dropping my hand to the side, I wondered why this had to happen to me. Why did I just snap one day, lose my mind and some of myself along with it? Early onset, they said, rare and fascinating. No family history, no prior symptoms, general ability to function otherwise, I was an anomaly and for that reason, this hospital room was my cage. The people here tried to make this easy for me, it was nothing like movies suggested. But still, I did miss the stars.

Closing my eyes, my mind drifted back to a time where I wore black, not hospital scrubs. Back when loud music was abundant and dreams of tattoos occupied my mind. A once upon a time that ended in big black boots and pocket chains, in traveling, in future friends and edgy romance and taking on the world. It was a time where my biggest concern was how much cooler than everything I was. I mean, I still was that way, but the hospital staff humored me very little. You could only be the big bad bump in the night, the edge-lord-extraordinaire, until you're on your knees sobbing because the voice is so loud it hurts and it's not even real. But I could pretend that I was a prideful badass and no one would call me out, they didn't have to. They all knew I was bark and no bite. At least now I could acknowledge the absurdity of my act, once it was my trashiest of truths.

Man, what it was like to be sixteen.

A sigh so deep it hurt took me.

Now I was twenty-one-years-old, I didn't have a singe tattoo and I couldn't even remember the last time I wore black. What I'd give, to just wear black again.

"Thaddeus,"

I opened my eyes to see Honore standing at my bed side.

It only took me seven second too long to jump in surprise, "Hey..."

She was smiling, that wasn't the most common thing in the world, "Run away with me."

Blinking at her as I sat up, my eyes drifted to my door to see that it was closed. How had she gotten in here without my noticing? "Come again?"

Sitting down on my bed next to me, her weight didn't make it shift at all, "Run away with me. I know you don't want to be here, let's leave."

"You and I both know that's not a good idea," I leaned back on my hand and studied her and her short flippy hair that was black but once bleached turned a shade of gold that matched her honey eyes, "are you supposed to be out of your room?"

"Have they really tamed you?" Her challenging tone was enough to earn my irritated glace as she went on, "I remember when they dragged you in, you fought the whole way. You had all hell in your eyes and now look at you, you're like a panther in a cage rolling over for treats."

"One can only fight for so long before you realize it's useless," I laid back on my bed and stared at the ceiling, raising my hand up above me, "I didn't want to believe my mind had broken, and I thought that if I was as difficult as possible, they'd just give up and eject me."

Laying down next to me, the Egyptian young lady in scrubs with recurring suicidal tendencies hummed quietly for a moment, "What if your mind wasn't broken?"

"If it never shattered?"

"No, what if it was never shattered?"

My brow furrowed as I stared at the ceiling, "You have lost me."

Turning her head to the side, she studied me so hard I could feel it, "What if you're not sick, what if you really see ghosts-"

I sat up, anger spiking through me so sharply it hurt, "Don't ever say that again,"

"But Thaddeus-"

"No." I stood from my bed, trying not to glare at her but I wasn't doing a wonderful job, "There is no such thing as ghosts. We are both sick, very sick," I extended my arms, gesturing to the drawings littering my walls, "No sane person could conjure up these things."

"You were so sure," she slowly stood, her cautious air doing its best to disarm me, "back then, you had so much bite, you just knew. You said there was a monster, one taking over everything. You said there was a boy, a shadow with eyes, what if those were all real?" She stopped right in front of me, a few inches shorter but that didn't hinder the intense eye contact, "What if something happened to you?"

"Something did," I rested my hand on the door knob, "I was struck with sudden onset schizophrenia and my life was destroyed."

Bringing her hand up toward the side of my face, she froze before making contact and retracted it, "I believed you back then, I always did. You believed it, too."

"That's because I was delusional, Honore."

As if she could see right through me, she stood there fearlessly despite my attempts at intimidation, "I still see it in you, that fight. There's a reason you're the way you are, but you're not going to find it locked up in here. When did this start?"

I didn't want to humor her, she was festering a wound I tried to sear shut with indifference, "When I was on a tour here in Evanesce."

She lit up, "Oh yeah, the ghost tour with that insufferable tour guide, what was his name again?"

"Algernon." I would absolutely never forget his name for I hated him.

"Yes, him," her smile was unfading, "you need to go find him."

I rolled my eyes, sighing as I leaned my back up against the door, "Not a chance."

"Maybe something happened to you there, that's why-"

"No, there's nothing more to this." I wished I hadn't raised my voice some, but alas, "Leave me alone, I'd prefer to pine over a life I'll never have in solitude," yanking my door open, I glared at her and she just raised a brow, unmoving.

She wasn't scared of me and that was utterly infuriating.

"Leave..." I deflated, eye dropping to the floor, "please?"

"They told you that you were broken," she approached me, making me look up to her as my front of anger started to dissolve into the insecurity it covered, "Thaddeus, they were wrong."

Hospital staff rushed down the hall, yells following them. Honore snickered which was strange but I didn't have a lot of time to think on it because I realized where they were running. Chasing behind them, I ran down the hall to see people rushing into Honore's room. My world jolted, ripped from its frame and sat in the between as I stared forward, vision shaking as everything around me roared to a screaming halt. Hanging from the ceiling vent, Honore's body was motionless, pale, spinning.

"Use this distraction," Honore said from behind me, making me fly out of my skin, "and run."

Staring at her, my mind stalled. I had to tell a doctor, I was losing it. Locked up, I was nothing more than a deer caught in the light of Honore's smile.

"You aren't broken." her hand passed through through my chest, "Run."

My heart crashed into my ribs and I fell away from her. A chill deposited in my blood, making me go numb where she touched as horror took over. My eyes jumped toward a fork in the hall. At the end of one was freedom, at the other was my room. Hazel sat in the corner of my mind that was darkest, it sat with the edge, with the boots and chains and leather and loud music, it sat with who I was- who I wanted to be. Sterile white, personable baby blue, that's what sat in the rest of my mind.

Colors that weren't me, colors I was forced to be. Looking down to the blue hospital scrubs, my mind was made.

The vibration of a bass started to drum up in my blood. Anticipation building as it grew in my ears, the hum of an electric guitar waiting to scream laced my muscles.

I never did look good in blue.

Honore beamed as she took off running toward the fire escape door in a massive lapse of judgment. Passing me, I heard Honore's laugh for the first time.

"Suck it, you guys couldn't keep me here forever," she ran right through the door, as if it wasn't there as her laugh echoed around me.

My mind wasn't computing much at the time, so that's what I'm going to blame.

Running right into the door, my world was thrown from focus as I fell backward. Employees froze and stared at me as I stared at them, all of us trapped in a moment of stunned confusion. Scrambling to my feet as they raced toward me, I shoved the door open and fire alarms went off in the hall behind me as I bolted. They yelled for me as I barreled out into the parking lot, running faster than I had in years. It felt so good, so exhilarating, the air was so brisk and the sun enthralling on my skin. Honore ran a few yards in front of me as she sprinted down the city sidewalk. Everyone stared at me like I was an escaped convict and I sort of felt like one. Yells grew from the direction of the hospital but they were drown out by the pounding of my heart.

I was free.

Honore gestured for me to join her around a corner in an alley and when I ran around it, I ran right through her. Shuddering as a chill took me over, I stumbled to my knees against the grimy back brick wall. She laughed at my discomfort, standing there smiling more than I had ever seen before.

"Does it feel creepy?" She looked at her hands, "I don't even look transparent, what's up with that?"

"You're dead?" I asked between pants.

"Finally," she laughed, "but what a surprise it was to still be here afterward. I realized then that if you could see me, then you weren't insane, and well, look at you now."

I crouched behind the dumpster at my side as I heard approaching yells. "Wanted, I'm wanted Honore."

"Yes, but you're free too." She spun around, arms out, "Now we just need to find Algernon."

"It has been five years," I said quietly, hoping to not garner any attention as search parties were already deployed, "I don't know if he'd even still be doing that job."

"Well there's only one way to find out," she stopped spinning and put her hands on her hips triumphantly, "lead the way to the tour,"

Sighing deeply, my annoyed eyes rested heavy on her and she seemed to shrink under them, "I've never left that hospital. It was the best one in the state so when I broke here in Evanesce on that family trip, I never left. I have seen Evanesce all of once five years ago and I was too cool to look up or whatever so I saw shit. I haven't the slightest where in the hell that tour was located."

She hummed, leaning up against the wall across from me. That didn't go as planned, I assume, because she fell right through it. Laying on the ground, her legs were the only part of her still on this side of the wall. Staring as I continued to catch my breath, I couldn't even believe what I was seeing. Maybe I should have just gotten up and surrendered to the search parties, there was no way.

"How do I know you're not just another hallucination?"

Sitting up, she pulled herself through the wall and rolled her eyes, "Why would you just randomly start hallucinating about me before you knew I was dead? Especially right after a dose."

"Well the medication never did work much,"

"Exactly," standing, she walked over and looked around the corners into the street, "because you were never sick in the first place," turning to look at me, she smiled, "I understand why you're apprehensive, I'm not particularly sure what's going on either. But you're just going to have to go along with me for now. I don't know much, but I do know one thing." Walking back up to me, her smile didn't fade, "In the five years I've known you, I always knew there was something about you. Like you didn't quite belong, not just in that ward but in this world. You're drawing, Thaddeus, and I can feel that pull even more now. You're subdued, but I still see the flicker in your eyes. Trust me," she extended her hand, "and let me help you ignite that spark again."

Staring at her hand, I didn't know what to think. I was either having a severe psychotic episode, possibly from the new medication, sitting in an alley talking to nothing, or I was talking to a ghost. I wasn't sure which was the scarier option.

"There's only one person in the world who may be able to help you. We just have to find him."

"Algernon," every letter of his name rolled off my tongue with pure disdain. I have hated many things in my time, but nothing courted my resentment quite like that patronizing tour guide.

Honore smirked, reaching her extended hand closer to me, "I can see it, the life that name digs up. Hatred looks good on you."

A laugh took me, chased by a sigh of defeat, "I'm still not completely convinced you're real,"

"That's okay, neither am I,"

I started to bring my hand up, "But I guess since I'm out, I might as well enjoy my escapade."

"Fantastic,"

The scream of music was still being held behind a wall, muffled like it was trapped under water. But I could feel it, right under my skin, itching to break free.

I tried to take her hand but mine went right through hers. Staring at our hands, we both stood in a quiet pause.

"I...I uh, don't know what I was thinking," she took her hand back and laughed, "this will take some getting used to."

A chill lingered on my hand as I took it back and looked around, "Likewise." my gaze returned to her, "Alright, if we're going to find Algernon, I can't keep walking around looking like this. Hospital scrubs aren't the most common place thing in the world."

Lighting up, she ran back to the mouth of the alley, "What street are we on?" she disappeared around the corner and left me just standing there, acutely aware of her absence, until she came running back a handful of moments later, "I know where we are, there's a thrift store a couple blocks west. I think you'll like it."

Starting back my way, she led me deeper into the alley and back way behind buildings. She was so excited, I almost felt bad for what I was about to do, but her bubble needed to be popped.

"That's nice and all, but one need money to shop."

"I have a plan," the mischief in her voice already had me worried.

But that's when I caught myself about to smile.

"So Algernon," she said, keeping a vigilant eye out around us as we carefully stepped around dumpsters and ran from alley to alley, "do you remember any of the stops on his tour? Maybe that could help us locate him."

I tried to pull that day back into focus in my mind, though I had done my damnedest to forget it.

"The area was really sketchy, dirty. There were clubs all over and I think he talked about a drunk ghost at one point. I don't remember it all that clearly, but the area was run down, dirty, and loud."

We stopped behind a pile of discarded construction debris as she looked out onto the street around it, "Did he talk about history at all?"

I ran my fingers through my hair, just thinking on that damn tour guide made my blood boil, "Something about some dead fireman, great floods, corruption and stuff."

A soft breath escaped her as she slowly turned to look at me, "I know exactly where you were."

Heart lurching some, eyes wide, I stared at her, "You do?"

She nodded and stepped around the derbies and motioned for me to follow, "I used to frequent the area, the underbelly of Evanesce.

Luckily it's not all that large, so it won't be too hard to locate him in it."

As we approached a store, the very heavy reality that I could possibly be faced with Algernon again turned my blood to stone and made my steps heavier. But that only possessed me for so long because then my eyes met with the store fully. Black, studs, fish nets and chains, this was unlike any thrift store I had ever seen. Staring at in with probably very obvious wonder, the different shades of black and leather enchanted me.

Honore laughed, "Come on, edgelord."

Stepping inside, I felt at home among the punk and grunge, among the safety pins, excessive zippers, and platform boots.

"Hey," I flew out of my goddamn skin when an employee approached me. Dead in his soul, he stared into mine, "looking for anything in particular today?"

"Something black."

The employee eyed me up and down, slightly raising his pierced brow as his eyes rose back up to mine, "Well you are in the right place." He turned and started to paw through a rack of glorious black skinny jeans, "Escape a mental institution or something?"

I nervously laughed.

Honore pointed to a shirt that had more rips in it than fabric covering the mannequin it sat on, "What about this one,"

"No, of course not."

The employee slowly looked over to me, "What?"

"Oh, I wasn't talking to you."

Taking out a couple pairs of jeans from the rack, he looked around. "No one else is here."

My eyes snagged on Honore and my gut started to sink.

A thick silence dragged.

Of course he couldn't see her.

"These look like your size," he shoved the pants at me, "the fitting rooms are in the back behind the shoe section. Let me know if you need anything else." With that he walked off toward the counter across the small store. Far enough away from me to make conversation awkward but due to the relative small size of the overall store, he was still close enough to make everything more awkward than I had already. Sinking into my shirt some, I started to dig through some of the other racks.

"I like that one."

I only spared Honore a glance as to not make the same mistake twice. She found that obviously amusing. Looking over shoes, it took me a while but I picked out a pair of combat looking boots with all the buckles for maximum edge. After meandering about the store, I ended up with a belt, several shirts, a couple pairs of skinny jeans and the boots. Taking all my items in hand, I carefully maneuvered around the racks, looking down, as I went to the fitting room. It was so weird, being out in the world. It felt like it had been so long since I was apart of society, in a store, interacting with an employee. I had to fight the urge to look for my mother, I was twenty-one now. As if I had stepped out of a pocket of time that had kept me frozen in place, I was suddenly an adult and that thought was terrifying.

The fitting room was small, several smaller rooms separated by bathroom stall-like doors. Stepping inside one, I glared at Honore as she made faces at me before I closed the door. Taking a deep breath, I struggled with removing the garments from the hangers. It felt nice, taking the scrubs off. Like I was stepping away from the halls that kept me contained, away from the personable blues and florescent lights that had tamed me.

Pulling the black and gray tank top shirt over my head, the first thing I noticed was that I liked the feel of the fabric. Slightly clingy, fitted, soft, black, it was a nice shirt. Stepping into the pair of jeans I liked the most, I didn't have to struggle with them at all. Once upon a time I would have said that means they weren't tight enough. Buttoning them and puling my shirt down, I looked up to the mirror. My breath left me. Staring forward, I almost didn't recognize myself. I no longer looked like a subdued patient, I looked like the person I pined to be. To anyone else, I probably appeared to be like any other needlessly angst ridden goth, but to me I was at home in my own skin for the first time in years.

A whistle came from behind me, making me jump and nearly stumble into the wall with the body-length mirror. Turning, I saw Honore partly fazed through the stall door of the fitting room, her eyes scanning my every inch.

"It's hard to tell from those scrubs, but you really grew up to be something."

"You're being creepy," I whispered, resiting the urge to try to shove her away because I knew it wouldn't work. "Get out."

She laughed quietly as she stepped back and out of the room. Taking another look at myself in the mirror, a light smile found its way to me. This was surreal.

"Hey, pretty boy," Honore said from outside the fitting room door, "when you're done staring at yourself, I'm going to try to cause a ruckus out there. When I do, you need to run. I'll meet you outside. You're going to need to run the opposite direction from where we came, the nightclub district is that way."

I folded up the clothing I didn't like as much and fought to put the boots on. I was struggling with that still when I heard a loud clang followed by an avalanche of sounds. The employee's sound of surprise was my cue but I still wasn't done lacing up my shoes. It had been forever since I had to do that. Taking my scrubs in one hand, the rejected clothing in the other, I hissed under my breath as I opened the door.

Setting the discarded clothing down in the designated area, I ran from the fitting room. The employee's back was to me as he fiddled around with the aftermath of a mannequin domino disaster, racks of clothing toppled over in the wake. Quietly, I bent over and crept around behind the racks. If I could help it, I didn't want to be seen. Honore laughed, somehow managing to manipulate things in the living space enough to knock over a shelf of shoes too. Closing in on the door, I was a matter of strides away when my eyes caught on it. A leather jacket unlike any I had ever seen, it called to me as it sat on a mannequin near the door.

Eyes jumping to the employee who hadn't noticed me yet, I quietly approached it. Sliding it off of the false body one side at a time, my hands shook upon making contact with the cold black shiny leather. Freeing it, I bolted for the door. The sound of my boots was a lot louder than I had anticipated, but I managed to make it out of the store without gaining the employee's attention. Running around the back, I let out a strained breath as I tried to shake the anxiety resting in my bones from the escape. Sliding on the coat, one sleeve at a time, I felt the cool silk of the inside against my arms and it made me shiver. Kneeling down, I finished tying up the boots and then stood. I finally felt like me.

Looking at the scrubs in my hand, the hospital slip on shoes and character-less blues, I felt a great dissonance. That color wasn't me, it never was. Walking up to the dumpster, I allowed my gaze to linger on the garments for a moment more before dropping them inside. I stood in a moment of pause, a sliver of silence that belonged to me.

"Nice addition,"

I flew away from the dumper as Honore fazed through it.

"Can you stop doing that?" I turned my back to her stubbornly, "You'll give me a heart attack then we'll both be dead."

"So you believe me?" She said, stepping around me as she studied the coat, "That I'm a ghost and not just in your head?"

"Well," I stepped away from her, "it would be quite difficult for a hallucination to knock all that over, now wouldn't it?"

Laughing, she looked at me as a whole, "It was difficult for a ghost to, just for the record. I think I'm starting to get the hang of this, though. Now," she turned toward the street, "we're only about six blocks away from the cub district, are you ready?"

Standing there, clad in boots, skinny jeans, a studded belt, black tank top, leather jacket, and a vengeance, I nodded. When I took that first step, I felt like I was falling back into my own and with that, the music exploded into my veins. Bolting down the sidewalk, earning the eyes of people as I passed by, my heart pounded in beat with the screams of a guitar, my boots hitting the ground in step with the drums. I was the most angsty motherfucker ever to walk the face of the Earth and I was proud of it.

My physical inactivity started to catch up with me, though, so we had to slow down.

"You're lame, I feel like I could just keep running forever."

I looked over to Honore, coughing through my pants, "You're dead, that's an unfair advantage." She laughed but that statement brought a raincloud into my vision. "Hey, Honore?"

We turned a corner, "Yeah?"

"Why?"

Her bouncy persona started to fade as we descended into a part of town that grew more distressed with each block, "I wondered how long it would take you to ask." Looking up, she sighed, "Why indeed. I've always felt like I wasn't supposed to be alive, that I needed to die. My life wasn't even all that bad, anyone else would have probably been happy in it. It was like something I couldn't understand was puling me to the other side. The world is a lonely place." She looked around as we started to enter into a more crowded part of town, the hum of club music in the background as the sun started to set, "So many people but so little connection. We all share this world but at the same time we are all stuck in our own, it's tortuous." We stopped at a crosswalk, "But," her eyes dropped from the sky to the disgusting filth deposited into the puddle pooling up by the sidewalk, covered in a rainbow sheen and littered with trash, "I regretted it."

The crosswalk signal changed and we started across it. "If you hadn't have become a ghost," I looked over to her in a stubborn display of humanity, "I would have missed you."

Looking at me, her smile was soft. "Honey, you're talking to no one right now and people are staring."

Jumping, I looked around to see a couple bouncers looking at me funnily as we passed. Looking to the ground, I quickened my pace. That's when my heart stopped. Staring at the ground, I saw a bit of street art. It was faded, but I knew what it was for I had seen it before. Looking up from the faded scene below my shoes, my eyes caught on a historic building at the end of the block.

"There."

I expected my feet to carry me forward, but instead they grew heavy. Answers could be waiting for me at the other end of that block, but so could Algernon. The thought made me nervous, though I didn't understand why.

"I'd shove you if I wasn't a ghost."

That managed to make me laugh a little. Making myself move forward, every step was harder than the last but at the same time, my heart raced with an excitement I hadn't been able to feel in my monotone hospitalized life. Cast iron front, the historical building sat in a similar disrepair to the rest of that part of town, but you could see the pride a once upon a time artist put into it to make it stand out. When I saw that the lights were on inside, my breath hitched. A sign sat outside stating that the next tour was to start at 9pm. Wanting to turn around and run, I was only stopped because Honore rushed forward. Watching her, helplessness crashed into me as she fazed through the door and into the lobby. Staring forward at the tall historic door, it took every ounce of me to will myself to step up the ceramic tile step from the side walk.

Extending my hand to the artfully crafted long metal door handle, I struggled with it for a moment but then it creaked open.

Old wooden floors, vaulted ceiling, pictures lining the walls, brick and dirty windows, it was just as it had been preserved in the memories that were burned into me. Terror deposited into my blood as I stepped inside, my boots making a hollow thud upon the old floors. I could feel sounds start to claw at my ears, but I didn't want that to happen again. Waiting in a line behind a group of people, my heart raced out of my chest. It was then that I realized I had gotten myself into a hell of a situation. I still didn't have money and there was no way I was going to get very far that way.

The group in front of me grazed further into the lobby after spending a few moments in front of a raised desk with a computer at it, probably checked in for the tour. My eyes rose and that's when the world ceased to rotate. Standing there behind the desk, silver hair, hazel eyes, personable smile, was none other than Algernon.

The years had done nothing but good for Algernon, even his entirely silver hair was absolutely gorgeous. His mere presence warped the space around him, standing out against everything else like he didn't belong. My eyes struggled to focus on him for very long, my gaze drawn to his left shoulder for some reason. As if something was there but wasn't, I couldn't look away.

"Hey, edgelord," Honore's voice shook me from my mind, "say your name is Conner Sean."

"Hello," Algernon's melodic tone carried me away with it as his eyes drifted over from the screen to mine. When his gaze locked on mine through his hipster glasses, my heart twitched. "Welcome to my humble ghost tour this evening. What is the name on your ticket?"

My eyes jumped to Honore as she stood directly behind Algernon, "Say Conner Sean."

"Conner Sean." I barely managed to say, not enough air in my lungs to speak.

"Oh?" he looked between me and the screen, "The office said that you had to cancel your ticket with us tonight."

"I was able to come after all," honestly I was a terrible liar.

A pause dragged by in which his mystical hazel eyes rested on me with far too much weight. A light nod took him as he clicked on the screen, "Alright, welcome," as Algernon went on about some logistics, I was captivated. The way he moved, the feel his words held as they pierced the air, he was otherworldly.

The ceiling light above us violently flickered for a moment before returning to normal. Algernon didn't even spare it a glance as he continued on, saying things I wasn't listening to. Anger and something else battled it out in my core as my eyes fell back down to him. When he smiled, saying I could make myself at home until it was time for the tour to start, anger won out. His smile was so patronizing. Years may have passed, but that hadn't changed.

Walking by him, I approached the other groups of people waiting in the lobby chairs that sat around the large brick fireplace, it felt like I was walking through the past. Walking into the single person bathroom that sat in the back of the lobby, I closed and locked the door. Honore fazed through it and laughed.

"He doesn't look anything like I expected."

"What does that even mean?" I leaned up against the wall, looking away, "What's the plan now?"

"Plan?" My eyes followed her as she explored about the small eerily lit bathroom, "I got you here, it's your job to figure out what to say to him." She stopped and smirked at me, "That is, if you can manage to not stutter enough to actually get a competent sentence out. What, was he more handsome than you remembered or something?"

I had never felt more attacked in my entire life, "I was just so overcome with unadulterated loathing that I wasn't prepared to speak."

She laughed a little, "Whatever you say, edgelord." Stopping by the door, she looked me over, "Just try not to cause a scene, okay?"

"No promises."

After leaving the bathroom, I sat down in a chair as far away from the others as I could. Everyone else played on their phones leaving me as the odd man out. Looking over the old fireplace, I remember a younger Algernon putting on a show before it. A conversation of past played through my mind, drumming up annoyance in my core. How dare he treat me like such a child back then.

Something feels off.

The voice that wasn't mine tore through my mind. I brought my hand up to my head, trying to hide how much pain I was suddenly in. It was way louder than it had been, somewhat distorted, two toned, like it was tainted by something. Teeth grit, desperately trying to not make any sound, I held my breath for a few moments. When it passed, I saw Honore kneeling in front of my chair.

"Are you alright?"

I gave a small nod, as to not draw any more attention.

She didn't look like she believed me.

"Alright, it is nine. Are we ready to start?" Algernon said a he walked before us, standing in front of the fireplace. When he got scattered nods in reply, that fucking smile flew to his face, "Welcome to my humble ghost tour, my name is Algernon and I will be your guide tonight."

The way he stood, the way his clothing fit, I couldn't look away. An ironed gray button down that had his company logo on the chest pocket, a thin black tie, dress pants and nice black shoes, Algernon commanded the air. A force of nature, his gravity was undeniable and I didn't even hear what he was saying, I was so captivated by him. His jaw line, his dark expressive eye brows that stood out against his silver hair that caught the light just right, his controlled and effective gestures, his precise movements and confident posture, even the temper of his tone was like that of a siren, casting a spell over the room.

Honore's voice broke the air, "Thaddeus,"

Suddenly I realized everyone was staring at me. Algernon laughed softly, approaching me some, "Did you hear my question?"

Shaking my head, I wanted to look away from his complex eyes as he got closer but I couldn't.

"On a scale of one to ten, one being 'I don't believe in any of this', and ten being 'I literally see the dead', how do you feel about the paranormal?"

"Ten-thousand."

The way Algernon blinked at me suggested he hadn't ever received that reply before.

"What about you? Where do you fall on your scale?"

Regaining his guide persona, Algernon walked back to his spot before the fire place and spoke before turning back to look at us, "Nine." Once he tuned, his eyes were on mine, "I know they're out there, I just can't see them. For some reason..." Clearing his throat, he was taken by that stupid smile again as he threw the definition of paranormal at us and handed out the same ghost hunting devices he had in the past.

This time I took one, though I did still feel too cool for it. Turning it on with a push of a button that sat in the center, the green, yellow, orange, and red lights all flashed to life then fell back into the green. As Algernon spoke on, an idea found me. Reaching my EMF detector out to the side where Honore was standing, I shoved it through her. She jumped, glaring at me but didn't move away. The detector lit up all the way up to the red and held there. Looking up to her with a small smirk, she just rolled her eyes as I took the device back.

We were summoned to stand and follow him toward the door. I wanted to hang in the back like some edgy shadow but I found myself sanding front and center, only a matter of steps away from Algernon as he went on about the electric panel. No one else existed, none of the nine other individuals on the tour, not Honore, not even myself, as Algernon ruled the world. I wanted to hate him, but I kept forgetting to.

Exiting the building upon his command, I found myself cursing my obedience when I realized how eager I was to follow his instruction. Like he held some sort of unseen force at his finger tips, his words wove laws in the air I was ready to follow before I even realized it. After locking up the door, he started to lead his tour down the sidewalk and we followed, hanging on every word. His tone rose and fell, bouncing and seamlessly keeping me entirely engaged. Why hadn't I noticed this the last time? Oh yes, I was too cool to pay him any real mind last time. It was like I was hearing the stories for the first time, falling into the settings he painted before us, of a time long since past.

We were no longer in the noisy night club district, we were in a once upon a time with drunken sailors, corruption and prostitution, a time of human trafficking and murder. Though what he said was awful, the way he said it was entrancing. As taken as I was, as we walked between stops, my mind drifted. He smiled a lot, almost constantly, but I knew it was fake. It was exactly what I hated about him once, that smile that felt so patronizing to a kid who was already sure the world was out to get him. But now that I was here again, looking at him again, his smile didn't stir up the sane animosity. It almost made me sad.

A man rushed into me, nearly knocking me from my feet. When I looked up to him, my heart slid into my ribs. Looming, dark and gritty, he was drenched as his long black torn up clothing hung from his gangly limbs. He yelled something at me that didn't make any sense, whether what was because of his accent, tone, or the fact that he reeked of alcohol, I didn't know. But as he stumbled off, I did know one thing: no one else seemed to see him. Looking around, my eyes picked them out among the crowd, people who didn't fit in this time. I had seen this before, heard these sounds. Looking around, no one else payed this any mind; well no one except Honore. All it took was a light nod from her to confirm what I feared.

They weren't from this time, nor were they alive.

Lights flickered here and there, earning the confused gazes of the other guests and an occasional eye roll from Algernon.

He was talking about the racist history of the police department when a group passed us by. It was a group of twenty something punkers, all very impressive with their tattoos and ripped up clothing. They were cool, all too cool, and I wasn't impressed. It took one to know one and with that said, it took a poser to see a poser.

One of the group, a young lady in clothing that was more ripped than there, buggered up from their group with all the belligerent grace of a hippopotamus, and raised her voice toward our group.

"Stop paying for tours, throw me twenty bucks and I can tell you all you need to know about Evanesce,"

Her comment was met with muttered laughs from her peers as they passed in a rowdy hoard.

I wanted to flatten her, the blatant disrespect. The amount of self-importance it must have taken to convince her that she somehow would be better at Algernon's job than Algernon must have been enough to kill every brain cell she had.

My eyes fell to Algernon's and that's when I saw it, a flash, a crack in his act. I had witnessed it before and I was witnessing it again. A storm of things raged behind his hazel, I could nearly feel the changing of the winds. But it all came to a moment where the mask flew back and with it came the smile.

"My goodness, I'd offer you a job but unfortunately you have to be personable to be a tour guide."

The young lady heard him as the group passed and curses flew wildly, but her cohorts dragged her away.

Algernon stood, eying them, obviously not impressed.

With each stop, I watched him closely. What was going on in the mind of the guide before me? I had spent so much time staring at him that I don't know how I hadn't noticed sooner, but he spent a lot of time staring at me too. Averting my eyes, I looked down the sidewalk. Starting to move as a group again, I felt myself walk in the same path I had before. Firemen, drunken ship captains, seedy history, shootings, these things were all reminiscent a tour long since passed, and if I remembered correctly, that meant that our next stop was the one that changed everything.

That was where my memory went fuzzy, when I entered that parking lot the first time. A light, pain, dizziness, an argument, the feeling of a tie in my fist. None of it was clear but it was engrained into me at the same time and I didn't understand why. Algernon sent us out to investigate through the parking lot, to look for a particularly high reading with our ghost hunting devices. I thought it was stupid, just like back then, and I'm sure Honore saw the disinterest paint me as I watched the others excitedly divide and search.

"Would it kill you to play along?" She asked, leaning over from my side to catch my gaze.

I looked around to make sure no one would see me talking to the air, "Yes."

"You never know, if you stopped taking yourself so seriously, maybe you'd have fun."

"If I don't take myself seriously, no one will."

A chuckle from behind me made me fly out of my skin. Turning, I saw Algernon standing there.

"You're peculiar, talking to no one in particular," he looked me over, walking around and right through Honore without knowing it. A shiver took him for only a moment before he regained full self possession. "Have we met before?" He got closer, a little too close, as he looked into my eyes over his glasses, "I feel like I've seen the chartreuse of your eyes before."

I was absolutely trapped in hazel for a moment as I felt his gaze dig into me. As if I was standing in a puddle next to a downed power line, a tingle coated me, making an anxious poison lace my blood. And though it was potent, the feeling Algernon invoked, I wasn't quite sure if it hurt or not yet.

"What did you say your name was, Mr. Believer?"

"Isn't it your job to remember things, Mr. Tour Guide?"

Honore whistled and sent a jolt through me. Glaring at her and her mocking smirk, it took me a few seconds too long to realize that was a mistake. Looking back to Algernon, he was searching for what I had looked at before slowly returning his gaze to me, the way his brow was ever-so-slightly raised left me helpless. Was he even alive? He was like a spectral staring into my soul from the great beyond.

My gaze was drawn away from his, tracing the side of his silver hair to his sharp jaw line, down his defined neck to the crisp shoulder of his blazer. My jaw tightened as my heart started to slow. Something was off about the space right above his left shoulder but no mater how hard I stared, it wouldn't pull into focus. As if it were camouflaged, I could tell it was there but couldn't fully see it. Though it was nothing more than an offbeat smudge in my vision, I had the faintest idea that it was black.

"What are you looking it?"

"I don't know," narrowing my gaze, I could almost see it, "but it's following you."

Algernon went stiff, staring at me in what appeared to be horror.

One of the guests gasped and Algernon turned around. At first his movement was suave, controlled like everything else he did, but then his eyes landed on the young lady who held up her EMF happily and that changed. Absolutely bolting from my side like a bat out of hell, Algernon all but crashed into her, pushing her a muddle of stumbled steps away from where she had been standing. We all stared at him as he stared at a spot on the pavement for a moment. After softly apologizing to the young lady, he retreated from her personal space and maintained his professional tone and distance as he called for us to gather around. We did as asked and we were left standing there, the air sideways, as Algernon gathered his words from the cloud of discomfort he had created.

"Welcome to a creepy dark parking lot here in historic Evanesce. We don't usually get readings over here, I apologize for my display. Allow me to elaborate, this stop was once simple. I would speak of a supposed burial ground underneath this lot, warn people not to park here and to pity those who do. But that changed one night, years ago." Algernon shifted his weight, his tour guide persona faltering as a flood light above us flickered, "Among us guides, this is considered the right of passage parking lot. That inevitably, eventually, something of a considerable paranormal nature will occur here. I honestly thought my coworkers were simply messing with me, trying to keep me on edge. But one night, five years ago, I had a tour. Five women, one teenage boy, it was ladies' night out and the kid did not want to be there. Sitter called in, he wasn't trusted to be home alone. The kid was done before we even started. Black skinny jeans, black band-merch t-shirt, black dyed hair. Darkness itself, the edgiest of edgelords, angst incarnate, he was sixteen and his name was Thaddeus."

I felt my stomach drop as Honore laughed.

"At the very beginning I asked him where he fell on my scale and he just glared at me with his chartreuse eyes and declared 'negative-ten-thousand'."

The group laughed. I did not. I could already feel the embarrassment take hold as I sunk into my leather coat.

"He groaned and sighed at every stop, making sure I knew just how stupid he thought I was. He was exceedingly done when we reached this stop and the ladies all went off and investigated, he rolled his eyes so hard I just about heard it."

He was so...just so...annoyed. Seeing my younger self through his eyes made me cringe, I truly was garbage. But, as I glanced around at the others, their laughs rarely subsided. Though he sounded annoyed, he had a light smile that was being a trouble to tame. I felt shame, but somehow, something about this was a tad funny to me too.

The floodlight above flickered.

"I was hanging back, watching as I usually do- making sure people don't get hit by cars and whatnot, when I suddenly felt ill. That's not the most uncommon thing for me, I'm rather sensitive to things so I brought my hand up to my face and braced myself. That's when I saw a bright white light flash so brightly, I saw it through my hand. I didn't want to deal with that, whatever that was, but since it is literally my job to deal with that, I took my hand from my face to see the group of ladies standing near where we are now. I approached them, as coy as I could possibly conjure at the time, and inquired as to what they were looking at. A sky beam, they said, a bright white light emanating from the ground into the sky, how did I not see the sky beam. And I didn't see the sky beam, though I wasn't surprised. I've been told time and time again that I am a psychic block, that there's something so wrong with me, I mess up their powers. And honestly, they all came together, it wouldn't be a stretch of the imagination that they could possibly be messing with me. So, humoring them, I took out my phone and took a picture, and, well, I unfortunately still have that picture,"

As Algernon took out his smart phone, I observed the expressions of the surrounding people. He had a gift, the ability to captivate. He was the center of every one's worlds as they hung on every word. The few moments it took him to pull up the image dripped in anticipation unlike anything I had ever experienced. He had us wrapped around his finger, it was a great power he held but as far as I could tell, he didn't abuse it.

When he held up his smart phone for all to see, the air dropped. Plain as it sat, stained in my memory, was a bright light beam in the dark parking lot, our shadow stretching across the wet pavement.

"What did Thaddeus say?" one of the tour guest asked, his tone quiet with shock.

Algernon was taken by a smile before he could smother it, "Well, that punk came right up to me and informed me that my photo editing skills were bad."

As the group laughed, so did Honore, "My lord Thaddeus, you were such a brat."

I wanted to tell her to be quiet but I wanted to look sane so I didn't. But I think it's safe to assume that my glare sufficed in communicating the message.

"I didn't even know what to do with this kid but then he started shoving me across the parking lot, saying that I was stupid and that this was stupid and ghosts were stupid and so on. His mother didn't do anything to help me and there we were, his fist full of my tie and our eyes locked. That's when his mother decided to speak up. She told us to get out of the sky beam."

A couple people sharply inhaled, their engaged eyes locked on Algernon.

The light flickered.

"So there we were, both standing in this sky beam neither of us could see, when I stated to feel awful again. It appeared that Thaddeus didn't feel well either. My memory is somewhat hazy of exactly what happened, but the next thing I knew, I was on the ground and the world was silent. For a moment, Thaddeus was the only other thing in existence and I don't think I'll ever forget it. I tried to continue my tour on like normal after that, though it was a struggle. I didn't realize it until later, I was so stuck in my own head. But after that stop, Thaddeus went silent. That was odd, with how vehemently vocal he was about his displeasure before that. When I brought up that night's happenings to a coworker, she told me that what we witnessed was a type of paranormal vortex. That this one opens up sometimes, and no one knows what triggers it. But there was something else she wanted me to know about it. That if the vortex ever opened up again on one of my tours, I needed to tell my guests that under absolutely no circumstances, should one ever..." his eyes dropped down to the pavement, "stand on it."

We all stared at the ground with him for an awkward beat.

"Why not?" I asked, slowly looking back up to him as dots cautiously connected in the back of my mind.

"Well," he sighed, looking away, "according to my coworker, if you stand on an open vortex you run the risk of getting haunted, of something attaching itself to you and destroying your life. Though I'm sure there's plenty of other unsatisfactory outcomes as well." A pause later, he regained his persona and looked back to us, "You've probably noticed this flickering light," he turned and looked up at it, "this only happens when I'm around. Ever since that night, I have been haunted."

The light went out and didn't turn back on.

The moon illuminated Algernon as he faced us, "Lights flicker, things fly off of shelves, cups fall off of tables, doors slam, things move, the list is perpetually growing. I had a roommate who was so freaked out by it that he moved out. My life is a living hell because of that tour," though what he was saying was dismal, the corner of his mouth was twisted up, "but I do find great comfort in one thought: I wasn't the only one standing in the open vortex. I hope Thaddeus is haunted, too. He definitely deserves it."

Laughter littered around me, Algernon's smile won out for a few moments. Standing there, staring at him as he stood across from the spot we once stood together, things slid into place.

"So that's why," Honore said, inspecting the place the vortex had once been, "it wasn't sudden onset anything, you were literally messed up by some ghost light."

"What became of Thaddeus?" I asked, unable to look away from Algernon.

He shrugged, "Haven't the slightest. But I am waiting, waiting for the day he returns. Waiting for him to realize the day it all went wrong was my tour and come back on it. But this time he'll hear me talk about him, and with great horror, realize that I've possibly told thousands of people about him and his bad attitude."

It was then that Algernon noticed that I was the only one not laughing.

The tour moved on and the spinning of my heart started to slow even further. The last five years of my life could be boiled down to nothing more than a single ghost tour stop. As we left the parking lot, the light turned back on. The following stops didn't catch me as much as the previous, more history heavy. What did hold my attention was the sound of every one of his steps as Algernon walked in front of me. Echoing faintly, it was like he was in a space far greater than this street side we occupied. A string of lights in a parking garage turned off, one after another, as he walked under them, then returned to normal as he passed. Trash shifted away from him as he walked by and it was a small enough thing that one could credit it to a gust of wind, but the air was still. Eyes locked over his left shoulder, I struggled to pull what was there into focus.

Algernon stopped and I only noticed when I ran into him.

Stumbling back, I apologized under my breath but it hitched and I didn't finish my sentence. His soft chuckle, his look of amused confusion as he studied me, it reminded me of how he looked at me once upon a time. When I ran into him, I caught a whiff of something. It must have been cologne and it was such a pleasant scent that it made me all but choke on my next breath. Confused, I hardcore averted my eyes and slid to the back of the group as the next stop started. My face felt hot, my jaw was tight, as I stared downward.

"What's up with you?" Honore asked, "I thought you hated this guy, do you remember how livid you used to get when he came up? Patronizing, you called him, patronizing and cocky and annoying and fake. What happened to all that venom?"

"I don't know," I said as quietly as I could, hopefully standing far enough away from the others that they wouldn't hear me, "he hasn't changed much I don't think." I watched the sliver haired guide happily talk of great floods and massive body counts, "Or maybe he has? He certainly...grew up."

"Oh?" The drawl of her tone confused me, as if she was insinuating something that went over my head, "I haven't seen someone fire you up like he did, perhaps there's a reason for that."

"Yeah, he was a patronizing asshole."

She laughed and I chose to ignore her after that. Following along the tour, more lights went out as we walked down the sidewalk. As we turned a corner, a street light went out, then like a disease, one after another they went out down the entire street. Algernon spared them nothing more than a passing glance as we entered the main street of the night club district. A netting of led lights were strung above us like a canopy of stars in the empty city night sky. As we walked under it, lights went out. The music blaring out of the clubs at my sides started to grow louder, the different colored lights pouring through the windows grew brighter and flashed. As if the entire street was experiencing a massive power surge, I had never felt energy in the air like that before. With every cool step, his hands in his pockets, his shoulders relaxed, Algernon was the center of the universe in that moment. The bouncers of the clubs nodded Algernon's way as he passed, the lights going out above him and returning to hum brighter when he was no longer near. None of the employees around seemed fazed, but the tour group was trapped in absolute wonder. While the others were looking up and around, I stared forward.

Algernon was an anomaly.

And I was captivated.

My gaze snagged on Honore as we left that area and started toward where we began. The way she was looking at me, soft with the sweetest of smiles, a kind sheen had taken her eyes as they held a slight glass. I didn't understand what it was for, so I just stubbornly ripped my gaze away from hers and it landed right on Algernon's back. He unlocked the door to the historic building we began in and with a gentlemanly gesture, he motioned for me to enter. Staring at him, it took me a moment to realize I was staring. Rushing into the lobby, face red, I couldn't get him out of my head. Like his aura was a tangible thing, I could almost feel it surrounding me. For the first time since I got trapped in the static between channels, I felt like someone else was standing there with me.

"Are we ready to hang out in a dark basement together?"

He earned laughs from the others as he led us to an opened door to the floor in the back of the business. Panic started to lace my movements, making my hands shake as I reached for the flashlight from the table near the stairs when directed to do so. Turning on the flashlight,

I stared down at the beam on the floor. This was the place my mind broke, or that's what I thought happened. But with the thoughts that followed that, more questions and fears were raised than I was prepared to compute. If what I saw down there wasn't in my head, then what the hell was it?

Algernon said some things I didn't hear and with that, the group followed him into the basement, descending into darkness in a single file line down the old stairs. Taking a breath, I followed in last. As I started on the second, smaller flick of stairs that led right into the basement, I hit my head on where the floor from above turned into the ceiling. Stumping down the next step, I hit my head on a light fixture too and ended up nearly falling down the last step when someone caught me. His hands were strong, far stronger than their bony appearance would suggest.

"I asked you to mind your head," Algernon's soft tone was tinted with a smile, "are you alright?"

I was until I realized that I was basically in his arms. Falling away from him, I backed up right into the brick and stone wall. What the hell was wrong with me? My heart raced, but not our of fear. I had never known this sort of racing, though. I wasn't about to break down, I wasn't about to punch someone. The only things I ever knew to hold power over my heart like this were fear and anger. After a moments pause, Algernon continued on with his monologue and I just listened, still standing in the back.

My EMF lit up and I jumped.

Honore tried to muffle her laugh but didn't do a good job, "You're high strung, all of the sudden. What's up?"

"This is where shit hit the fan for me before," I followed as they started further into the basement, "being here again just makes me nervous."

I totally wasn't scared but as we circled up and extended our EMFs out before us, I wondered how long I'd be able to keep lying to myself.

"And, for dramatic effect," Algernon said, holding his detector out like the others, "let's turn off our lights."

No one was too pleased by that but they all obeyed and we were left in total darkness, the only lights in the world those of our ghost hunting equipment. One was brighter than the rest, the one Algernon was holding.

"Hey, uh, Algernon," Saying his name out loud again just made it settle in more, we were standing in that basement together again, "switch with me?"

"You want to see if mine is rigged?" He said as his EMF moved over to me, "You wouldn't be the first."

Switching EMFs, the moment mine met his hand, it lit up and his dimmed upon meeting me. Gasps came from the darkness around but among them was a saddened sigh, a long drawn out breath that sounded like it deflated the owner.

"It has been five years, I promise, I've done every test I could possibility think of. But ever since then, things with me have just been off."

"Well at least it makes your job interesting," one of the guests said and though the others did, Algernon did not laugh.

"Is anyone down here with us tonight?" He asked, his tone far more reserved than it had been in that rare display of personality from him, "We have a nice group, would you like to come say hello?"

The lights went up from the low green to the slighter darker green and held there.

"Huxley, are you there?" His tone was careful, kind, almost unrecognizable from his tour guide persona, "Do we want to say hello to him?"

Algernon managed to convince ten people standing in a circle in a dark basement to say hello to nothing and that in itself was quite a super power.

"Hello Algernon. Yes I'm here. I'm always here. I cannot leave. I've told you this."

I remembered that voice, the voice of a young boy as it came out from behind me, manifesting alone in the shadows. Slowly turning my head as fear threatened to take hold again, I saw a young boy. Again his features were concealed by the darkness, but I could see his outline for it blocked some of the light coming faintly through the floorboard above.

"Huxley," I said, earning the boy's attention. "You're trapped?"

The EMS lit up in an affirmative reply when Huxley continued to speak, "As I have told you guys, over and over and over again, I am not trapped, just stuck."

He walked right through me, making me shiver as he stood in the center of the circle. The light green of our devices lit his face up some and again saw saw the charmingly childish smile on I face.

"Algernon," I tried to keep my voice steady as I stared at the boy, "what do you know about Huxley?"

"He is ten,"

"And a half," Huxley said, turning to face Algernon, "get it right, that half a year really matters."

I barely had any breath to speak with, "Anything else?"

"His favorite color is red, he likes Halloween but not Christmas. He especially doesn't like Valentine's Day because both girls and boys are icky. He's afraid of the dark..."

Huxley whined some, spinning around in the middle of the circle like a bored kid, "And yet you keep turning off your flashlights."

"He misses his mother and siblings, his favorite creatures are butterflies and he thinks I'm annoying..."

Snorting, Huxley stopped spinning and faced Algernon, "Because you are. Down here every night, asking the same questions. Do you even have a soul left after repeating yourself so much?"

Bewildered, I stared at the boy before me. Though fear was my initial response, something was being created in my core. A new feeling transmuted underneath the pressure of darkness and fire of fear, it forged something I hadn't known before. Comfort.

"Huxley," I said, commanding the silence, "are you alone down here?"

The EMFs didn't fluctuate, "No I'm not, rarely am. Though some alone time would be nice."

"Huxley, I'm sure you've noticed but," I glanced around, "some may be afraid of you. Are you ever trying to scare people?"

The EMFs yet again sat in negative stillness, "Never."

A pause passed, I wasn't sure what to do with myself. He was real, right there in front of me, answering my questions in full detail and no one else could hear him. Honore at my side, Algernon at my other, I was in the presence of the dead and unlike last time, I wasn't terrified.

"Huxley," Algernon broke the silence, "you said you weren't alone."

"Yes I did," Huxley reached forward and tapped the end of Algernon's EMF and sent it up to the red, "I'm here, that new girl over there is, and like always, so is Doug."

"Doug?" I realized too late that I had repeated his word out loud and earned the eyes of all in the darkness. Though I couldn't see them looking at me, I could feel it.

"What did you say?" Algernon asked, lowering his EMF some.

"Did you hear me?" Huxley approached me.

"I, I uh," my breath got stuck in my throat, images of personable blues and pills flashing through my mind, "I said Doug."

Huxley stood right before me, reaching out to my EMF to make it light up too, "You did hear me. Can you see me, too?"

I nodded, hoping that no one other than Huxley would see me.

"He can see ghosts," Honore said, "but no one else knows that."

"Is that why you're with him?" Huxley said, studying me, "I've only been seen once before, by a younger guy."

"Chances are that was him, too. He was here a long time ago and got so scared he bolted." Honore's laugh wasn't appreciated, "His name is Thaddeus."

"Thaddeus?" Huxley said, crossing his arms, "As in *the* Thaddeus Algernon is always going on about?"

"He talks about me?" Again I was swept up in the moment and realized too late that I was talking to no one in the company of others who were standing in silence.

"Who are you talking to?" Algernon stepped into the circle and approached me. Huxley got out of his way as he stopped right before me, "You said Doug, how did you know that name?"

"Who is Doug?" The lack of space between us was heightened by the darkness shrouding us. I could just feel his presence, his warmth, his aura. I couldn't breathe without catching his cologne and I was paralyzed.

"Doug is a shadow person, or so the legend goes. He haunts this area, tall glowing red eyes, not exceptionally nice, he is the most powerful presence we come into contact with down here. But I didn't speak of him, I rarely do, so how did you know?"

The temperature spiked downward in a sudden rush. Algernon grunted, hand up to his face as he lost his footing and fell to his knees. The pressure in the room was nearly unbearable as a deafening scratching sound erupted against all the brick walls surrounding us. Turning to look into the infinite canvass of the darkness, I saw a shape starting to take hold. I had felt this before, it was what sent me out of the basement. But this time I didn't want to run.

Flashlights were turned on and when their beams passed over the shadow man, he hissed and jumped away, holes being left in him where the lights had touched.

"Oh look what you went and did," Huxley said, standing at Algernon's side with his hand on his back, "You know better, Doug. Algernon is too sensitive for you to just show up like that."

"I was summoned," a dark gravely voice thundered from the shadows as they puled together into a tall gangly figure, "was I not?"

"Someone just saying your name doesn't mean you were summoned, you big doofy oaf. Now shoo, Algernon has a job to do."

"Understood," Doug's voice started to fade as his figure dispersed, "It was nice to meet you again, Thaddeus."

With that, the pressure disappeared and Algernon coughed. Kneeling down, I put a hand on his back and he jumped. The tour group turned on their flashlights in a grand hurry and illuminated Algernon as he stared up at me. As if something lit up in his mind, his eyes locked on mine with intent but it was suddenly interrupted when a guest asked if he was alright.

He didn't accept my help as he shakily stood, "I am, I apologize. I don't often even dare to speak his name because that particular presence is a little much for me to handle."

Not again.

The voice that wasn't mine tore through my mind, causing me to lace my fingers in my hair and let out a pained hiss through my teeth.

Why does this happen.

I fell against the wall.

I'm going to fall over.

Opening my eyes, they would barely focus as I watched the rest of the group quickly leave the basement room we were in and start toward the stairs. I did my best to follow, unable to see much or hear anything other than-

This is his fault.

I walked right into that same damn low hanging pipe that I had once upon a time. Someone may have inquired if I was alright, but I didn't hear them as I gathered myself and tried to follow them out. Barely able to climb the stairs, I got to the seat where I started and there I was, watching Algernon in front of that fireplace once more.

Smile.

"You all survived a ghost tour, good job," some laughed at that, others sat there and stared, dead eyed, at Algernon as he smiled, "We may never have the answer, if ghosts are really out there or not. But I know that if they are, they aren't trying to scare us. We all harbor some fear toward the unknown, it's simply natural. But it is our ability to overcome fear that makes us humans so special. I truly do believe that ghosts are good, and that if we're able to see beyond that fear, we may make a friend on the other side. They may be just as scared as you are."

He almost lost his footing when he tried to shift his weight.

Don't fall over.

Regaining his footing, he went on, "Could you imagine being totally alone, isolated from the rest of the world? So close and yet so very far from everyone else, for all eternity?" When he paused, his smile faltered, "My name is Algernon and thank you so much for joining me tonight."

He gave a slight bow and with that, it was over.

We clapped, all of us, but I couldn't feel my hands doing it. That wasn't what I expected him to say, the note he would leave us on. It was surprisingly heartfelt, almost sad- desolately so. It was parading around as hope, but the reverberations of his words held nothing other than agony. People stood, awkwardly handing Algernon folded up money as he leaned against the fireplace. I was just starting to gather my mind again when Honore popped up in the side of my vision,

"Here, give this to him," she said, setting a folded up twenty dollar bill on the arm of the chair when no one else was looking. I opened up my mouth to speak but she cut me off, "Don't ask me where I got it, not in front of everyone. Just give it to him."

Taking the money into hand, I pushed myself up from the chair and waited for everyone else to approach Algernon and head for the door before I did. I extended my hand and he took it.

"You seem to have a reason for being a ten-thousand," Algernon said with an attempt at a smile as the handshake broke and he was left with a tip that surprised him.

I glanced over at Honore then back to him, "You could say that, yeah."

"Well," he paused, the lack of a name to address me by becoming painfully obvious as he walked back toward the front desk, "I hope you found my tour to be informative."

"It did answer one of my questions, but," I followed him, heart starting to race again, "it generated so many more." Starting for the door, I couldn't bring my eyes up from the ground. "Hey, may I ask you one last thing?"

"But of course," he did some things on the computer at the standing desk.

"What do you think of Thaddeus?"

"I hate him,"

He hadn't missed a beat, his statement the most assertive and definite thing I had heard him say in the last two hours listening to him speak.

I took a step back, "Hate him?"

"Indeed," his eyes dragged over to me from the screen, with every passing moment his guide persona faded into something far more jaded, "with every fiber of my being."

When I backed up into the door, I startled myself. Eyes jumping from his to his shoulder, I again saw something jarring there, a layer pasted on top of the world and out of place blur in my vision. He may have said something to me, but I wouldn't have heard it over the muddled whispers that took over my ears. Shaking hand finding its way to the old metal door handle, I opened it behind me and stumbled backward. The last thing I saw before bolting was the hazel of Algernon's eyes begin to dull.

Leaving the door swinging open behind me, I ran down the sidewalk and away from that place, away from him. I hated him, I had spent years hating him, so why, why when he said he hated me too, did it hurt so much?

I wish he would die.

The voice in my head was loud, too loud, so loud that it took me to my knees and when I made contact with the ground, I could feel my core fracture.

3

ANOMALY

"Thaddeus,"

When I opened my eyes, personable blue stained my vision for a moment.

"Thaddeus, what's wrong?" Honore's voice echoed, bouncing around me until I realized the reverberation only existed in my mind. Bringing my hand to my face, I tried to gather myself.

"Thaddeus," Huxley's voice came from in front of me, making me fall back into the dirty sharp concrete, terrified for a moment.

Staring at him as he stood before me, blue drained from my vision and left me sitting there, stiff. "Hello."

"I knew you'd come back," in the streetlight, I could see everything about the young man. Chocolate hair, bright blue eyes, soft features and modern clothing, he looked like any other schoolyard little boy. "You have to help him."

"Help who?" Honore asked, studying the little boy as she walked around us, "We came here in hopes that Thaddeus could find help."

"It's not every day, or like ever, that someone can see us. Something is amiss here, and it's just getting worse. I think it has something to do with Algernon, and," he leaned over to be eye level, "with you."

The shadow of the dumpster at my side started to jolt and jump, morphing into a human like shape. When red glowing eyes blinked to life on it, I scooted away some. "There are whispers of a darkness, a force out to taint everything it can touch. It was unleashed five years ago and has only been growing stronger."

I wondered if Doug would ever not scare me. "Five years ago?"

"When you were here." Huxley watched as I stood, "I don't know where or what it is, but it's messing with everything."

"Living and otherwise," Doug's voice was like a fork in a garbage disposal, screaming in agony as it was torn apart, "If you were somehow involved in the start of this, you can be involved in the end."

"What do you mean, things are being affected?" I looked around the corner of the alley and out into the night club district as night settled heavier on my surroundings. "It looks like a normal sin neighborhood to me."

"At first glance perhaps," Huxley walked up next to my side, "but if you look a little too long you'll start to see it."

"Something is wrong here," Honore said, approaching us, "I can feel it too."

"What am I supposed to do about it?" I asked as I leaned back, still having no idea what Huxley was talking about.

"You and Algernon need to be on the same side," Doug's shadow stretched across the ground to get closer to us, causing me to step away, "I don't think anything can be done on your own."

"Did you hear what he said about me in there-"

"Every day." Huxley sounded anything but amused by this, "He goes on and on and on when he thinks no one else is listening."

"That punk Thaddeus did this to me, my life is falling apart because of him. If he had just stayed away from it, then maybe things would be okay, maybe Malus-" Huxley stepped on Doug on the ground, causing him to stop. As we stood in pause, the shoe

Huxley used to step down with lit up in a rainbow pattern for a few moments.

"Algernon is troubled," Huxley smiled brightly, "there's no arguing that, but he's terribly alone."

I averted my eyes, lowering my tone, "Perhaps that's why..."

"Oh like you're one to talk," Honore laughed as she started to walk back toward the entrance to the alley, "so what do you propose we do, kiddo?"

"Earn his trust, somehow," that's when Huxley's brilliance started to fade, "I've been trying for years, but there's only so much I can do from the other side."

"But you're stuck in between," Doug said, squirming out from under Huxley's blue and gray sneaker, "you can see us, and touch him. You're the only one who can help."

I was going to argue, to debate the likelihood of me being able to come anywhere near befriending Algernon, when the front door to the tour office opened. Algernon said goodnight to no one and locked up. Walking past the alley I was standing in, he glanced over but didn't see me because I had jumped behind the dumpster.

"Go, follow him," Huxley said as he leaned up against the wall next to me, "I can't, I'm stuck to this building." Huxley faded through the wall and out of sight.

"Good luck." Doug's voice echoed as his shadow dispersed and no longer held the shadow of the dumpster hostage.

Honore and I stood in silence and she gestured for me to start moving. It took my everything to will my foot forward but once I started, I didn't feel like I could stop. Eyes on Algernon's back, I loosely followed him through the winding grid of downtown. I had no plan, but that hadn't been the first time that day that I found myself without a plan. Algernon's gravity was strong, his allure dramatic enough to draw me from meters away.

He started to slow in his pace and I was taken by a sinking feeling. Stepping around the side of the building we were passing, I barely looked out. When he came to a stop, he turned around and stared for a few moments before sighing and continuing on. Following him, I was jumpy that every movement of his was a moment away from being discovered. We started to pass a bar that was painted in rainbow lights and boasted rainbow flags. Upbeat music poured from the seams as it sat, lively in the night.

Algernon visibly stiffened as we grew closer, quickening his pace.

A young man stepped out of the bar, or more stumbled. Looking up, he perked and raced forward, "Non-non," his voice was slurred, too loud, clumsy, like his movements, "lemme buy you a drink,"

Algernon shoved the young man away with surprising force and shivered as he created distance between them again, "Leave me alone Andrew, you're drunk."

"And you're not," Andrew, the young man of medium build and golden bouncy locks, said as he slumped over, slinging his arm around Algernon, "we can fix that." Pushing Algernon into the brick wall of the building, he hovered next to Algernon's neck, "You also must be lonely," he kissed Algernon's neck, making him seize up, "we can fix that too."

Algernon all but punted Andrew into the road and stepped back away from him. I expected to see fear paint him, but no, resentment did, as his hellish eyes locked on Andrew, "Stay, the fuck, away from me. I left you for a reason," he wiped off his neck with his sleeve, "You're a useless lush who doesn't take no for an answer. Now go die of alcohol poisoning or something,"

As Algernon stormed off, Andrew stumbled after him and I had no choice other than follow as Andrew yelled out, "If I die, I'll haunt you."

"Ghosts aren't real, Andrew. Grow up."

Algernon's words made me pause in my step, nearly tripping myself. So he really didn't believe what he said? There was a distance to his tone, a layer I couldn't quite grasp. I wasn't sure what it meant, but I had a feeling he hadn't meant it.

As I passed Andrew, his hazy gaze locked on me, "Stay away from him, he'll break your heart."

I shoved Andrew away when he reached for me and quickened my pace too. Algernon didn't even turn around, perhaps he hadn't heard that last part? Or maybe he didn't care. I continued to follow, doing my best not to step on any of the scattered trash, I didn't want to alert him to my presence. But with each careful step, I started to wonder what in the hell I was doing. What was I going to do when he saw me? What could I even say to him? My eyes rose and locked on his back. I wanted to hate him.

But, as I saw the way the moonlight reflected off of his silver hair, I knew I couldn't.

Not after hearing him say goodnight to the ghosts he can't see.

I stepped on a can.

Freezing, I locked up and Honore jumped to hide, despite her being the one of us he couldn't see. Algernon didn't seem to notice, and after he was a few steps further, I let out a deep breath and shot a glare Honore's way. She just giggled and started stalking with me again. Winding about the dark, perpetually moist streets of the city, I wondered where we were going.

Stopping at a crosswalk, I hovered around the corner of a close businesses as he stood there, eyes down. I studied the backpack he wore, it was decorated with buttons that I'd have to be closer to be able to read them. Though some of them were quite colorful, which came as a surprise to me. When the signal changed, he crossed the street and took a sharp left which created a problem for me. If I followed, he'd see me. So I stayed, unsure of what to do. He stopped across the street and pulled out his phone. When his attention was taken I bolted across the street, nearly stumbling over strange metal dips in the road, and hid around the corner of another building. What was he doing?

Dings took over my ears and I glanced one way, saw nothing, glanced the other way, and was then blinded by lights. A train rushed by, just on the street like a car or some shit. Flabbergasted, I stared as it slowed to a stop. The doors opened and Algernon, without even looking up from his phone, stepped on. Anxious nerves took me as I cautiously approached.

I froze before stepping on.

"What's wrong?"

"I have never," I looked over to Honore, "been on a train before,"

A voice from the ceiling of the train announced that the doors were going to close as lights started to flash. Panicked as the doors started to close before me, I jumped in but was caught between the door doors. Red lights flashed and the train beeped unhappily at me as the doors opened again, allowing me to fully enter the train and I stared at them close again, pretending like I hadn't just made a scene. I received passing glances from people on the train but no one said anything to me. Looking around, I saw Algernon sitting in a seating area facing away from me, he hadn't noticed me yet. Stretching some, I stifled a groan. Being closed in those doors hurt.

"It says right here that you need valid fare to ride on this," Honore said, pointing on a large informational sticker on the wall next to the doors with a slight, but evil all the same smirk on her face, "Better hope no one catches you."

I couldn't reply to her so all I could do was roll my eyes and lean up against the wall like a cool guy.

The train started to move with an alarming jerk and sent me stumbling. Honore laughed at me as I dejectedly held onto one of the hand rails in defeat. We rode that train for a long while, people getting on and off, sparing me odd passing looks. We started over a bridge and my breath was stolen. Staring out the glass doors, I saw a cityscape at night, skyscrapers like stars in the sky, reflections in the river that cut the city in half. It was unlike anything I had ever imagined and it was absolutely beautiful.

As if I had spent the last five years in numb status, I was starting to feel the colors of the world again.

Algernon got off a couple stops later at a large building, like, it was ginormous. I didn't even have the words to describe its size. Honore must have seen the wonder on my face as we loosely followed him in.

"What," she fazed through the glass door at my side, "you act like you've never seen a mall before."

"A mall?" I glanced around the inside of the stone building at the endless storefronts all connected by vast hallways and vaulted ceilings, "The malls we had at home were outdoor storefronts and were not nearly as huge."

"Welcome to the city, dork. This is the Erickson Center," she paused, looking around, "and Algernon is going to the ice rink."

"Ice rink?" I followed her, "What? Inside a mall? There's no-"

When we turned around a corner, I saw it. A massive indoor ice rink, literally just on the ground story of the four story mall. How was that even possible? The room wasn't even cold.

Staring at the ice, I was bewildered, "Witchcraft."

Honore just laughed as she approached the side glass wall containing the rink like a fence. I followed, cautiously at first, as I studied the skaters going about in circles. They looked graceful.

Someone ate it in front of me, sliding across the ice in a slow, painful display.

Well, some of them looked graceful, anyway. Others struggled, throwing their arms out like a panicked bird for a few moments before regaining their balance. I had never gone ice skating before, I wondered how difficult it was. My eyes scanned the rink but I didn't spot Algernon. Was he getting skates on? I glanced up to a clock hanging across the way. It was so late, I was surprised that the rink was even open still. As a few minutes passed, Honore and I stood in silence. I didn't have much of any plan, and I was starting to feel the weight of that uncertainty.

My mind drifted out of focus.

My eyes snagged on someone as they skated in front of my vision.

Black sleek skates crowned with black skinny jeans led up to a black button down shirt that was leashed with a silver tie. The fabric clung nicely, showcasing every movement, his silver hair shining in the lights from above, glasses reflecting the surroundings, Algernon paused time. His movements were sharp like his bones, his hazel eyes determined as he wove around other skaters. Black gloves made his hands stand out against the ice as he gained speed and I was left, watching every moment hanging on the next.

When Algernon jumped, nothing else existed.

Landing, the crisp sound of the blade of his skate against the ice echoed in my head. He was captivating on his tour, but he was something else on the ice. Was there a word to describe a state beyond captivating? Entrancing perhaps, but that didn't even feel like it gave justice to that feeling. What was that feeling? Heart racing, eyes locked on him, unable to look away, I didn't know the right word. But I did know that it was unlike anything I had ever felt before. Or no, maybe once, once a long time ago my heart had jumped in the same way. Though I couldn't remember when.

"Hey," I startled and looked to her when Honore spoke, "anybody home up there? I've been talking to you and you're just staring off."

I blinked at her and she just sighed.

"Since you're alive, you're going to need to eat at some point."

Suddenly I was acutely aware that I hadn't eaten in an uncomfortably long while. I may have never noticed, had she not pointed it out, and withered away as I stood, trapped in Algernon's wake.

"There's an ATM upstairs, follow me," when she started to walk away, I didn't follow, looking back to Algernon, "we'll come back, don't worry. Then you can stare at him all you want."

"I'm not staring," I followed her in a huff toward an oddly placed staircase.

Looking up from the ground when she laughed, I jumped back. Were those stairs moving? Honore stepped onto them and yes, they were moving upward. The city was just full of wonders. I couldn't let on that I was scared of the moving doom stairs, cool guys aren't afraid of no doom stairs. So as I approached, I did my damnedest to maintain a poker face, but I hesitated before stepping on and perhaps winced some once I did. For a brief moment I felt success race through me and was able to bask in the glory of my bad boy facade but then Honore smothered a laugh, turning away from me. Dejected, I followed her off of the doom stairs and through the second level. I found that my eyes kept dragging back away from the floor before me and over toward the rink on the floor below. Algernon was nothing more than a black silhouette of a person as he glided around the ice, jumping and landing perfectly, but I knew exactly which ant he was down there.

I wasn't paying attention, that's why I walked straight through Honore when she stopped. A transcendent shiver took me over, shaking me down to my very bones as I stumbled away from her and apologized. She lightly rolled her eyes away from me and toward the ATM mounted on the wall in the corner of the food court. Taking a step toward it, she extended her hand and after a few moments, she fazed her hand through a section at the top. I approached, watching as she fiddled around and I probably appeared quite strange to those around me as I studied the ATM with such intent. It made a disgruntled humming sound and that's when I caught on.

"You're not trying to-" I stopped, choking on my words as I looked around for a moment then lowered my voice to a whisper, "you're not trying to rob that, are you?"

"Of course not, the goal is to keep you from being locked up." She looked back to the machine, "I've messed up the camera, we can't have you showing up on it using my account. That's how you get caught and suspected in murder." gesturing for me to approach with a nod of her head, she just smiled, "I didn't have a lot saved up, but I had some. It's not a lot of use to me now, so you withdraw it and stay alive."

I was going to debate that, and also point out that I'd need her card to withdraw, but that would mean more talking to nothing so I simply did as told. She listed off numbers for me to type in and I did, trying to look as normal as possible as the machine groaned in protest. After putting in a third set of numbers, paper bills started to eject from the lower slot and when they were finished I just casually shoved an uncomfortably large wad of money into my leather jacket pocket and walked away.

Honore snorted as she caught up with me, "Could you possibly look any more suspicious?"

I didn't reply because the answer to that was yes and she knew it.

After obtaining food and trying to appear as normal as possible, I quickly returned to the rink and found a seat. I barely remember eating my sandwich, I was so caught up in Algernon. It didn't even occur to me that he could eventually notice me staring, I just continued to do so. The scraping of metal against ice, the crisp click of a clean landing, the hollow thud of someone falling, every sound occupied my mind and left very little room for much of anything else.

I can't always be afraid of this.

Jumping, I grit my teeth with the shot of pain that came with the voice that wasn't mine as it tore through my mind. Honore looked at me but I just looked around.

It hasn't happened in a long time.

The voice grew louder, hurting me more as I laced my fingers through my hair, doubling over some and trying to keep myself quiet.

I'll be fine.

Honore said something to me that I couldn't hear.

I won't fall again.

Suddenly the pressure in my mind released and my hearing veered back to me. The voice was so loud, echoed so much, it was barely audible in the first place, but it had been getting louder, so loud that it could blow out a speaker as it shook my skull. Algernon skated by in a flash of black and captivated my attention. Like some sort of specter, he stood out against the boring backdrop of the rest of the world, an actor center stage. Reaching the middle of the rink, the most unoccupied area, he stopped, scraping his skates against the ice. He took a couple deep breaths, running his fingers through his hair as he looked down.

I was left, hanging onto every moment, every moment, every breath, in that moment of pause.

Skating around, he gained speed then when he returned to the center, he drew in his arms and executed a spin so tight, it made me dizzy watching. The sound of skates spinning on the ice became my favorite sound.

The lights flickered.

Scattered gasps erupted around the mall.

The lights went off.

The sound of skates spinning stopped, as if the sound had been torn out of the air.

The lights turned back on but now the world held a red hue. Devoid of all sound, the silence was utterly crushing. Looking around, that's when my breath hitched. Everyone was gone, everyone except Algernon. Shadows crawled toward me from the corners of my surroundings, the racing of a heart the only sound fading back into existence. Turning, I could see Algernon spinning faster and faster, not making a single sound as the shadows started to claw closer. I had felt this before, as if I were trapped in a separate View-Master slide.

Whispers started to rumble in the silence, saying things I couldn't understand as they came from everywhere and nowhere at the same time. I couldn't find my voice, as if every breath I took was toxic. Running up to the rail surrounding the rink, hands tightly clasped onto it, I forced myself to speak no matter how much it burned.

"Algernon,"

My yell echoed around but was then cut off mid reverberation as if someone had sliced it with scissors. A vacuum of silence threatened to destroy me until it reached a crescendo of oblivion. A whisper, so loud it could hardly even be called a whisper, broke my mind. It was so close, it was like it was right up next to my ear.

"It's only a matter of time before..."

The heartbeat stopped.

The lights flickered.

The blood dropped from my head, taking me to my knees.

The lights went off.

My vision blurred as the lights turned back on, the sound veering back in a sudden explosion. The cool air stung my lungs as I coughed, holding my face in my hand. Honore asked if I was alright and that's when I heard the thud. Jerking my gaze up, I saw Algernon laying on the ice. He had hit the ground so hard, I felt the vibration in my knees. Unmoving, staring at the ceiling, Algernon garnered the attention of surrounding skaters.

What had just happened?

I managed to bring myself to my feet and stumble around a large support beam, hiding from view of the rink. Leaning against it, I tried to catch my breath. "Did you see any of that?"

"I didn't see anything out of the ordinary, other than you falling over."

"Did I yell?"

Honore's concern only grew, "No?"

Leaning around the beam, I watched as Algernon refused to accept any hand up and stormed from the ice. Ripping his glasses off, he wiped his eyes as he disappeared around the corner of the skating locker rooms. Muffled conversation took over the rink, words thrown around until they eventually dispersed and continued skating around in circles.

"Did you see the lights flicker?"

Honore nodded as she leaned against the beam with me, "What did you see?"

"A world, just like this one but darker and empty. There were only two people in it, Algernon and me. I think this has happened before, the day this all started."

"The vortex story,"

"Yeah," I kept a watch on the locker room door, "just like last time, it was only him and I. But if you're a ghost and you didn't see it, what could it possibly have been?"

"Unfortunately death doesn't come with ultimate knowledge. It's really not all it's chalked up to be." She stepped around the beam, "So, what are you going to do with this information?"

"I don't know," my eyes locked on Algernon as he raced out of the locker room, "but I'm going to have to figure it out."

Following loosely, my eyes locked on his back, I was determined to understand what was going on here. Of one thing I was sure, this had something to do with the both of us. Lights went out as Algernon waked under them, only turning back on after he was fully out from under them. The automatic doors flew open and away from him as he approached and nearly slammed shut on Honore and I as we followed. With each step of his I could see him growing weaker, shaking and trying to hide it. I could feel his frustration in the air, it was nearly a tangible object that I could reach out and touch the pain radiating from it.

Getting on the other end of the train car from him, I kept my eyes on him. Chances were that he was going home, his address would be good information to have. My mind hadn't really formed much more of a plan from the time I got on that train to when we got off and to my surprise, we were back at the same stop we had gotten on earlier.

Tracking Algernon became harder in the crowds of the nightclub district, livelier than it had been earlier, but I managed. His silver hair stood out, even if his dark clothing didn't. The further we got from the pulsating lights and vibrating concrete the sketchier it got. Piles of trash about, people sleeping on the stoops of businesses, needles caught in the sidewalk cracks, I was starting to grasp the haze that hovered in the air there. A screaming argument broke out a block away the shrill tones are sharp words echoed between the buildings and into the night. Something about drugs, it was distracting to say the least. Maybe that's why I didn't notice when he stopped.

A hand around my neck, my back shoved into the brick wall of a side street alley, the wind was knocked out of me with such force my vision blurred. When it dragged back into focus, what was left of my breath was stolen. Parlaying hazel froze my blood, the tight grip of slim fingers around my throat, the shining of silver in the moonlight, Algernon had me pinned against the wall.

My heart stopped and for some reason, it didn't hurt.

The streetlight flickered as his grip tightened.

"Why are you following me?"

"Following you?" I choked some, "Whatever do you mean?"

"Could you make it any more obvious that you're flying by the seat of your pants?" Honore's commentary was not appreciated a she nonchalantly leaned against the wall next to me, "Shit, he looks really mad. He might even kill you. What are you going to do?"

"You were on my tour and have followed me ever since," he closed the gap between us, stepping through my legs and pressed me into the wall further. It looked as if he were about to spit fire when his eyes softened as they searched mine, "Why do you look so familiar?"

"We've met before," I didn't know where that sentence would end when I started it. Something told me that I shouldn't tell him what had happened, but my nerves won out and opened the floodgates, "I came on your tour, the one five years ago."

"You're going to have to be more specific," sarcasm was sharp on him, "I have given a lot of tours in my time kid."

There was a moment, one in which I could have said any name, apologize and left Algernon alone in that alley. This was the point of no return and as I stood there, staring him in the eye, I knew there was no way I could do that. I couldn't turn away from the only answer I'd ever find.

"I'm haunted, too." His blank stare ossified me, "I'm Thaddeus."

He flew away from me as if merely being near me caused him physical pain. Crashing into the opposing wall, wide eyed and recoiled, Algernon was taken by visible horror. "No."

"You were right, standing on the vortex did do something to me. Now I see ghosts, plain as day."

Terror snapped into anger as he stepped toward me again, making me want to step back but I was already against the wall, "Did Andrew set you up?"

"What?" My mind flashed back to the lush, "No, of course not, I'm serious-"

His anger quickly drained into something else, but I wasn't sure what remained underneath; I couldn't peg it. But whatever it was, it ruled his every breath. "Leave."

"Algernon," I tried to maintain composure but then reality snapped back into focus, "I can't, if I go back, they'll lock me back up-"

Stepping away, he studied me, "You escaped from prison?"

"No," I looked to Honore, at a loss for words, "a hospital." Taking a shaking breath, I dragged my eyes back to him, "I'm not

messing with you. I don't know how to prove it, but I promise.
You're haunted too, and we're connected. At the rink, before you
fell, I saw it too."

"Saw what?" While those words could have taken on so
many different tones, anywhere from accusatory to sharp, they
were painted in desperation.

"The whole world, it went dark. There were voices, but we
were alone. It was just you and me, just like back then."

The way he stared at me, as if every truth in his life was
shaking; I didn't like it.

The street light flickered, strobing and making his
movements look jagged as his dark tone chilled the air. "If you've
known this whole time, then why did it take you five years to come
back?"

All sorts of things backed up those words that I didn't
understand. It was like I was trapped in the middle of a magnetic
storm and the pressure was going to rip me apart, "The last time I
saw you was the last day I saw the outside world. You surly
remember, I had a breakdown. They put me I a ward that day and
never let me back out." my tone started to falter, the rock inside
my chest beginning to outweigh the pressure from outside, "They
told me I was sick, that I was broken, they kept me in a room and
the medication never worked. It wasn't until my friend died there

that we realized that I wasn't sick, just seeing ghosts. So we ran away and I found the tour. I don't know what's going on, but I do know the only person who can help me figure it out is you."

Rain started to drop from the sky.

The light flickered on and left in its ray was Algernon, all hint of animosity wiped from his features as his eyes dug into me, "They locked you up for five years?"

A few drops then suddenly, all at once.

Five years of numbness, five years of hopelessness and haunting art, five years of loneliness and pills, those five years crashed back into me like the extension of a coo-coo clock, clicking back into my chest where no one else could see it but I could feel it in the void. With that came a wave of emotion I was anything but prepared for. Everything had been turned upside down and I was scared. I was faced with the unknown, standing in an alley with a stranger that I knew very little about. If he just turned and walked away, if he left me alone out there, what was I going to do?

I nodded, bringing my hand up to my face in bitter frustration. Silence sat between us as I desperately tried to gather myself until he broke it, his tone even once more.

"I hate you."

"I know."

With a sigh, he looked away from me, "I live in this building. Let's not stand in the rain."

Staring at his back, I was bewildered for a moment before Honore gestured at me to follow him. Nearly tripping over my own combat boots, I walked around the corner and to the front of the building. Watching like a shy puppy, I observed Algernon slide his wallet out of his pocket and bring it up to a black plastic rectangle on the wall next to the glass double doors of the apartment complex. A beep and click later, witchcraft happened and the door popped open. Following Algernon in, I glanced up at the skyscraper I was entering. I had never been in a building that tall before. I wondered what floor we would be going to as we walked through a sketchy lobby. The outside would suggest that this was a nice building, though the interior would beg to differ. A security guard sat at a small desk near the elevators, a few computer screens sat about with jumpy security footage displayed on them. I tried to not make eye contact with her but I couldn't help it when I saw the way she was undressing me with her eyes, glancing between Algernon and I.

A groan escaped Algernon as he reached for the elevator call button. The moment his finger made contact, the floor lights above the elevator dropped violently, as if the elevator was literally falling out of the sky. The dings that came with each floor passing sped up as the elevator approached and when it hit the last one, the whole lobby experienced a power surge, causing the lights to flicker.

"Welcome Algernon," the guard laughed as she leaned forward, hitting the side of one of her computer screens, "that never gets old."

"Evening, Tasha," the door to the elevator opened and Algernon stepped inside. "And it's not what you think."

Tasha hummed in disbelieving sarcasm as she sat back in her desk swivel chair and I cautiously followed Algernon. Stepping into the elevator, I pondered if this was how I died, considering what I had just witnessed with the elevator. But as the doors closed, my eyes were drawn to Algernon and I felt like things would be alright.

Somehow, someway, someday.

The elevator shook, and while I hadn't been in a ton of elevators in my years, I was pretty certain that wasn't the most normal thing in the universe. The lights flickered and a moment later we shot straight up without refrain, as if we were on a carnival ride. As suddenly as it had started, the elevator came to a dead stop on the fifteenth floor. A light ding later, the doors shook open and I all but ran from the elevator. Algernon was so nonchalant about it as he strolled out and into the musty narrow off-white hallway. Running his fingers through his hair, I found myself staring at him as he passed me and continued on.

"Well damn," Honore said, smirking at me, "this guy is something."

All I could do was nod in reply as I started to follow him. We stopped in front of a door just like all the others, but as he took out his key, I smiled at that little, knowing that it was his door. Catching myself in the middle of that thought, I stopped and probably appeared visibly confused because I earned a questioning glance from Honore. Shaking my head, I dropped my eyes to the ground. When the door opened, it tried to fling all the way open but Algernon caught and stopped it. He looked back to me and gestured for me to enter. Walking into the darkness carefully, I wondered what my mother would say about me going into a stranger's dark apartment alone at night.

The door slammed and Algernon sighed when it made me jump, "I'm sorry, it just does that."

We were not in the dark for much longer. A hum took the air and the lights flickered to life, flashing a few times before growing too bright then dimming to a normal level. I was left, standing there in the middle of an excruciatingly neat and sterile apartment, staring at Algernon in his black clothing, his glasses reflecting my black clothing, his eyes prying me open.

"Welcome to my every moment."

The chandelier type light above us swayed, the clocks on the microwave and oven flashed different times; each moment it was a different hour, a different minute. A hum of electricity in the air, it felt as if it would shock me at any moment, but at the same time, I didn't think that would hurt all that much.

"Sounds like an interesting life."

He rolled his eyes so hard I heard it as he walked away and sat down in the living room. I was proud of myself, using his phraseology in my internal monologue, as I followed and sat own at a couch across from the coffee table from him. Black, fake leather, the couches appeared to be of the build-a-chair variety along with the other furnishings about. There was a small television, a bookshelf that was nearly spilling over, a couple black doors that were closed, and a modern shiny kitchen. His apartment was much different than anticipated, by the way the lobby looked.

Pulling away his glasses, he ran his hand over his face as he leaned his elbows on his knees as he sat across from me, "So you broke out of a psychiatric hospital to come tell me that you can see ghosts? Do you understand why I feel the need to call your validity into question?"

"Of course," I ignored Honore as she laughed, "and I'm still calling my own validity into question."

"How long ago did you run away?"

I had to think about that, "Well, since I can't tell the time from any clock in here, I'm not exactly sure. But it was some time earlier this evening."

That looked like it alarmed him, "Are they looking for you?"

"Potentially..."

A blank stare, that's what I got, but then it slowly dulled into annoyance, "You're going to have to give me a really good reason to not call that hospital right now."

My blood jolted, "I don't know how-" my voice cracked upon the fear that deposited in me. Clenching my jaw, I tore my eyes away from him, "The possibility that I wasn't sick for the last five years only entered my mind earlier today. I haven't had all the time in the world to figure it out. But I'm not alone with you, Honore is here too."

"Honore?" He sat back in the couch, his hazel eyes lingering n me in a display of analysis that made me feel my every move.

"Yeah," I looked to her, "she was in the hospital with me but then she killed herself and instead of fading into nothing, she's still here. She's standing right here," I said gesturing to her, "but if you can't see her, I don't know how to prove she's here."

"Let me try something," Honore said as she started toward the bookshelf.

"What, no," I stood and walked after her, "leave his stuff alone-"

She reached out for a book and concentrated for a moment as Algernon slowly stood. I stepped back, really hoping she knew what she was doing, as I shoved my hands in the pockets of my coat. Taking a book, she was able to carefully slide it out and she flashed a smile but it only lasted for a moment. The rest of the books on that shelf violently flew out and scattered all over the floor. Holding one book, she looked around and laughed a little. My eyes wandered up to Algernon and that's when the world stopped.

Standing there, staring forward at the book Honore was holding, he must have been able to see it floating there. "No fucking way." Stepping forward, he waved his hands around the book and when his arm went right through Honore, they both shuddered. "It's so cold right there," he cautiously stepped back, "but how..."

"Neither of us are sure, but she's dead and I can see her."

"How do you know?" With each syllable, the toxicity he

had carried washed away.

"I saw her body before I ran, I know this for sure." Kneeling down, I started to gather the mess of books, "At first I thought she was another hallucination, but then I saw that and realized that she was dead, just as she had said, before I knew she had died." When I reached for a book that had been knocked open on the floor, my hand paused. It was a photo album, the open page covered in images of Algernon, smiling, in the arms of another young man. A picture of them kissing, one of them watching fireworks, holidays, birthdays, what looked like years of love was displayed between the two pages before me.

I didn't get a close look at the other young man because I was too busy looking at Algernon in the images. Algernon knelt down and snatched the book up, slamming it closed before he forcefully returned it to the shelf.

"What other ghosts have you seen?"

While that interaction was weird, I had other things to worry about as I continued to gather books from the floor, "The first ones I saw were in the basement on your tour five years ago. A young boy, a shadow-like person with red eyes," my hand lingered on the next book before I picked it up, "and there was another, something that wasn't really a person. It was more like a feeling. Dread with white glowing eyes." Standing, I carefully returned my armful of books to the shelf, "There are other things, too. People that appear and disappear who look like they're from another time. A drunken sailor man, a disembodied voice that hurts every time I hear it, sounds from a past setting, and..." I looked to his left shoulder, "There's something about you that makes you feel like you don't belong." I picked up a few more books, "And earlier, at the rink, I saw it too, what made you fall." Sliding the last book on the shelf, I forced my eyes to his, "Are you alright?"

The lights flickered.

He looked away from me, "I am. It hurt like hell but that's not the first time something like that has happened." He leaned up against the wall, crossing his arms, "That day five years ago is when it all started. I briefly listed off some things on my tour, but there's honestly so much more. I've been assaulted countless times, been injured, ill. My personal relationships have crumbled and things are only getting worse with time. The further I get from this part of town, the weaker I get. It's like I'm a walking anomaly, disrupting everything around me."

It's too much, I want to give up.

I nearly fell from my feet when the voice that wasn't mine shouted in my head. Bracing myself as to not fall, I couldn't hear anything else beyond the ringing of my ears for a few moments. When I looked up, I saw a similar sort of concern paint Algernon that had the day we met years ago.

The lights flickered.

As I stared into his eyes, endless hazel surrounding me, a thought took over.

That wasn't my voice...

But what if it was...

"Are you okay?"

I wanted to speak but I couldn't. Algernon's hand on my shoulder, his voice soft, I was struck dumb as I stared at him.

What is going on?

The voice was louder this time, I was unable to stay on my feet.

Why can't it just all end?

Algernon's hand on my back was the only thing I could feel other than the pain.

I want to die.

I may have yelled out, the blood I tasted would suggest so, but I couldn't hear anything, I couldn't feel anything. My heart about to explode, my mind about to implode, every nerve on fire as those words burned into my soul, I felt the intent behind every letter. And when my world faded out, I was left with nothing more than the skeletal remains of the emotion of another. When I hit the ground, the lights flickered and mine stayed out.

4

PROPHECY

Burnt bridges leave behind haunting embers.

"Your mother is here to visit," the nurse said to me as he had may times before.

I remembered sitting there at the window in my hospital room that afternoon, looking out as apathy settled in my core. "Tell her I'm not well and can't take visitors."

He leaned in the doorway, sighing, "How many times are you going to make me do this?"

"If she wants to see me, she shouldn't keep me locked up here."

"It's what's best for-"

"Best for me?" I slowly turned to look at him, my disturbing art lining the walls and framing him in my vision, "That's what you keep telling me." I looked back to the window, looking at the family car as it sat in the parking lot, "How convenient for her, she had a trouble child who is trouble no more. Subdued here in a tower, locked away from the world. Her only responsibility is an occasional visit to see me. Isn't it strange, you'd think she'd fight to see me every time I turn her away. She doesn't have any other children, so it's not like I have a sibling to occupy her time, and father is never home. I wonder what she's always off doing when that car drives away. When she leaves, she's able to pretend like she doesn't have a son, and I get to stay here and know that I don't have a mom." I stepped away from the window and leaned against the wall next to it, dead eying the nurse, "I'd probably be in prison by now if she hadn't put me in this one first. I think I'd prefer prison to this, though, I could get tattoos in there."

A wayward chuckle escaped him as he started from my room, "I look forward to who you'll become when you're not an edgy teenager anymore."

As my memory faded into black when the nurse closed to door to my room, my mind was stuck in that past, that day back when I was only seventeen. I was young, too young. I was still too young, too lost, but also too old, too cold. The clinking of a dish startled me fully awake and I flew up. A blanket fell from me as I sat on a black fake leather couch. My mind slowly reeled back to me and that's when I turned around. Standing in the kitchen, light flickering above him as he stared at me, was Algernon.

Standing, I got tangled in the blanket and nearly stumbled over myself. Eyes jumping to the window, I saw that it was daylight. My mind was stalling, pulling the last day and the unbelievable truth that my world had become back into painful focus.

"You collapsed last night."

Untangling the blanket from my legs, I set it on the couch and that's when I noticed that I didn't have my coat on anymore. My eyes lingered on it as it sat on the next couch over, nicely folded. Honore sat on the same couch and waved at me with a slight smile.

"I'm sorry," I picked my coat up and put it on, "I don't know why that happened,"

"What did happen?"

He was doing something with cups but I wasn't exactly sure what as I brought my hand up to my eyes, "There's a voice that isn't mine, it yells so loudly sometimes I can't bare it. But I don't think it has ever been bad enough to make me collapse."

"What did it say?" He started into the living room with two cups in hand.

I was surprised when he handed one to me. It was warm. "I don't...remember,"

Sitting down, I racked my brain but I couldn't fathom what the last thing I heard was, I just knew that it wasn't my voice saying it. Taking a drink after quietly thanking him, I felt the warmth take me. Tea, I hadn't had hot tea in so long I had nearly forgotten the warmth.

"I'm sorry, I didn't intend on being such a burden to you," my hand tightened on the cup as I stared down into the tea, "I can leave."

Taking a drink, Algernon's eyes relished in the suffocating pause as he looked me over, "And go where? Do you have a family?"

"I do but..." I took another drink as I tried to gather my words, "They're not much of a family, if that makes sense. If they found me, they'd send me back."

Every cog in his head turned, I could just see it. Something about him was different from the night before, like he was a little livelier, less exhausted, more vivid. "Do they believe you're dangerous?"

"I don't think so, though they'll claim otherwise," sitting back in the couch, I continued to fight to slow down my thoughts, "I think they used this as a convenient way to not have to deal with me,"

He snickered as he took his next drink, "I can't imagine why they wouldn't want to deal with that sixteen-year-old punk I met back then." He set his cup down on the table, brow still raised, "You were a pleasure, truly."

I didn't say anything in return, I couldn't, as I took another drink.

"So you're, what, twenty now?"

"Twenty-one,"

He hummed, his eyes rarely leaving me, "And, unsurprisingly, you still dress like the antichrist."

I laughed, killing some of the weight in my core.

The lights flickered and Algernon's cup of tea slid off of the table. Without taking his eyes from me, he lifted up his hand and caught it by the handle. I stared in utter amazement as he sat back in his chair, taking a sip.

"I've spent a lot of time wondering about you, Thaddeus."

I choked on my tea, coughing and somewhat flustered for some reason, "You have?"

Honore tried to hide her laugh, but she didn't try very hard.

"Indeed," He sat there in his black button down, silver tie, blazer, black dress pants and nice shoes, his perfectly combed hair that fell over in a swoop that rested just above his black frames and dark bows, studying me. The sunlight highlighting the spirals in his eyes and his smirk carving his perfect face into mischievous wonder, he must have been twenty-five now. "I wondered if maybe you were suffering too." Standing, he offered to take my empty cup, "Wonder is perhaps the incorrect word," he started into the kitchen, "I hoped you were."

"Yeah," I glanced away from him and out of the window, "Huxley said something along those lines about you."

When a dish clicked, I looked back to him to see him staring at me.

"Huxley?"

I nodded, a tad confused, "Yeah, you talk about him on your tour. I spoke with him later, he's the one who suggested that I follow you, so blame him for that."

"What else did he say?" As if a childish wonder had been ignited in Algernon, his tone was devoid of his previous edge.

"He called you troubled."

The way Algernon laughed, I will never forget the way Algernon laughed. Genuine, sweet, entirely out of the character I saw him display. "Well, I suppose he's not wrong."

"Doug and Huxley think something is wrong and that we're the only people who can do anything about it."

"Doug's real too, huh?" He started out of the kitchen and to a closet, "Well, I agree with them. Something is wrong. But I haven't any idea what and what we could possibly do about it."

I stood from the couch and approached him carefully, "They think it has something to do with you. They said that you're alone and-"

A towel was shoved my way, cutting me off. As if the conversation had been decapitated, ending right in the middle of my next breath. Algernon smiled at me with that tour guide mask, "The bathroom is right around the corner if you want to go get yourself together for the day. I'll make us food then you can accompany me to the store. There's a spare tooth brush and other guest toiletries in the second drawer down on the left. I have a feeling we'll have plenty of time to discuss this matter, since I'm stuck with you."

"I don't have to stay-"

"You have nowhere else to go," he turned from me and started back into the kitchen, "and I'm not about to let the only piece of this puzzle I've ever found go." He shot me a cold glance, "No matter how much I hate him."

Eyes slowly moving to the bathroom door, I stood there in stunned shock for a few more moments before scampering that way. Quietly closing the door, I just stared at it. Honore fazed through, startling me and causing me to step back into the counter.

"He did not like what you just said."

"He's a dick," I set the towel down, my voice hushed as to not be loud enough for Algernon to hear, "it's not my fault that we've been cursed by some sky beam thing."

"I'm not so sure, you did push him into it. And I think you're jumping to character conclusions," she watched as I took things out from the second drawer down on the left side, "One moment it's almost like he's a person, the next he's frigid and closed off. Someone doesn't just become that way for no reason. He reminds me of a friend I have, someone who puts up a front but is struggling with himself on the inside."

"That friend sounds like a mess," I fought with the shower to figure out how to turn it on.

"Oh, he is, but, he's a good guy under all that. He's just been through a lot. He's not sure who to trust, or even how to trust sometimes. But you know what? He has a favorite color like the rest of us."

Leaning against the counter, looking to her as the shower heated up, I could just sigh, "How am I supposed to deal with that though? If he's going to violently fluctuate from human to whatever the hell that other thing is, I don't know how I'm going to get on his side."

"What I've learned about people like him from my friend is that the first step to understanding the present is to decode the past. It's a lot easier to pick apart a motivation with a backstory. I think if you can do that, the rest will follow with him. He's alone now, but perhaps he wasn't always? And perhaps he doesn't always have to be." She shrugged, "That's just my two cents, he does seem like a hard one to crack."

A beat passed as she stared at me and I stared at her.

"Thank you for your insight, Honore, but... can you like... leave so I can take a shower?"

"What, and go out there with him?"

"He can't see you, what does it matter?"

"But what if I knock something else down?"

"Don't touch anything and it won't be an issue."

"But..."

"Honore."

She giggled, waving at me with that shitty grin of hers as she fazed through the door, "Try not to think about it too much, but you're about to be in Algernon's shower."

Glaring at the door after she was gone, I grumbled to myself. Of course it was Algernon's shower, this was Algernon's apartment. What was that even supposed to mean. Holding my face in my hand in the shower, I tried to not think about it, but I didn't do a very good job of that.

I got myself together for the day, as quiet and painstakingly as possibly as to not make too much sound. I couldn't stand the thought of existing while simultaneously dressing as obnoxiously as possible. As I combed my wet hair back, the fact that I made absolutely no sense was very apparent to me.

The last time I was out in the world I was sixteen, I could legally do jack-shit. I was tall for my age but now I was even taller, I had filled out and could wear whatever intimidating nonsense I wanted. But really, for the first time in my entire life I could do anything and no one was here to tell me no, to keep me on a schedule or make me bend to their rules. The fact that I was excited about this realization proved that I was still far too much of a child to be allowed these freedoms, but I also didn't care. So I suppose that just went to prove the aforementioned point even more.

I came back into the apartment like a scared puppy, trying to not make noise with my steps. I was hoping to catch a glimpse of him when he thought no one else was looking. Algernon was a king atop his wall, what did he look like without that guard up? Stepping around the corner of the hallway, I leaned over a tad to look into the kitchen. Pouring another cup of tea, Algernon looked no different than he had before. Uptight, flawless all the same, but he still looked as if he was tied into knots.

"I hope you were able to figure out the shower?"

I jumped out of my skin, nervously laughing as I walked into the living room more. "Yeah,"

Honore snorted from where she sat on the couch.

I glared her way.

That was a wonderfully awkward meal. Sitting there, looking up to him on occasion, I tried to fathom words to say.

"So," I said after taking my last sip of tea, "what's your favorite color?"

His eyes radiated 'fuck off' so potently I could nearly hear him say it as he glared at me from over his cup. Taking his dishes into hand, he got up from the garnet island in the middle of the kitchen. "Bring your dishes then we'll leave."

I did as told and put my leather coat back on as he tied his shoes. The silence was heavy but it didn't seem to bother him any. As we left the apartment, the lights flickered and the door slammed shut behind me without anyone touching it. We got into the elevator, the silence following for only a moment before the lights got brighter and an electric hum took over the air as the elevator free fell. Holding onto the rail, startled, I looked over to see Algernon not even somewhat fazed. A demented ding took over my ears as the doors creaked open and a we stepped out, I could feel my heart racing. As we walked toward the door, the security guard Tasha eyed me wildly. Looking away, I pretended like I didn't notice though it made me shiver before we managed to leave. I heard her laugh quietly in the background as the door closed behind me.

We walked in an uncomfortable quiet through the city that looked far different during the day, but still felt off. Like there was a toxin that laced the air with latent electricity, about to snap at any moment. My eyes started to get a better look at the historic district, I could see the dirt sticking to the walls, the building in disrepair, the stains on the sidewalk. I could feel agony floating through me, see huddled people quivering in the stoops of the businesses as we passed. Their mumbles made no sense to me, some sounded scared, others sounded delirious. It was easy to not see them as such, but they were people.

They had a favorite color like everyone else.

Algernon walked with such efficient speed it was hard to stay by his side, "Did you grow up here?"

"Born and raised." The tone he took as we approached a train platform was so cold it made me shudder.

Looking to Honore as we got on the train, she just gestured back toward Algernon.

"Have you traveled much?"

"I used to."

Standing next to him on the train as it started to move, I stared at the ground and tried to maintain a personable tone to counteract his sour one, "Do you have a favorite place you've visited?"

"Yes."

A beat passed, a beat that should have been filled with his elaboration but was simply filled with the silence he very obviously placed there.

I withheld my sigh, "Where would that be?"

"A lovely town really, it's small and on the coast," his eyes locked on mine, "it's called none of your fucking business."

A random man on the train whistled.

I was left, staring.

"Well damn," Honore said walking around Algernon as she studied him, "what a front he's putting up."

I rolled my eyes away from her, "I tried."

"Who are you talking to?"

I looked to Algernon, annoyance flattening my tone, "None of your fucking business."

The lights on the train flickered as he looked away from me.

Honore would have died laughing had she not already been dead.

Sharp silence sat around us, prickly in the way that it stung even if you breathed. People occasionally glanced our way, as if waiting for another installment to our bantering but when none came, they eventually lost interest. We got off a couple stops down and approached a store. The automatic doors flew open with unnatural speed as we walked up to them, causing people to spare us wayward passing glances.

"You have to keep trying," Honore said as she walked happily by my side, looking about the store, "he's obviously not going to just let you in."

I wanted to voice my opinion that trying to force my way in is breaking and entering and that shit was illegal but I didn't want to talk to nothing so I stayed quiet. Algernon picked up a hand basket and I would have offered to carry it if he hadn't been such an asshole.

We entered an aisle of boxed goods, crackers, cookies, cereal, as I tried to stay in step with Algernon, "Does your family live here?"

"Yes." He took a list out of his wallet from his pocket and refused to make eye contact with me.

I watched as he put a box of something I didn't get a good look at into his basket and continued onward, "Do you have any siblings?"

We rounded the corner into a new aisle as he picked something else up, "No."

"What about a family pet?"

"No."

I followed a few steps behind as he picked up other items, "Do you have a favorite holiday?"

"No." He quickened his pace as I tried to keep up.

"A favorite movie?"

"No."

"Favorite season?"

"No."

"Favorite animal?"

"No."

The lights flickered in the store, causing scattered gasps as he stopped and looked at some bottled item on the shelf. I caught up, quickly reaching a point of exasperation.

"Man, you're really a delight, you know that? I'm honestly surprised that you have a partner, with that attitude."

His eyes shot to me making me take a step back for they held all hell in their hazel swirls, "I don't," the lights flickered, "not anymore." he took a step closer to me, his tone growing darker with the lights as they dimmed slowly all around us, "What are you trying to accomplish here? I didn't think I could possibly hate you

any more than I already did but you're quickly proving me wrong."
He backed me up into the aisle and things started to fall from the
shelves all around, "If I were you I'd back the fuck off before you
force my hand and I turn you in."

Mere inches away from me, his eyes locked on mine, for
the first time I felt like I was actually seeing him. Not as the nasty
display he was shoving at me, no, I could see something else in
those eyes of his. I couldn't pin exactly what it was, but it made my
heart ache. Reaching up, I was about to put my hand on his
shoulder, about to say something in an attempt at apology, but
that's when they approached us.

"Death."

Algernon and I stared at each other for a moment before
both looking off to the side. Standing there a few steps away from
us was the most colorful individual I had ever had the displeasure
of laying eyes on. As if they obtained every article of clothing they
had on from a kid's tie-dye birthday party, they were a disaster of
clashing neon colors and muddy designs. Their eyes weren't on us,
not at first. For the initial few moments, they were most definitely
looking at Honore.

Algernon stepped away from me, "Pardon?"

They walked right up to Algernon, making him stumble
back and drop his basket in surprise, "Death."

"Death." I repeated, studying the person with matted hair so long it nearly reached their knees.

Lifting their hand, they brought it up over Algernon's shoulder and carefully analyzed the area before jumping back in terror. "It's following you. Death."

"What's following me?" Algernon's sudden desperation was both concerning and surprising as he appeared more genuine than I had ever seen him behave, "Can you see it? Please, tell me what it is,"

"Death," they looked between Algernon and I, "it's growing stronger."

"How do I make it go away?" Algernon's voice cracked, breaking my heart with it. I wasn't following what was going on, but I knew it was important.

The unique individual before us stared at him, but then a moment later, their terror drained and they snapped into a distant daze, "Hearts intertwined, you're running out of time," they grabbed Algernon by his blazer, their tone holding hints of a growl in their chest, their words not much more than a harsh whisper, "The anomaly will obliterate all that it isolates. A king lies in wait, ready to seal your fate. A key that is locked in its own safe, a love since past, it's nearly too late." With every passing word, the lights above swelled brighter, the tension in the air grew with the horror on Algernon's face, "Beware the apple of emotion, for once it is in your eye, your demise rests in your devotion. Where it started is where it will end, an outcome that you won't intend. When shadows in the night lay, prepare, for that will be judgment day."

Every light bulb hanging above us exploded with a violent blast of electricity.

Items flew off of the shelves as glass rained upon us.

Screams echoed around.

They let go of Algernon and ran away.

Apple.

The voice yelled in my head so loud it made me stumble over into the shelf, hand to my face as my ears rang. An announcement shouted for us to evacuate but I could barely catch it through the echoes in my ears. The cracking of broken glass made its way to my senses before the warmth of the hand on my wrist. Being dragged, they brought me out of the darkened store and into the parking lot before I noticed that it was Algernon.

A hand on my back, my world was too dizzy to compute what was going on. Why had this become so debilitating? I couldn't remember it being so bad, not since since the first few times. What changed?

"Thaddeus," Algernon's voice broke the static taking my mind, "are you alright?"

Hazel calmed my blood.

I nodded.

Algernon looked around, "Where did that person go?"

There was no sign of the rainbow vomit stain, but their words sat on my skin like slime. People poured out of the building, some were cut and bleeding, the echoes of sirens started to approach. I had never witnessed anything like that before, the amount of raw pressure in the air, a release so violent. It felt not of this world, something too powerful for this world. As if the weight that had been building since that morning had been lifted, the hum in the air was absent as I looked to Algernon.

"They touched you," my mind settled, "are you okay?"

"Yes," he brought his hand up to his blazer where they had grabbed him, "but what they said, we need to write it down." Taking out his phone, he started typing, "Death. Hearts intertwined, you're running out of time."

I leaned over, looking at his cellphone with quiet wonder. It was more advanced than the last smart phone I had seen, "The anomaly will obliterate all that it isolates."

We both stood in pause then he looked up to me, his color draining, "What did they say next?"

"A king lies in wait, ready to seal your fate." Honore said from my side, startling me.

She laughed a I repeated the phrase and he typed it into his phone.

"A key that is locked in its own safe, a love since past, it's nearly too late," Algernon mumbled to himself as he typed each word with a vengeance.

"Beware the apple of emotion," I paused to think, "for once it is in your eye, your demise rests in your devotion."

"Where it started is where it will end, an outcome that you won't intend."

"When shadows in the night lay, prepare, for that will be judgment day." Silence followed my last word and it hung, dully in the air, as Algernon finished typing.

Algernon didn't look up from his phone, he just stared at the words on the screen.

"Am I missing something?" I looked over his shoulder.

"Wasn't that strange?" He started to walk from the parking lot, not looking from his phone.

I followed, "Well of course it was. I've never met a pothead in the flesh before."

Scoffing at me as we stopped at a stop crosswalk signal on the street, Algernon wasn't the slightest bit amused, "That person, they were looking at someone." He looked up to me, "Someone that I couldn't see."

Honore jumped, "Yes, they totally were looking at me."

"And I know you've been locked up for a while, but lights don't just casually blow up like that, Thaddeus."

"I know..." I followed a few steps behind as he raced across the street, "But what they said was nonsense, right?"

"At first glance, maybe, but," we turned a corner and I could see a familiar location in the nearing distance, "some of it made sense to me."

Bolting, he took off and I struggled to keep up with him, calling out as we ran, "What, do you really think that was some sort of fortune?"

"A prophecy, perhaps," he stopped, panting in the parking lot that changed our lives five years prior, "and they could see it," he started toward the area we stood on his tour.

"See what?"

He stopped, pointing to his left shoulder, "What's haunting me."

Staring at his shoulder, I couldn't pull it into focus, but there was something there, "Death..."

He nodded, turning away from me and looking back down to his phone, "Maybe we can activate it again,"

It took me a moment to catch up as I stepped to his side, "The sky beam? What does that have to do with the prophecy thing? You're not sounding the most...tethered at the moment."

Slowly looking up to me, Algernon raised an irked brow, "You're the one who sees ghosts."

Honore waved, "Hi."

I glared at her and sighed, "Alright, fine."

"Here, it says something about where it began." He pocketed his phone, "And this is where things went wrong."

The parking lot was rather deserted, the nigh club district wasn't the most popping place in the middle of the day. Glancing about, I thought back on that night long since passed. Walking over, I retraced my steps from once upon a five years ago. Stopping, I looked up.

"Hey, Algernon, come here for a second."

To my surprise, he didn't question as he walked up to me.

When he was standing there, his back to the location of the sky beam, I locked my sights on him, my tone toxic, "Do you enjoy getting paid to lie to everyone?" Algernon's utter confusion was a bit more satisfying than it should have been as I grabbed him by the shoulders, "You don't even believe what you're saying," shoving him, he didn't fight as he stumbled backwards, "You're the worst kind of person," I shoved him again, Honore standing there watching with a lofty smile, "Stop taking advantage of people's stupidity and go do something productive with your life."

Stopping right in front of him, I took a fistful of his shirt and all but lifted him from the ground in my grip. I was all grown up, taller, somewhat stronger, and definitely more intimidating. I saw those things reflect in Algernon's glasses a I held him there, inches away from me, my grip unwavering, my edge sharp enough to be cut on.

There we were standing in the exact same spot we had been when this all started, but nothing was happening. Though at the time, I didn't notice. I was too busy getting lost in hazel. His eyes were wide on mine, absolutely defeated by my display of dominance. The fabric of his shirt in my fist felt nice, I could feel his warmth through it. His breathing had stopped, as if I had broken him. And as we stood there, nothing else existed. Not because I was caught between slides of a View-Master, but because I was caught by him. His face was red and something about that was utterly adorable.

We were so close.

Never before in my life had I felt so inclined to do something. It crashed into me with such potency, it nearly possessed me. Grip tightening, my mind entertained the idea for only a moment before I let go of him, breaking the enchanting eye contact and stepping away. Staring at the ground, I felt my face burn. His cologne smelled nice.

I absolutely refused to face him as he cleared his throat, "Well, that didn't do anything."

I would have disagreed with that, that definitely did something. It was something I had never felt before, something that dripped into my blood and had passed through my entire body. Running my hand through my shaggy hair, I couldn't bring my eyes from the ground. But there was one thing that shook me more than anything else as I followed Algernon out of that parking lot.

I couldn't stop smiling.

"What was that about?" I nearly flew out of my skin when Honore spoke.

Looking over to her, I was able to express my question without speaking.

"Oh, so you want me to believe that you just sanding there, holding him close and gazing into his eyes, was just normal?"

I wasn't pleased with the leading mockery of her words as I looked away and to Algernon's back.

"You know, even though you were a punk back then you were horribly cute." she said as we started across the street, "I was honestly surprised that you had never had a girlfriend."

I stopped walking.

She stood at my side, smiling more than she should have been, "There was only ever one person you talked about, this pretentious tour guide who treated you like a child and pissed you off, but all the same, you made sure to tell me that he had hazel eyes."

Algernon stopped and turned to see me standing there, staring.

A beat passed that was filled with the beating of my heart.

A car honked and I jumped, looking over to see that I had stopped walking right in the middle of the crosswalk. Running to the other side, I was flustered but that got even worse when I heard Algernon try to muffle his laugh as we went along. Was Honore right? I suppose I had never thought about it before, having been so preoccupied with being the darkness and all that. There was only one person who managed to maintain my attention, regardless of the tone of said attention, and he was walking two strides ahead of me. Approaching the old hotel that he ran tours out of, my memories snagged on hazel.

Opening the door with a key from his lanyard attached to his belt loop, he looked up to me, "You can talk to them, right?"

The caution in his words was curious to me, "The ghosts here? Yeah." I followed him in as he tucked his keys back into his back pocket, "Would you like me to ask them what they think?"

"If you would," Algernon looked away as he started through the space and toward the back corner, "I would but I'm still processing the fact that they've been here for the last several years, just listening to me say the same things over and over again."

The existential crisis was real and I could just laugh as I closed the door behind me. "Alright," I slowed in my step when I saw that he was picking up flash lights, "Wait, we're not-"

"Well where else do you think they are?" he handed me a flash light, "There's a reason we talk to them down there."

"No, I call bullshit. I know thy don't have to stay down there," I watched as he started down the stairs into the abysmal basement, turning his light on, "I've talked to them in the alley, we don't have to-"

"Well," he stopped at the platform between sets of stairs, looking up at me, "do you see them up there?"

I looked around and deflated, "No..."

"Then come on," he disappeared into the darkness, "unless, of course, your royal edgyness is afraid of the dark."

"I'm not..." I turned on my light and started down the stairs, "I just feel like this is how stupid white people get killed horror movies."

"Good thing I'm not white," Honore said as she followed me down.

"Yes, but you're already dead Honore," I shined my light through her, "look, you don't even cast a shadow."

"She's here too?" We both looked at Algernon as he stood off in the darkness, the light in his hand pointed at the stained concrete ground.

"Yeah, she's been with us the entire time. But I've refrained from acknowledging her as to not be annoying."

"It's quite rude, really," Honore started to explore.

My eyes followed her, "He can't hear you..."

"What did she say?" He went further into the basement.

"That I'm rude," I bashfully followed him.

"Well," he ducked under a pipe covered in bubble wrap, "she's not wrong."

I quietly grumbled to myself as I followed. Standing in the smallest and darkest room of the basement, silence settled. Taking a deep breath, Algernon turned off his light. I wanted to protest, but I didn't and soon my light followed suit. The silence started to grow into a roar, my every breath too loud in the absence of other sounds.

"Huxley, Doug, anyone, is anyone down here with us?"

"We have some questions for you," I added, trying to keep my tone even, "you told me you can't leave so you must be here."

"Boo,"

Algernon jumped because I jumped. Wheeling around I turned my flashlight on and standing there in the darkness, grinning, was Huxley.

"Hello, you called?"

"Why did you do that?" I watched as he walked between Algernon and I.

"I am a ghost, aren't I? I'd be failing my ghostly duties if I didn't scare the daylights out of someone from time to time." Crossing his arms, he looked up to Algernon, "What can I help with?"

When Algernon did nothing but stare at me, I realized it was my cue, "Huxley is standing right there," I gestured, "he wants to know what he can help with."

Algernon's eyes carefully fell to where Huxley stood, "Good afternoon, Huxley." His tour guide persona had tamed as he knelt down, "I think you were right to send Thaddeus after me. Today we were approached by someone, they told us something strange. It may be a prophecy of some sort. Since you seem to know something about what's going on, I was wondering if you'd like to try to decode it with us?"

Huxley laughed, "Does he realize he's talking to a wall and I'm over here?"

"Uh, Algernon," I took a step closer to Huxley, "he's right here."

Algernon's eyes lit up and he turned away from us entirely, holding his face with his hand, "How about you just do the talking...It's not like they want to talk with me anyway."

Huxley's smile flattened, "What does that mean," he looked back to me, "Ask Algernon what he means by that."

"Huxley wants to know what you mean by that."

Dropping his hand from his face, his head hung low, Algernon still didn't face us. "I've spent so much time down here, throwing questions into the abyss, asking, no, begging, you to show me a sign, to do anything, that would show me you're here. But I've been met with nothing more than silence for years. Why would you do that to me, if you've actually been here?" He took a shaking breath, "Why did you leave me totally alone?"

Algernon saying goodnight to nobody the night before played through my mind and along with it came a wave of heartbreak. Huxley shared the sentiment.

"I tried, but I'm not powerful enough. I can't interact with the environment, only Doug can." His voice cracked, "I'm sorry Algernon, I've been here with you every night, and when you say goodnight to me, I say it back."

Silence sat in the air and Huxley deflated.

"I wish he could hear me."

I leaned against the brick wall, "Huxley says that he's not powerful enough to do anything on this side and that he has says goodnight back every night."

Algernon turned around and I only saw it briefly in the beam of my flashlight, but I think Algernon was crying, "You do?"

"I'm sorry we've made you feel that way, I had no idea." Huxley wiped his eyes with his sleeve and extended his hand out in front of him, "I've been with you, you were never alone."

A light smile took me as I walked up to Algernon's side. Without a word, I took Algernon's hand in mine and lifted it up to Huxley's. Algernon flinched away when we made contact but then relaxed.

"It's so cold..." His voice barely above a whisper, he stared forward, "Is that?"

"Yeah," I let my hand linger on his before loosening my grip, "he's smiling at you."

Algernon smiled too and I was trapped.

Holy shit.

My heart jumping, I looked away and derailed my spiraling thoughts, "But what excuse does Doug have then?"

"I didn't want to scare him,"

When that rumble of a voice came from the utter darkness outside the gaping door that led to the rest of the basement, I flew into the opposing wall. Algernon, startled, stared at me and I stared at him before rolling my glare toward the deep space of the basement.

"Could you guys just make a normal entrance please? If you keep this up I'm going to have a heart attack and end up joining you." I pushed myself up from the wall and leaned in the doorway, looking into the darkness, "So you don't do things because you don't want to scare him?"

"Yes, just look at him,"

I glanced over my shoulder to see Algernon staring into the abyss, wide eyes and stiff, "What...what are you talking to?"

"Doug," I smiled as I looked back to the darkness, "Alright, point made."

"What point?" Defensive looked silly on Algernon.

"That you're a scardy cat."

"I am not," he stormed up to my side, boldly looking out into the dark room with me, "I'm not afraid of you."

Doug sighed.

A shadow hand emerged, a darker shade of darkness than the surroundings, as it reached forward. Carefully, Doug pinched the nose piece of Algernon's glasses and slid them right off of his face. They hovered there in the darkness, I had never seen anything like it before. As if his brain had broken, Algernon stared. A moment later, terror clicked and he went jumping back, but then the most curious thing happened.

He jumped behind me.

Standing there, looking over my shoulder at him, a mellow warmth took me with my smile, "Isn't this your job?" He just stared at me as I reached forward and plucked his glasses from the air, "Of all people, I thought you'd be able to handle something like this." Slowly and carefully, I slid his glasses back on him.

It was then that I realized there was little space between us, but I didn't mind. Pushing his glasses all the way up his nose, I admired the way they framed his eyes, even if they were stupid hipster glasses. Maybe Honore was right, I never could forget that hazel. Algernon didn't move away either, in fact, something about the closeness felt magnetic, like there was a mutual gravity. It set my blood on edge, but the sting felt good as it tore through me.

"Thaddeus?" His voice was so soft, it didn't even sound like him.

I hummed in reply, enjoying the view.

"How are you not terrified?"

A smirk took me, "I am darkness itself, the edgiest of edgelords, angst incarnate," I messed up his silver hair, "remember?"

A guy cleared his throat that was neither Huxley or Doug.

"Oh no," Huxley's hushed voice made me shudder but when I turned around, the room dropped violently in temperature and that shudder turned to shaking.

Standing there, as if he wasn't apart of this world, or any for that matter, was a young man. Somehow darker than Doug, but outlined in a blue glow so he popped from the backdrop, this young man captured my gaze and held it hostage. But he wasn't enchanting, no, he was a car crash you couldn't look away from. He was the morbid fascination, the call of the void, the moment before the trigger was pulled. Shorter than me but still larger in presence, he was of wider bone build but fit in tone. Every visible inch of skin up to his head was decorated with tattoos, a chain hanging from his belt to his back pocket, his grungy punk aura was something to worship. Eyes such a dark blue, they absorbed the darkness around us, his hair messy and black, crowned with a black round brimmed hat, he was the sort of person I wished I could be.

I wasn't one for religion, but I'd worship that.

"Return to the darkness from whence you came," Huxley said, walking up to him, "we were just starting to have fun, you don't need to show up and ruin it."

"Ruin it?" his voice like the vibrato of a bow against the thickets cord on a cello, it was both melodic and deeply unsettling at the same time, "Can I not join in?" When his eyes slid up to mine, I felt my heart stop, "Fascinating," he started toward me, "who might you be?"

Before I could answer, he reached out for me. I wasn't expecting him to be able to make contact so when he did, it took little effort for him to slam me into the brick wall and away from Algernon. Coughing, I tried to tame the terror taking over my core.

"Thaddeus," I said through clenched teeth, locking my glare on the demon of a guy before me, "and you?"

"Thaddeus, in the flesh huh?" he traced my jawline with the tip of his finger, the rest of his fist closed over his black fingerless spiked gloves, "you've caused the guide a lot of trouble, or so the legend goes." his finger dropped to my throat and he loosely laced his other fingers around my neck, "What could have possibly possessed you and instilled the audacity required for you to dare to come back?"

"Leave him alone," Doug slithered our way across the ground then crawled up the wall next to me, "fate has brought him here."

"Fate," the young man scoffed, "no such thing."

"Really," Huxley said, standing next to Algernon, "they have a prophecy or something they need help with."

"Oh?" the way his eyes dug into mine made it feel like he could see my every secret, even the things I didn't know were a secret yet, "do tell." Shoving me away from the wall, he took on a cocky stance, smirk nearly tearing his skin as he looked down to me, "It's about time, things have been painfully dull around here."

He left every sort of bitter bad taste in my mouth as I regained my composure and looked to Algernon, "There's another ghost."

Algernon looked shaken as he shifted his weight and ended up closer to me, "What is their name?"

When the ghost was absolutely set on simply standing there looking like an arrogant asshat, Huxley spoke instead, "The name he gave us is Mela, we don't associate with him much."

Doug slid to the wall closer to me, "He just showed up one day, acting like he became a king when he died. We don't even know where he came from because he won't tell us. But it's no use asking him, he likes being a mystery as if it somehow makes him intimidating or something."

Mela chuckled at that, leaning against the furthest wall in the small room.

After a moment of eye-locked tension with Mela, I looked back to Algernon, "Mela, and I think he has you beat in the asshole department,"

He shoved me and that brought a smile to my face.

"So," Mela's tone was so sharp, it sliced the air, "prophecy?"

I didn't want to oblige him simply because it was him but I had to, "Algernon, would you read the prophecy thingy?"

Taking out his phone, he blinded us both when he tuned the screen on and it blared white light into our faces. Tapping a couple times, he dimmed it then opened up what looked like a digital notepad. Written there were the words we had heard but a half-hour ago, though it felt like so much longer.

"Death." his voice ruled the basement, "Hearts intertwined, you're running out of time. The anomaly will obliterate all that it isolates. A king lies in wait, ready to seal your fate. A key that is locked in its own safe, a love since past, it's nearly too late. Beware the apple of emotion, for once it is in your eye, your demise rests in your devotion. Where it started is where it will end, an outcome that you won't intend. When shadows in the night lay, prepare, for that will be judgment day."

"How dramatic," Mela laughed, "I love it."

"It's not dramatic," Huxley said, stomping his little foot and lighting up his sneaker, "it's bad."

"Who told you this?" Doug asked, jumping to the wall behind Algernon.

"A random person," Algernon looked at me as I replied to something that he couldn't hear, "they approached us at the store and grabbed Algernon by the coat,"

"They said they could see whatever is haunting me," Algernon said, bringing his right hand up to his left shoulder, "but they wouldn't tell me what it is."

"This must have something to do with the shift in the air ever since Thaddeus showed up," Huxley looked up to Algernon, "Could you ask him what the symptoms of his haunting are? I've only ever heard him talk about it in passing to tour guests as they leave. I knew something was shadowing him, but I can't see it."

"Huxley wants to know what the symptoms of your haunting are." I watched as Algernon stiffened some, "He says he can't see it, though."

"Well," Algernon looked down, "there are the obvious that you've already witnessed Thaddeus, electronic devices act strange around me. Lights flicker, power surges, cellphones lose connection with me regularly, radios flip through channels when I walk in the room. And non-electronic things act up, too. Books fly off of shelves, cups fall off of tables, stools slide away from me, doors slam, the air gets so cold at night that I can barely sleep."

As I stood there watching him recount his life the last five years, I couldn't help but feel responsible. If I hadn't been such an asshole, none of this would happen to him.

"But there are other things I can connect to the haunting, but I have less proof. Ever since, my mind hasn't worked the same, things got darker, harder, I have perpetual nightmares. At times I feel so sick and dizzy I can barely stand, and it comes in random spurts. I'm exhausted, even when I don't do anything, like something is draining on me. Some of my more charged thoughts bounce back around in my head, like feedback on a microphone, and sometimes," his eyes met with mine, "it feels like I'm switched out of this world, dragged into a parallel one but there everything is dark and there is someone there. I've never seen them, but their voice threatens to take me away."

The air grew colder.

Algernon's eyes dropped back down, as if he was shrinking into himself. "But perhaps the most notable is what happens to those around me. Whenever someone gets close, they get sick. Like this haunting is contagious, it has destroyed the few relationships I've had since running away from home."

My heart was paralyzed, my blood still my body so cold I couldn't shiver, as I reached out toward him. "Is that why-"

"I know what's going on," Mela cut me off in such an obvious and hokey way, he was just trying to provoke me, "it must have attached itself to him when you pushed him on the vortex."

"We already know that," I took a step in front of Algernon when Mela started to approach, "and here you made me think for a moment that you actually knew something."

A brow raised, his smirk burned on his face, the car crash of a person dropped his tone, "But I know *what* it is." He stepped around me when I couldn't move, stuck in shock. "What he's describing is nothing short of a demon parasite."

"A demon parasite?" When I repeated that out loud, Algernon looked at me with such horror I wished I hadn't.

"Yes," Mela stopped uncomfortably close to Algernon and the poor tour guide had no idea, "It has latched itself to him, buried deep into his soul and is surely going to eat him up until there's nothing left."

"You're running out of time..." Huxley took a step away from Algernon, looking right up at him.

Doug got closer to Algernon as he stood there, staring at the ground, "The anomaly will obliterate all that it isolates," his glowing eyes turned on me, "things have been getting worse for him since he's been alone. He wouldn't be so alone if Malus hadn't-"

Huxley stepped on Doug's shadow tail, cutting him off as his shoe lit up, "We don't talk about him." Exhaling sharply, he looked back to Algernon and I, "The part near the ending may be referring to the vortex, that's where it started, right? The outcome may be what's going on right now, it's not like you intended for you to both end up haunted. But as for that judgment day thing, I have no idea."

"I don't think there's a safe here," Doug said, puling his shadow tail out from under Huxley's shoe, "nor is there a king. Who's stupid enough to lock the key in its own safe?"

"The apple of emotion," Mela said as he continued to hover too close to Algernon, looking right into his hazel eyes, "demise, devotion." A thought lit him up like a fire alarm, so startling it made my blood jolt, "Algernon is dying."

"What?" Algernon looked at me when I jumped and he probably could see my color drain, even in the darkness.

"Yes," Mela waved his hand over Algernon's shoulder and a black scribble, a ball of mangled black lines jolting about, faded into my sight, "that's what the prediction is saying. That Algernon is dying because he's alone. He has locked himself away in a place he thinks no one can get to because he's afraid of hurting others. Demons feed off of emotions, and he's been great at repression them all this time. Honestly, I'm surprised that he has lasted five years." He looked up to me, "That last line, when is the next full moon?"

"Who just knows that off of the top of their head?" I could barely muster the breath to speak as I looked to Algernon, "Hey, is there a calendar upstairs?"

"...why?"

"We need to know when the next full moon is."

Despite the tension, Algernon chuckled softly as he took out his phone and tapped around on it, confusing me. "It's on the thirty-first, so twenty days from now." He stepped back when he saw my hand fly to my mouth, "What, what does that mean-" he jumped, looking down to his phone, "When shadows in the night lay...judgment day,"

"Exactly," Mela stepped around Algernon and right up to me, "Algernon is going to die in twenty days if you don't do something about it."

"What can I possibly do?"

Mela seemed satisfied by my obvious distress, "Didn't you guys just meet? My, what an emotional reaction you're having about the death of a complete stranger. That is, unless," he brought the tip of his finger up to my chest and the moment he touched me, cold spread through my muscles, causing them to tighten and make it harder to breathe, "you care about him for some reason. He's really dismal, not much redeemable about him. But if you're into trash, you may be the only thing that can save him."

I wanted to yell at him, to somehow banish him to the seventh ring of hell, but I couldn't, not yet. "And how do you suppose I do that?"

Turning from me, he shrugged, "Invoke the most powerful positive emotion in him, that may drive the demon away."

I blinked, thinking for a moment, "Unadulterated rage?"

Mela actually stopped and slowly turned to look at me, brow furrowed as if I had shattered the dramatic moment he had woven in the air between us. Algernon looked equally confused as he stared at me and I felt bad for him, I'd have to explain it all later.

"No, for fuck's sake Thaddeus," Honore stepped forward from where she had been silently lingering in the shadows, "love."

Mela groaned as he started to disappear into the darkness, "Algernon is doomed."

"No he's not," I took a step after him, "I'll do it."

"Yeah well I wish you luck," Mela started to fade into nothing, "Algernon is a mess. He'll be the death of you."

When he evaporated away, no longer gracing us with his toxic presence, Huxley huffed. "Like he'd know, he's never even been around for one of the tours. He doesn't know the first thing about Algernon."

Steps creaked on the wooden floor above us, making all of us jump, ghosts included. For a moment I feared I was being sucked to a past setting again, to a time when this was a bar and not a tour agency, but then Algernon spoke.

"It's most likely another tour guide. Their shift probably starts soon," he looked to me, "but that's our cue, we can't be hanging around down here when a tour is going on." a pause later, Algernon looked around, "I'm sorry I can't see you, and I don't understand what is going on yet, but thank you for your help."

Huxley smiled, totally not about to cry, "We'll save you Algernon,"

Doug started to fade away into the darkness, "Somehow."

As Huxley started to fade, too, he looked up to me, "Algernon does know how to love, I've seen it. He's just been alone for so long, it may be hard to get to him."

Mulling over the words of the prophecy in my mind, I think I knew where to start. "I won't let it come true," I started to follow Algernon out, "I promise."

Following Algernon through the darkness, all I could do was lock my eyes on his back. Every step he took was elegant, the strength to his shoulders great, he had ruled my thoughts for the last five years. The light from the stairs caught on his silver hair, and for a moment, he was the brightest thing in the world. Stopping, I could just stare as he ascended each step as he had many times before, I'm sure. But he had always been the last one out of the darkness, this time I was the one left in the shadow. And as I took that first step out of the basement onto the stairs, I enjoyed being in his shadow.

The anomaly will obliterate all that it isolates.

If Algernon's anomaly was that scribble floating above his shoulder, then I would just have to make sure it couldn't isolate him any longer. That way the only thing it'll obliterate will be itself. If I could make just one line of that prophecy unwind, then the rest was sure to follow. The key thread to the tapestry was a sting attached to Algernon's heart.

When he turned to look back at me as I continued up the stairs, the warm hazel of his eyes bled into my colors. I wondered what would happen if I tugged on that string, what would be waiting for me on the other side? Standing mere inches away from him atop the stairs, a smile took me.

"Chartreuse,"

I raised a brow in question.

His eyes didn't leave mine, nor did he step away from me, "Earlier, you asked my favorite color."

Cocking my head, I wasn't impressed, "What the hell even is chartreuse?"

His moment of softness turned to deadpan annoyance, "Green."

"Green?" I followed him back into the main room of the box office, "Why, of all the wonderful colors in this world, is green your favorite?"

He stopped, glancing at me over his shoulder with a smile, "That, Thaddeus, will follow me to the grave."

I wanted to laugh but suddenly, that wasn't funny.

5

PROMISE

"A... seance?"

"Yes," Algernon said, his tour guide persona flying high as we stood there, faced with his horribly confused coworker, "we were just chilling in the basement with the dead."

His name was Robert, or that's what his name tag would suggest. He looked old for a young guy, maybe it was that grimace that left wrinkles he wore it so often. Salt and pepper hair, matte brown eyes, his fashion sense wasn't anything to write home about either. All around, he was an underwhelming, somewhat grouchy, presence that sort of dragged down the air and I couldn't imagine him being a tour guide.

"You know Algernon," Robert clicked around on the computer, not bothering to look at us, "something about that is hard to believe."

"Now why is that?" Algernon started to casually move toward the door and nonchalantly signaled for me to do the same.

"For an actor, you've never been good at lying."

I laughed but tried to cover it up quickly. Algernon glared at me for a moment but then his eyes lit up and he laughed too. Robert just stood there, looking at us like we were the most annoying little shits in the whole goddamn universe. But it was funny, too funny, because though what Algernon told him may have sounded like a lie, he was telling the truth.

"I think you need to recalibrate your lie detector," with a wave, Algernon started for the door, "Have a fun tour tonight,"

"Yeah," Robert clicked on the computer, "fun."

I followed as Algernon quickly left.

Standing outside, I was jarred. "There's no way it's this late."

Looking up to the starry sky, Algernon pulled out his phone, "This says it's still three in the afternoon."

I glanced to his screen, he was correct. Turning around I saw that the sign in the window that said the next tour was at 9pm.

"And if Robert just got in, that means that it's eight thirty or so."

"We lost five hours?" I turned back around, "But how?"

"It's an anomaly..." Algernon mused as he started to walk toward a crosswalk, "You said you're 21, right?"

Catching up to him, I was surprised by how well he was taking our time traveling, "Yes."

"Have anything on you that can prove it?"

"No?" I fell into step with him as we crossed the street, the moon climbing high and making my blood curdle, "I've literally been locked up since I was sixteen."

He hummed to himself as we approached a building. Its walls were pulsing, leaking the beats of dance music as lights flashed through the tinted windows. Rainbow flags flew high above it as a woman sitting on a stool outside the door looked to us. Flawless makeup, a knit hat, her blonde braid hung out from underneath it.

"Algernon," she beamed, standing up to hug him. When she sat back down, her eyes jumped to me, "Oh, and who is this?"

"Thaddeus Beau," he said as he showed her his ID and took out a ten dollar bill, "He's a run-away who is staying with me." handing the bill to the man standing by the door in a similar red outfit to the woman, he looked back to her, "With that considered, he didn't have time to take his personal effects. It was a volatile situation. When he showed up, he literally only had the clothing on his back."

"So what you're telling me," the woman's eyes rolled my way, "is that he doesn't have ID?"

"Precisely," Algernon smiled, knowing that he was causing trouble but that the same time, obviously not caring at all. "Though I've known him since he was sixteen, so I can vouch."

After eying me for a few moments, she sighed and smiled, "Alright, I trust you Algernon. Let me see your wrists." Algernon held out his right wrist, I did my left. The lady took out a stamp and stamped his wrist then picked up my right wrist instead and stamped that one. "Go have fun."

"Thank you, Christa,"

She just smiled and shook her head, shooing us through the door. I glanced behind me to see Honore waving, not following us in. When it closed behind me, I froze up. It was so loud, lights pulsating, bodies dancing in a mass as one, a huge wall of alcohol bottles, male strippers grinding on cage like bars attached to a median on the dance floor, I was stunned. Black lights above me didn't do much to my leather and darkness, but it lit up Algernon's silver tie like an amethyst in the night. It was actually sort of funny.

"Welcome to Refuge," Algernon walked up to the bar, gesturing for me to accompany him as he sat down. When I sat next to him, he went on, "This is the only place down here worth going in. We have the most strip clubs per capita in the world, and all the nightclubs to boot. But none of them are as good as this one."

A guy shoved another guy into the wall and a moment later, they were making out. That made me look around to see that the majority of the people in there were male swinging, a few drag queens scattered about. My eyes accidentally drifted up to the strippers as they did their thing and I stared for a moment before jumping and looking away.

"I know the bouncers well,"Algernon waved at a bartender from across the way that I couldn't see from where I was sitting, "I've spent a few too many nights here."

The most magnificent person I have ever seen approached us. While I knew drag queens existed, I had never met one. Lime green hair that stood nearly a foot in volume up off of their head, yellow eye shadow, green full lips and long lashes, their piercing blue eyes sat like gems in their flawless face. The sequence dress was over the top, but their bedazzled nails upstaged it. I wasn't sure how to describe this person, but a god was a good start.

"Algernon, love, it has been too long." Their gaze set to me, "Oh my, look at him."

Algernon looked at me from the corner of his eye as he slid his glasses back into place, "This is Thaddeus."

When they lit up, that person radiated glory, "What? No. *The* Thaddeus?" Bending forward to be eye level with me, they studied my soul, I could just feel it, "He's hotter than I had expected."

"Stop being a creep," he took out his wallet, "he's just a kid."

They hummed the sassiest shut down I had ever heard, "He don't look like no kid no more."

"Well..." Algernon smiled a little, "he was a kid when I met him," he looked away, "just a kid."

"Oh honey," they laughed, "you're too much. What can I get you handsome young men?"

I was officially lost as I looked to Algernon while he handed his debit card to them over the bar.

"What do you like?" Algernon turned to face me fully but when I just blinked at him, his brows raised, "oh wait. You've been..." a smirk found its way to his face, "We have a drink virgin on our hands here, Lady Spectra."

Lady Spectra laughed as they started to mess around with bottles and fruit and ice and all I could do was watch in horror. What in hell's name did he have planned for me? Algernon's smirk hadn't washed away as he watched them work, apparently enjoying himself.

Leaning over, I whispered, "What pronouns does one use to refer to a drag queen?"

"You usually used the pronouns of what they're presenting as. But it's also chill to just ask. Lady Spectra uses she and her."

"And outside of drag?"

He struggled, still watching Lady Spectra work, "I've never met her outside of this building."

Leaning away from him, I just watched in awe as she created two colorful concoctions and slid them over the counter to us. "Enjoy you two," she gave Algernon a look and he returned it in ten fold as she went to go interact with others at the bar.

Mine was pink-ish, his was electric blue.

"You don't have to drink it, but it's there if you want it." He took a sip of his through a red straw.

Looking down at it, I pulled the drink closer an after a moment of hesitation, I took a sip through my red straw. A shudder took me over as I brought my hand to my mouth. Wincing, I recoiled for a moment before swallowing properly. Algernon laughed which just made me embarrassed as I looked over to him.

"What do you think?" he took another drink.

I glared down at my cup, "It tastes how nail polish remover smells."

Algernon choked laughing on his next sip.

After regaining composure, he propped his chin up on his palm and just looked at me, all of me, "What you have there is a raspberry vodka. It won't knock you on your ass, a good first drink. But this," he gestured to his, "this is an AMF and if anyone else offers you one, say no," he took a drink, "people only ever buy these for someone they want to watch make bad decisions later."

I attempted another sip of mine but shivered despite my best effort not to, "What does AMF stand for?"

He raised his glass and I raised mine too. Clinking them together, he said, "Adios Motherfucker." Setting his glass down after a drink that was perhaps a tad too large, he looked back to me. "So, what was going on down there as I stood in awkward silence?"

"Well..." I thought over my words and took another drink to stall for a few more moments, "Between the four of them, I think we pieced something together. Can I see the text?" He took out his phone and brought it to the right screen, setting it on the counter between us, "Alright, so," my eyes scanned the screen, "The gist of it boils down to one thing," I looked up, "you."

"Well I figured as much." He took a drink, "The place where it started is the vortex and the thing about shadows is referring to the next full moon, but what else did you guys figure out?"

"Mela had a theory," I stopped myself, looking into his warm hazel eyes, debating my next words, "he thinks that you have a demon parasite attached to you and that it's what is making you feel so terrible and causing all of the strange things around you."

"Yes, I did catch that part too..." he paused after his next drink, "Did he have have ideas on how to get rid of it?"

I took another sip to stall, "He did," I took another sip and by that point it was painfully obvious what I was doing but I did it anyway, "he said that it feeds off of negative emotions, but that you're really good at repressing everything. That hasn't made it leave, so he suggests fixing the problem to chase it away,"

"Problem?"

I took a drink that lasted far too long, with each it burned a little bit less, "You didn't like it when I said it before, but you're lonely."

He set his glass down, making me jump. But what he said next startled me even more, "Yeah, I am."

I was ready to defend myself, to support my claim, to cite my sources, but then I was just left to sit there, and stare.

"I used to have people I held dear, a family, lovers, friendships that existed outside of the walls of a club. But one after another, they've all blown up in my face. I noticed the pattern, so I cut everything out. I didn't want to watch it happen again, I never want to watch it happen again. I can't." He took a drink then looked back to me, "I'm sorry that I'm such an asshole, I don't even know how not to be one anymore." He ran his hand over his face, messing up his glasses before fixing them with a sigh, "Of the two of us, you're the one who got nicer. What the hell happened to you?"

"Even a lion can be broken if it's kept in a cage long enough," I ran my finger down the side of my glass, drawing a line in the condensation, "I only acted all piss and vinegar back then because I thought in my teenage narcissism that it would somehow demand respect. My family couldn't really have given a shit less about me, so I made them give a shit. Albeit that shit was dedicated to shutting me up, but it was a shit all the same." I sat in pause, allowing the beats of the club music to fill it for me, "Then when they locked me up, I learned real quick that my attitude wasn't scaring anybody. I'm still too much of that sixteen-year-old than I'm willing to admit, though."

"I like it," he took a drink, "Thaddeus Beau, the most spitfire little punk I have ever met."

I took a drink, looking down to the counter, "You remembered my last name?"

An exasperated laugh took him, "Of course I remembered." His eyes lingered on mine, "I remembered everything about you. Your name, where you came from your age, what you were wearing, the feeling of your fist clenching my tie. I held onto those things, hoping that one day you'd come back."

I couldn't look at him, "But I thought you hated me?"

"I do," he looked up, leaning back in his chair, "but in the way that we hate a storm. We hate the wind and the rain and the snow, but do we, really? They just make us feel something out of our comfort, they make us feel alive in the most uncomfortable of ways. And as much as we say we hate them, the world would be incomplete without them." he tuned his head to the side, his hair falling somewhat out of place when he looked to me, "I spent years hoping that you were haunted, too. Not because I hate you, but because I didn't want to be alone. It's selfish, to wish suffering on another so that you can stand in solidarity. But I've been alone for so long, it was the only hope I could cling to."

I had to make sure I was still sitting in that stool for it felt as if his words had physically moved me. It took me a few moments to gather the thoughts he had scattered, surprising me with his soft tones and profound ideas. "I understand why you do it, push others away and keep up that wall. I do the same thing. But I can't help you if you don't let me. If we want to chase that thing off, we have to take away what it feeds on."

He lifted up his drink, "And what is that?"

"Your broken heart."

Sitting there, glass frozen in the air as he stared at me, Algernon was put on pause.

"I would try to let you in, but you'll just get hurt. It's only a matter of time."

I took the nearly empty glass from his hand and set it on the counter, "I take that as a challenge."

Sitting there, his hand in mine, little space between us, the pulsating lights framed him in rainbows, the music vibrated my chest in tune with my heart. I could feel it, the tug on the string of his heart, the beginnings of an unraveling tapestry.

I wonder what it would take for him to fall in love with me?

What an audacious thought. I let go of his hand and took my cup in grip instead, taking a drink. What even was love, anyway. Was it creepy to even think that I could win someone over? That was like insinuating they were a prize. I knew more than most that prizes can be earned, but love, no matter how hard you try, can never be earned. Someone has to give it to you, it doesn't matter how hard you try. A child with a cold parent will never earn the prize of love, regardless of effort.

But then how did one fall in love? Did they have to decide to, allow themselves to? I had a feeling that I was over thinking all this but I didn't know what else to do.

I looked over to him as he took off his glasses and rubbed his eyes.

Did I love Algernon?

No.

But could I?

I took another sip.

I think so.

"Non-non,"

I watched Algernon seize up so quickly it looked like it hurt as his eyes locked on someone approaching.

"Andrew," Algernon stood from his stool, any bit of vulnerability he had shown me before was gone, "I've told you before, you need to stay away from me."

"But Non-non-" Andrew was nearly falling all over himself, reaching out for Algernon.

"Don't call me that," he lifted his arm, keeping Andrew at bay, "why are you this drunk already? Go home."

"Home is lonely without you," Andrew forced himself onto Algernon, shoving his back into the bar.

The shiver that took over Algernon was visible as he tried to push Andrew away from him. Standing, dark fire snapped in my mind. Grasping onto the back of Andrew's hoodie, I yanked him back. He choked under the force, stumbling away. His glazed eyes locked on mine and I was ready for a fight. But for some reason, fighting didn't appear to be in his nature as he just stared.

"Andrew," my smile was all sorts of toxic as I stepped up to him, "let's go talk over here while Algernon uses the bathroom," Locking my arm around his neck, I yanked him into a headlock and started to drag him away.

Algernon didn't argue, storming off and disappearing into the dark backdrop of dancers and flashing lights. I took Andrew around the bar and made sure Algernon was out of sight before I let him go. He didn't fight much other than discontented whines then was left, staring at me.

"Who the fuck are you to Algernon," his eyes scanned me in the most uncomfortable of ways, "he said he was done with relationships,"

"And yet you still force yourself on him?" I pinned him to the bar, "What did you do to him that made him so closed off?"

As if I had lit the alcohol in his blood, he caught fire, "I didn't do anything to him," he shoved me back, "I just loved him, I loved him so much, but one day he changed."

Seeing his anger flair was sobering, "How long ago was that?"

My interest seemed to put him on pause, "Three years ago."

"Three?" I looked down then over toward the back to make sure Algernon wasn't near, "Would you mind telling me about what happened?"

With a roll of his eyes, he plopped down on a stool, "Yeah, I'll save you before you make the same mistakes as me."

"Oh, story time?" Lady Spectra said as she leaned over the bar and slid a drink Andrew's way, "Are we gossiping about Algernon?"

I slowly sat down, really hoping that Algernon wasn't coming back soon.

"I met him earlier that year here in the bar, he had told me that he just got out of a relationship he thought would last forever. So I knew from the start that I was a rebound, and at first I was okay with that, but there was just something about him," Andrew took a startlingly large gulp of his blue drink, "We'd come here often, dink, make out, it was great. He started staying over at my place, he said his would be weird because that's where his last had guy lived with him. Things were great, I had never been happier and really, I was thinking it would last forever too." He took another drink, nearly half of his glass emptied, "But then he stopped wanting to come here, so I'd go alone. He'd get upset with me for drinking so much but it was him that would go out drinking with me all the time in the first place. He called me an alcoholic but I hadn't been before I met him-"

My stomach dropped.

Dots started to connect.

"Did he leave you?"

"He did,"

"And he drank himself into a stupor afterward," Lady Spectra said as she cleaned the counter with a rag, "I had only ever seen him that bad once before," she swatted Andrew's shoulder with the rag, "He really did love you, you just refuse to get your shit together."

"No," Andrew took one last drink, "he was just playing with me."

"You don't mean that," Lady Spectra took the glass away from him once it was empty and turned to leave, "I'm cutting you off."

Andrew whined at her and I just sat there, eyes down, "Hey, Andrew," he got quiet and looked over to me, his blond curls disheveled and somewhat in his reddened face, "you said you were a rebound? Do you know anything about Algernon's relationship before you?"

The heartbreak that painted Andrew was so potent, it shaded the room darker. He was about to speak when someone else did.

"They lived happily ever after." We both jumped to see Algernon leaning there, arms crossed, but not particularly annoyed in appearance. It was more somber, bittersweet, mellow, as he spoke on, "You've been cut off, it's time to go home."

"Fuck you," Andrew stood but only manged to take one step before losing his balance and falling over.

Algernon laughed, but it was almost sort of cute as he bent over to help Andrew up.

"I'll call a cab for his ass," Lady Spectra said as she walked back and leaned over the counter, "it wouldn't be the first time."

"It's alright," Algernon got Andrew to his feet then continued to be his support, "he lives close, we'll take him back."

Lady Spectra looked right into my soul as I helped Algernon with Andrew, "Do not leave Algernon alone with him, he can't be trusted."

The air was chilled by her words and I could just nod in reply. Andrew didn't appear heavy, but when drunk and stumbling, he was a handful. It didn't help that my steps were becoming sloppier, the drink I downed a little too quickly starting to kick in. I noticed the same in Algernon as we walked down the sidewalk. Honore was no where to be seen but my mind wasn't with me enough to fully realize that.

"Why are you doing this to yourself, Otter?" Algernon shifted his weight to support Andrew better, "There's no way you really enjoy this."

"What would you know," he shoved Algernon some, nearly knocking all of us from our feet, "you don't have any claim to my life anymore,"

"This is true," while one would expect Algernon to be annoyed, his voice was nothing but soft, caring, a nostalgia and past bond so apparent in every syllable that it made the chilly night feel a little fuzzy, "but that doesn't mean that I don't still care about you."

Andrew scoffed, "Whatever, you're just drunk."

Algernon laughed, "And so are you, dear."

The groan that escaped Andrew was too funny, but I didn't mean to laugh. By the time I realized that I had laughed, Algernon had joined me. Looking over to him, his face somewhat red, his silver hair disheveled and shining in the moonlight, his glasses a little crooked and a soft smile, he was a sight to see. I was staring, maybe that's why I nearly walked us into traffic. I nervously looked away when I noticed Andrew was looking up my way.

"Hey, Algernon," Andrew started, his tone far more mellow than before, "who is this guy to you?"

Algernon's smile didn't fade, "Remember that guy I used to complain about, the one who was such an asshole on my tour that I'd never forget him?"

"Thaddeus Beau from Blazing Star, sixteen-year-old punk dressed in all black who was the most disrespectful piece of shit you've ever met; and if you ever meet him again, you'll kill him." He looked over to Algernon with a light chuckle, "How could I possibly forget?"

"Well, that's him."

"What?" His word was so drawn out it nearly faded into the night as he turned his head to look my way, "No. I thought he was sixteen."

"He was," Algernon led us around a corner, "five years ago."

"Oh." Andrew blinked at me like he knew that was supposed to make logical sense but at the same time like his brain was too inebriated to compute it, "That's no fair, why did he have to grow up to be hot?"

"Tell me about it," the way Algernon laughed, man I'll never forget it.

Wait.

Did he just call me-

I tripped over my own foot and almost took all three of us down.

"Are you alright, was that drink too much for you?" Algernon looked my way, genuinely concerned but I didn't know how to reply so I just shook my head.

Staring at the ground as they went back and forth about Andrew's drinking problem and his liver, I could feel my heart beat in my ears, the red on my face like I had been burned. Was it the drink doing this to me? Or was it something else?

Approaching a modest apartment building, Algernon reached into Andrew's pocket and took out his wallet. Running the wallet over the box by the door, it clicked unlocked and I reached out to open it. It was an adventure, sprinkled with laughter and stumbling, to get to the elevator. As if Algernon had done this many times before, he didn't have to ask which floor or which room, and with that came a sadness that dripped into my blood. It was cold, the sort of feeling that accompanied loss, but not just any loss. It hurt to lose something yourself, but it hurt to see that someone else has lost something and there's nothing you can do.

Eyes stuck on his door, the name plate below it looked as if a second name had been removed from under it. Andrew Otter and a scratched up blank that told a story no words ever could.

My mind caught up to the present when I saw Algernon had a key to Andrew's room on his key ring attached to his lanyard and was unlocking the door with it.

"I'll take it from here," I took on all of Andrew's wight as Algernon looked to me from the opening door.

"I don't think he'll try anything when you're here," Algernon watched as I walked Andrew into the dark apartment.

"I don't care, he apparently has in the past and he's not to be trusted," I looked back at Algernon for a moment, "he has lost the privilege of your private company,"

Algernon stared at me.

The lights in the apartment flickered on though no one touched them.

I struggled to get Andrew down a hall and it took a couple tries, but I found his bedroom. I turned on the light and that's when I froze. Pictures on the walls, on the dresser, on the desk, they were all of Andrew and Algernon. They looked so happy, in love, unbreakable. As Andrew fell over onto his bed with a heavy sigh, I couldn't help but let my eyes linger. He hadn't been this way before he met Algernon, and once he started, he couldn't stop. My mind dragged back to what Algernon said about the haunting and the way it has destroyed his life, his relationships. Was what haunted Algernon responsible for Andrew's tailspin?

Was Algernon alone because he didn't want to get close to people and have this happen again?

I was starting to step out of the bedroom door when he sat up, "Thaddeus,"

Stopping, I turned to look at him, "What is-" my words caught in my throat when I saw the tears taking him over.

"It was my fault. My drinking destroyed my relationship with Algernon, I drove him away. He begged me to stop and I couldn't, I tried but for some reason, it just has a grip on me. He said I didn't love him without the alcohol, and that wasn't totally true, but I couldn't seem to love anything else without it anymore. I don't know what happened to me," his breath hitched, running his hand over his face, "The night he left me, we got into a fight and it was like I was possessed, but I hurt him. I can't forget it, and I don't know why I did it, it wasn't me. But it was me, I raped Algernon," his voice cracked and he devolved further to sadness, "He's so frail, he couldn't fight back. I'm a monster and I'm happy he left me. But now he's alone. He was alone when I met him but now he's even more so and I'm so worried about him. I'm terrified, terrified that," he took his hand away from his face, looking up to me with desperate despair unlike anything I had ever seen before,

"terrified that he's going to step in front of a car or something."
Standing, he swayed, "Please save him from himself, I can't."
Stopping right in front of me, he put his hand on my shoulder, "I
think he could really like you, he likes bad apples."

His saddened laugh broke my heart.

Bringing my hand up to his back, I tried to make sure he
wasn't about to fall over, "But you don't seem like a bad apple,"

"Nah, I was an honor roll band kid. But the one before me,
he was as bad as they get."

"What happened to him?"

Andrew stepped away from me, "He killed himself,"
turning, he looked into my soul with his tired eyes, "and he wasn't
just Algernon's boyfriend, they were married."

My world fell out of rotation.

"His name was Malus and Algernon tried to follow him, it
just didn't work." leaning against the wall, he ran his hands over
his face again, "I'm scared I'll wake up one day and he'll be gone,
just like Malus left him."

Walking up to him, I tried to keep my voice steady, "I will
save Algernon, but you need to promise me something." he looked
up to me over his hand with glassy eyes, "Save yourself. No one

can do it for you, you have to. I think Algernon would be happy to see that, see you clean this act up. If you don't, you may be the next one to leave him behind."

Brows furrowed, another wave of sadness crashed into him a he nodded his head, a harsh shuddering breath escaping him. I pat him on the shoulder and started back out of the room.

"Algernon is being dragged down by a monster, and I'm going to slay it." I stopped by the door and did my best to smile at him, "I promise."

"Take care of him," he said, sitting on his bed, "I saw the way you look at him, don't you dare break his heart."

"The way I..." my eyes dropped to the floor, "I was just looking at him though."

"That's what is so magical about it," he ran his fingers through his hair, dragging it out of his face as he smiled at me a little, "you think it's just a look like any other, but everyone else can see what you do just by looking at you."

"But I just met him and he just met me, there's no way that I could lov-"

"Hey, dude, chill," He cut me and my flustered rambling off, "I can promise you one thing, he never stopped talking about you. I was actually jealous. Even back then, I had a feeling in the back of my head that you'd come back. It's like you two have a connection." He flopped over, "Get back to him, it's only a matter of time before he crashes and he's a sad drunk. The timer is going down."

Every step that I took out of that room shook more than the last. Algernon had loved someone enough to marry them and that person had the audacity to leave him behind? And if he had tried to follow Malus before, was he capable of trying again? While I took this seriously before, a new layer of seriousness had draped over my world. It was different than before, before it was laced with determination. It was the sort of challenge that I felt like I could fight and win against. A demon was nothing, but a demon inside Algernon's head? I didn't know how I could fight that. It was the sort of dread that took me upon realizing what Honore had done, and how I couldn't do anything to make her want to stay. If she hadn't become a ghost, I would have never seen her again.

If I didn't stop it, would the demon drive Algernon to...

Standing in Andrew's front door, eyes on the ground, Algernon looked like a statue. Every line of him was highlighted by the shadows, his silvery hair shining in the light, a reflection obscuring his glasses, he was captivating. Looking up to me, I could see the exhaustion in his eyes. It was like he was fighting a war I couldn't see. How was I supposed to fight something I couldn't see?

We were silent until we got out of the building, like something was weighing on him.

"Are you alright?" I looked over to him from the dark sidewalk before us.

"Are you...bothered?"

"Bothered?"

A beat passed as we waited for a cross walk signal, "Yeah," he dragged his gaze away from me, "I'm sure you saw in his room, the pictures he refuses to put away."

My heart shuddered, "No, I'm not bothered," we started to cross the street, "not in the slightest."

"Are you just saying that because you don't want things to be weird?" I could hear it, the tug of sadness taking down the last sound of his sentences, "I understand if you think I'm weird. You do hail from Blazing Star, it's not a place that's known for its, uh, tolerance."

I may have sighed a little too hard as we rounded a corner, the pulsating club rattling my ribs as we passed, "I know it's not, and I always hated it for that. But no, I promise Algernon, I'm not bothered, not at all..." I trailed off as I debated my next words and logic was too intoxicated to swoop in and stop me, "I'm actually starting to question my ability to walk in a straight line."

A moment passed.

I couldn't believe I just said that out loud, staring forward and unable to look his way.

Algernon was smiling, I could just hear it, "I think that's the alcohol."

I really needed that laugh, it helped me breathe again.

I hadn't realized how close we were to Algernon's apartment, maybe time just moved differently in comfortable quiet.

Or perhaps it was the alcohol.

The lights flickered as we walked in to the lobby, a different security guard gave Algernon a nonchalant nod and didn't seem too bothered by the hideous sounds the elevator made as it came screeching down to the ground floor. The doors opened with a demented ding and we got inside. I lost my balance when the elevator shot up and went stumbling to the side. Catching myself, I had Algernon pinned against the wall. His crooked glasses, his hazy hazel eyes, there was something I wanted to do.

I hovered there a moment too long.

Flying away from him, I held my face in my hand.

I knew that was the alcohol.

When the doors opened, I rushed out. It took him a few moments to follow. While I was on edge, he appeared chill, one hand in his pocket and the other spinning his key ring as he approached his door. Though I realized quickly that I was was witnessing wasn't chill, it was the moment before the meltdown. Hand shaking, he wasn't able to unlock his door. A hushed curse under his breath, he leaned his head against his door.

Walking to his side, I gently took the keys from his shaking hands and unlocked the door. The moment it was unlocked, it absolutely flew open with such force it made me jump out of my skin. The lights flickered violently, a plastic cup slid off of the counter in the kitchen, the cupboards opened and closed, the radio turned on, flickering through channels, every visible clock freaked out, it was like we had stepped into a poltergeist movie. Algernon walked through it all, the lights getting brighter as he passed, the static growing in volume as he walked by the radio.

Honore waved to me from the couch. I entered, closing the door carefully and locked it before following Algernon into the other room. I was lucky that my reflexes worked faster than my mind because before I knew it, I had caught Algernon when he went stumbling backward. Steadying him, I found myself not wanting to let go. Helping him sit on his bed, I sat down next to him.

The lights mellowed out to normal.

"I'm sorry," he fell backwards onto the bed, staring at the ceiling, "it has been a while, that drink was a little too much for me."

Looking down at him and his crooked glasses, I leaned over and took them off of him, "It's alright," folding them carefully in my hands, I looked down at them, "I'm surprised I'm as functional as I am,"

He snorted, "That's because you had a kiddie drink,"

I looked over to him and was about to bark back in banter but I was caught by his eyes, his silver bangs in his red face, the slight smile he wore.

He sat up and started toward his wardrobe, "You're a lot more grown up than I'd expect of someone who lived in one room for the last five years,"

I watched until I realized he was taking off his tie, then I looked away, "When they locked me up, my family all but abandoned me so I had to manage somehow. Though going in at sixteen and coming out at twenty-one when the rules inside stayed unchanging has been quite a culture shock. I'm like, an adult and shit."

"And your vote counts as much as mine," he turned to look at me as he unbuttoned the top button of his shirt, revealing the chain of a necklace, "Who is our current president?"

I stared at him blankly.

He laughed.

Hanging up his blazer and taking off his shoes, I wondered why he was just casually doing all that in front of me. I kept my eyes down as he got back on his bed and leaned up against his headboard. Standing, I swayed some, "I should let you sleep,"

"Can I talk with you a bit more first?"

That sentence sent a shock through me as I turned to see him making space on the bed next to him. My heart sky rocketed as I knelt down to untie my shoes. I internally cursed myself for stealing boots with so many goddamn laces. Why was I so edgy. Trying to hide the underlying buzz of my heart, I climbed up and leaned against the headboard next to him. Glancing over, I saw that the necklace Algernon wore under his shirt held a ring on the chain.

"I don't know all what Andrew told you, but it was probably true."

"He just said that he hurt you and that he's worried about you."

The sad chuckle that took him made me look his way, "I worry about me too."

Knives bloomed in my stomach, "Why is that?"

He slowly brought his hand up to his chest, "Do you ever feel like you have a hole, right here?" He grasped at the fabric of his button down, clenching it in his closed fist, "I worry about Andrew, too. I miss him. He made me feel something. I haven't felt much of anything since I left him. It's like this hole grows every day and one of these it'll out-grow me. I'll become more hole than person, perhaps I'll implode into the abyss." He slid over and leaned his head on my shoulder, making me jump as he put his hand on my chest, "I want to feel things, I want to be happy. But I'm scared. Every time things are going well, something happens. I lose them. I don't think I could survive it again, if things went bad." He took his hand back but stayed on my shoulder, "You make me feel something."

My voice was barely above a whisper, "Is it something good?"

"I don't know. At first it was hate, I was livid with you for doing this to me. But as the years passed, I realized that maybe you were just like me. I waited for you to come back, hoping that you were haunted too so that I wouldn't be alone in this. And now that you're here, I don't know what to do with myself. I don't know what you're doing, but please," he put his hand on mine on the bed between us, "please don't stop. I don't think I can save myself on my own from this, and I feel it destroying me. It's like soon there won't be anything of me left. Please," he tightened his grip on my hand, "make me feel something."

Sitting there, his hand on mine, his head on my shoulder, I stared forward. I wanted to take what he said and keep it, but as his words ran free in my mind, painting pictures that hadn't quite pulled into focus, a thought passed me by. It made my heart slow, my blood a little colder, my mind a little more sober. It was a humbling thought, one I wish I hadn't had. I didn't let go of his hand, though, despite it. Leaning my head carefully onto his as his weight grew heavier on my shoulder, I spoke softly.

"Algernon, you're drunk. Do you even know what you're saying?"

"Not really, but," he laced his fingers through mine, effectively sending my heart right back up into my throat, "I think that's exactly why I mean them. I'm so goddamn uptight all the time, and I don't even know why. Maybe if I could just say what's on my mind, even if it's nonsense, I wouldn't have these issues." His weight grew as he leaned against me as if he was starting to drift off, "You can disregard what I'm saying, sober Algernon would properly disembowel me for daring to open up even a little bit. But even if he'll never admit it, sober Algernon needs you to help him."

His hand was so fine, so delicate, so beautiful, as it sat, intertwined with mine. I realized as we sat there, that was the first time I had ever held someone's hand like that. I liked it.

"I'm not much of a protagonist but," I allowed myself to relax some, "I'll slay the dragon."

"Please don't let it eat me," his words became quieter, less sharp, as he went on, "Hey Thaddeus?"

I hummed in reply, feeling myself start to drift, too.

"What is going to happen on judgment day?"

Silence sat in the air.

I had a choice to make.

His grip on my hand grew looser.

My words were numb as they left me, "I don't know."

The lie stung to my very core.

He didn't reply.

The moment my eyes closed, I was out. I didn't dream, it was nice.

I wondered if that's what death felt like, you just close your eyes one moment, and the next you're gone.

6

ANTICIPATION

It was like I blinked, it was dark one moment then day the next, I hadn't moved all night.

My hand was in another. Looking down, I saw Algernon's hand tense, his grip tightening on mine. That's when noticed that he was trembling. Slowly sitting up from where I was leaning on him, I saw that he was still asleep, but trapped in an obvious nightmare. That look of distress, of fear, of turmoil that he wore, it made the room feel colder. When the sunlight coming in the window caught on the tears streaming down his face, a thought crashed into my mind. When Algernon welcomed me, he welcomed me to his every moment. Waking was nowhere in that sentence.

"Algernon," I gently jostled him, hoping to not startle him, "it's just a dream,"

I stopped.

I was about to say that if he woke up, everything would be fine. But images of the night before flashed through my mind, ripping like a TV show being warped by static. The things he said spun around in my head, darkening my thoughts with the weight of each one.

He flew awake, scaring the shit out of me as I jumped too.

Staring at me for a perplexed moment, it shattered when Algernon realized he was crying. Turning away from me and bringing his hand up to his face, he sighed harshly through clenched teeth. I was about to ask him if he was alright wen my ears screamed, ringing as my head pounded. Groaning, I brought my hand to my face, too, and we both sat there, writhing.

"Why are you in my bed?" His words were more of a groan than words.

I quickly stood from the bed but ended up stumbling into the wall. My head had only hurt this badly when the voice would yell at me, I had no idea what was going on. "You invited me and I must have passed out, I'm sorry,"

"I invited..." Algernon slowly turned around to look at me then sighed, "I'm so sorry." Standing, obviously stiff, he continued on that irked tone as he picked up his glasses from the nightstand where I had set them, "I'm useless when I'm drunk. Please ignore anything I said or did and I am deeply sorry if I made you uncomfortable in any way."

Standing there against the wall, I just stared at him. Pointed, well-spoken Algernon was back in stark contrast to the vulnerability I had seen the night before. His plea echoed in my mind and found its way to my heart. Pushing myself up from the wall, I followed him out of the room but I was barely able to make it to the couch before I had to sit back down. The sunlight coming in from the windows burned my very soul.

Honore laughed from where she was sitting on the next couch over, "You two were absolutely plastered last night. Now look at you, you're so hungover you can't even walk."

"Hungover?" I repeated, looking to her through my fingers. I had heard that word before, perhaps in passing or in some movie. I never really understood what it meant, though.

Algernon chuckled from the kitchen, "Indeed we are," he walked over and sat down on the couch next to me. Handing me a cup of water and a couple pills, he sat back into the cushion, "take those and drink that, it'll hopefully help."

I did as told.

"I certainly didn't miss this," he took his pills and after a few sips of water, he looked over to me. "Did I say anything particularly idiotic?"

I leaned back into the cushion next to him, "Do you...not remember?"

"I haven't been black out drunk in so long, I forgot it could happen," he ran his fingers through his hair, "I really am sorry, that was so irresponsible and unbecoming of me to do. I'm the adult here and I should have acted like it."

"I don't know," taking a drink, I smiled a little, "I had fun."

"And you don't regret it? Not even now, with this hangover?"

"Nope," I looked away, "I'll never regret last night."

The way he stared at me, the horror, made me nearly choke on my next sip.

"We didn't..." he looked to his clothing, checking the buttons, "did we?"

I was confused.

"Tell him I said no, you didn't," Honore sat there, smirking so wildly I really wondered what was going on.

"Uh," I looked back to Algernon, "Honore wants me to tell you no, we didn't."

Relief washed over him as he exhaled and stood, holding his forehead in his hand, "Holy shit..." a light laugh took him as he walked back into the kitchen, "Thank goodness. Remind me to never drink again."

"You haven't..." Honore sat back and crossed her legs, smiling, "yet."

I took another drink, utterly lost and too hungover to catch up.

"You cannot say things like that," he said as he filled up his glass with more water from the sink, "you'll give me a heart attack kiddo."

"I'm not a kid," I smiled a little, "but you're an old man."

"Ah yes," he returned and sat down next to me, now with a remote in hand, "you're just envious of my beautiful hair, aren't you?"

My smile wouldn't leave, "Definitely."

I was pleasantly surprised, I hadn't expected Algernon to be someone who maintained good nature, even while in great discomfort. Turning on the TV, we both recoiled when the volume was up too loud. He hit the mute button on the remote with a vengeance. Honore smothered her laugh and Algernon and I groaned. I glared at her, making her laugh more.

"I'm sorry," she whispered, "do I need to haunt quietly? Boo~,"

Eyes drifting back to the screen, I choked on my water. Right there staring back at me was a picture of myself. Algernon fumbled to unmute it and when he did, it was too loud again, making us cringe. Lowering the volume, he set the remote down.

"It has been two days since Thaddeus Beau, 21-year-old schizophrenic, escaped from the Evanesce care facility he was being treated at. He is considered off of his medication and dangerous, do not approach him. If you see him, call 911 immediately. Please keep an eye out, his family is concerned for his safety and well being."

I set my empty cup down and leaned forward on my knees, watching the screen as it flashed from a news room to an outdoor interview in front of what appeared to be a police station. Standing there, all the mics in her face, was my mother. She was loving the attention, I could just tell.

"Thaddy, baby, come back. It must be so scary out there. We can help you, but you have to stop hiding. We miss you and we're worried, please," her voice cracked into tears, "please come back."

A tip line flashed on the screen, leaving us all to stare at it.

"Was that your mother?" Algernon's eyes were glued to the screen as he muted it again.

"Unfortunately," I stood and walked to the kitchen, "funny how she only cares about me when it brings her attention." Filling up my water, I stared at the level as it rose and desperately tried to fight back my temper rooted in hurt.

"She's not even putting on a good act," Algernon said, standing and joining me in the kitchen, "it's distasteful, really. You obviously didn't get your charm from her." He earned a small laugh from me as he opened the pantry, "I'm sorry they're talking about you like that, saying that you're dangerous."

"They've been talking about me like that for years," I turned off the water, "but this is the first time that I don't believe them."

"Thaddy," Algernon muttered to himself as he started to mess around in the kitchen and I leaned up against the counter.

"She has never called me that in my entire life." Taking a drink, I looked down, "She doesn't even know how to pretend like she cares."

"Families are overrated anyway," he clicked a burner to life, "I never had much of one either. I'm sorry you're saddled with a shitty one, but that doesn't have to hold you back."

As I watched him meddle about, I felt bad, "Can I help?"

"I have it under control," he turned to look at me briefly, as if I had surprised him, "but thank you."

I wondered how open sober Algernon would be with me, "What happened with your family?"

He opened the fridge and grabbed some things, "Well, they were horribly abusive, beat the shit out of me, and cared more about a book than their son's life so, I ran away and never looked back."

"Was it hard, being out all on your own?"

He paused in what he was doing for a moment but didn't turn to face me, "Of course it was. I was in a new city, alone, with shockingly lacking life skills and not a whole lot to my name. But I came here for a specific reason."

"And what was that?" I tried to speak as little as possible, I didn't want to accidentally say the wrong thing and close him off since he was being open.

"The Ghost Tour," he walked back to the pantry and retrieved something, "I've always been drawn to the paranormal, but what I really love about it is the people. While I enjoy telling the ghost stories, I love hearing them more. So many different people come through that door, from so many different places with so many different lives behind them. The experiences some people share with me will stick with me. I'm uniquely situated, a story teller who is also a collector of stories. I feel like I keep a small piece of the people who give me their time, and I hope they take some of me with them, too." He did something on the stove then turned to look at me, "That way, even when I'm dead, I won't be, not really."

My blood gelled. I turned away from him, starting back to the living room, keeping my eyes down, "You come off as the sort who hates everyone,"

"Oh I do," he laughed, continuing on in the kitchen, "don't get me wrong, I find human kind to be a dumpster fire. But I'm still drawn to the heat."

He sent me off to go get ready as he made food. Before he did, he handed me some clothing.

"Andrew never did come to get back some of his stuff he had left here. You're way taller than me, but similar to him in build. These will hopefully fit you."

Something in me wasn't too pleased with wearing Andrew's clothing and was a tad disappointed that I was too tall to wear any of Algernon's. My mind wasn't with me, it was stuck on him. Was there truth in what he had said to me the night before, or was that simply the influence crushing him? I didn't really understand how this all worked. Had I said or done anything I didn't mean? If you did it while under an influence that stripped away your inhibitions, did that mean what you did was meaningless, or meant more?

I got soap in my eyes in the shower.

Hissing to myself, I ran my hand over my face, the hot water puling me out of my mind.

It didn't matter how much I thought about it, I wasn't going to find an answer.

But I had to find an answer.

Algernon greeted me, laughing at Andrew's clothing. They fit perfectly but were all sorts of lame. Not a shred of it was black. A gray button down and jeans, it was a crime really. I could feel my atoms rejecting every fiber.

We ate and I thanked him. He seemed proud of his cooking skills, it was endearing. Like he enjoyed playing house, as if he hadn't been able to in a long time. And before I realized it, sitting there across the coffee table with him, something felt warm in my chest. It was a feeling I had only briefly known. Maybe I had felt it once a long time ago before mom was a stranger, before dad was swallowed by work. It sort of felt like family.

"So," Algernon sat back, taking out his phone to look at the time, "since your face is everywhere, we're going to have issues in public. We need to do something about that," he studied me making me greatly aware of my every inch. Sitting forward some, he reached out to my head and ruffled my hair, "How do you feel about a haircut?"

I barely heard him, my heart rate vaulting more by the moment. His fingers in my hair, his playful touch, his hazel eyes, it was too much, way too much. I wanted him to never stop, to perhaps even tighten his grip. With that sensory came a flood of intrusive, yet simultaneously wonderful, thoughts. But it was right about then that I realized I needed to reply and not just be taken by his fingers in my hair.

"Would a haircut help?"

"Well," he ran his fingers through my hair again, dragging my bangs back and out of my face. Staring at me, he was definitely about to say something but for some reason, he was put on pause. Standing, he quickly turned his back to me, "You're getting a haircut." Starting out of the room, he headed toward the bathroom, "And more clothing. You look ridiculous in Andrew's."

When he disappeared into the bathroom, I was just left staring. What was that about?

Honore hummed, sitting back in the couch and crossing her legs, "Well look at you, you've got him going red."

"I what?"

Her mischievous smile, her raised brow, I didn't like where this was going, "I figured you'd end up with a thing for him, but I didn't expect him to develop the same. This is quite the plot twist."

"You're full of it." I kept my voice lower on the off chance that Algernon could hear me. "I just met him, there's no way I could have feelings for him." The shower turned on and before I could stop it my mind ran with that thought a little too far before I brought my hand up to my face and groaned.

Honore snorted, "You're so funny to watch. Someone who spent years locked up is now free and faced with a handsome guy. You must be so pent up, it's not even funn-"

"Honore." Standing, I took the dishes with me and all but stormed into the kitchen.

"I'm sorry, this is just too entertaining to watch." She situated herself around on the couch to face me, "So, what are you going to do?"

"About what?"

"The prophecy. Mela was pretty clear, the only way to save Algernon is to mend his broken heart. And from the look of it, you may stand a chance at that. But you're also right, you guys just met. So what can we do to help this along? You don't have the time to play courting games."

It took me longer than I'll ever admit to find where Algernon kept the dish soap, "But doesn't this seems weird, plotting to win someone's affecions like this is some sort of game?"

"It's not like you have any real control over his heart. But people like it when others treat them well and try for their affection. And I'm sure you'd treat Algernon nicely, so what's so bad about giving him reasons to like you? If he doesn't like you, and never will, then there's nothing you can do about that. You can't force someone to love you." She laughed, watching me wash dishes, "That's actually audacious, when you think about it. You're worried that you could somehow force him to like you just by your sheer charm."

"That's not how I meant it," a dish nearly slipped out of my hand but I managed to catch it, "I just feel like all the motivations here are wrong."

"Why do we do anything, really?" She stood and walked into the kitchen with me, "I'll help you turn today into a date and before you know it, I bet you two will be on the same romantic page."

"But-"

"You heard him last night, I know you did. He asked, no, he begged you to make him feel something," she got too close to me, "are you really going to deny him that?"

An uncomfortable shudder took me as I set the last dish on the drying rack and turned to face her, "Why are you still here? Can't you go move on and be happy or something?"

"I have a job to do," she started back into the living room and I followed her, "at first I wasn't sure what it was but I figured it out."

"Oh?" I sat down, "And what is it?"
"A secret."

She laughed when I rolled my eyes.

"I don't even know where to start, though," I leaned forward onto my knees, "I haven't exactly been in the whole romance game before."

"Let me teach you a lesson." She got up and knelt down right in front of me, "There is one key element to romance, without it you'll fail. It's one word... twelve letters... it's..." she got closer to me and hovered mere inches away from my face. I couldn't move away, trapped by her eyes. She seemed so comfortable in the moment, enjoying the eye locked silent tension. I found myself holding my breath, trapped in her gravity. It was like it lasted forever. Bringing up her slender finger, she broke the moment when she poked my nose and whispered, "Anticipation."

Bouncing back away from me with a small laugh, she returned to her seat. I was left there, fingers up to my nose, staring. She had commanded the universe in those few moments, it was like magic.

"Since you're so worried about unethically swaying him, leave the definite move up to him. You just have to do everything but. Build the tension, stack anticipation, until the ache is too much and he has to release the pressure. Not only does that leave the ball in his court to assuage your concerns, it'll be a challenge. Because while you'll be building the pressure, you can't fold under it no matter what. He has to be the first to give."

You know, I felt like there were some very dirty connotations to what was being said but I was too sheltered to catch exactly what she was throwing at me. Though I think I had the general idea. Leave him hanging over and over until he falls.

That way, if he does fall, it will be because he wanted to, not because I pushed him.

"Don't worry, I'll give you pointers since he can't hear or see me. You'll just need to make it not obvious that you're listening to me."

"What makes you an expert?" he got up and walked over to the mirror attached to his wall next to the book shelf and looked over my hair. It was long, flippy, and honestly a mess. When you live in one room, looking like a shaggy mop isn't really an issue, I suppose.

"Well of the two of us, I've kissed someone, you haven't." She stood and joined me, "So I may not be an expert, but I'm still better than you."

I brushed my hair out of my face where it had fallen when I was messing with it, "That's not a high bar."

She laughed, walking away, "You said it, not me."

Staring at myself, I realized something, "Hey, Honore. What color is chartreuse again?"

"Uh," she sat down, "green?"

I stared myself in the eye, standing there by the mirror.

The bathroom door opened up down the hallway and I jumped, quickly returned to my place on the couch. He got ready far faster than I had expected. Phone in hand, he walked back into the room and leaned in the doorway from the hallway. Sitting there, I could barely look up. I could smell his cologne and it was amazing, just... shit.

"Seems like Andrew saw that news cast also," he looked up from his phone, "he says he won't tell anyone about you and will ask the same of Lady Spectra and Christa."

I could feel the tug from the darker corner of my mind trying to pull me back to the personable blues that scared me, "What did he think about what they said about me?"

A pause held the air as he put his phone away after typing something, "That he didn't believe it, after meeting you he knows that it's not true." He walked up to me and I stood from the couch, "But unfortunately the rest of Evanesce hasn't had the pleasure of meeting you, so they won't see the same. Fear is a strong monster, people treat it like it holds the truth. So we'll just have to make you not match the pictures they're blasting everywhere."

"Will I be able to stay in hiding forever though?" I followed him as he started toward the front door, "I don't mind, I just don't know how realistically possible it is."

"Possible is a funny word," He stopped at the door, turning to look at me, "It's not like I'm going to let you go. You saw me drunk, if you try to escape I'll have no choice other than to kill you." When he saw the way I was staring at him, his serious tone cracked into a laugh, "I'm kidding," opening the door, he started into the hallway, "I think."

He laughed as I closed the door and Honore fazed through it, following us to the elevator. In suit, the elevator screamed up to his floor, lights flickering.

"Does anyone else ever notice this?" I followed him into the elevator when the door shook open.

"If they do, they've probably driven the maintenance staff out of their goddamn minds with complaints."

"But what about your friends?"

The elevator dropped faster than it had before, nearly knocking me from my feet upon reaching the ground floor.

Exiting, his tone was soft, "What friends?"

The lights flickered, following us out of the building until we were outside.

"You must have friends," I got up to his side as we walked, "there were the people at that club?"

"They are the only ones, and I just see them in that context," we rounded a corner, "I had casual friends once, nothing too deep. I can't seem to form deep friendships, there are just three kinds of people in my life: strangers, lovers, and lovers who are now strangers. I envy girls from time to time," we stopped at a cross walk, "I'll overhear their conversations, their topics that actually hold substance. Not always, but more than any male friendship I've had." We started to cross the street and he stretched, lacing his fingers behind his head, his blazer moving up with his arms, his black button down crumpling, the green threading of his tie catching the light, "why are we so fucked up?"

"I think we're afraid of getting too real, like the moment we show that we are actual human beings that is too far, too close, too real, and we need to backpedal."

"Yes," he looked up to me, dropping his arms back into place, "but why is that?"

"I don't know,"

He laughed a little, pocketing his hands, "It's ridiculous that I have to be sleeping with someone for them to be genuine with me. Isn't it tiring, holding up all these masks all the time?"

"Like you're one to talk."

"Oh?" He glanced my way, a mixture of challenge and amusement painting him, "whatever do you mean?"

"You have an acting job."

"Yes, well, I'm more me on those tours than I am anywhere else." He started toward the front doors of a building but didn't enter, just stepped off to the side, "As hard as it may be to believe, I do enjoy making people smile."

His tone made me smile. When his eyes caught on me, he smiled until he was able to regain total control of his expression and look back at me. Was he secretly adorable? I had no idea what I was going to do with myself if he was secretly adorable.

"Alright, so, Thaddeus, I have a very important question for you." before I had even fully looked at him, he had shoved me into the wall of the building we were standing next to. Leg between mine, grip on my collar, eyes sharp and dark, he stole my breath away has his tone plummeted into seriousness, "Do you trust me?"

I was about to inform him that it was hard to trust someone who just randomly assaulted me but then Honore jumped up and down in the background.

"This is a prime flirting opportunity. I'd bet money that Algernon is a bottom so this is just a front."

I wanted to ask her what she meant by 'bottom' but I couldn't because Algernon was still pinning me to the fucking wall.

"You have to overwhelm him with confidence," she stood right off to Algernon's side, "maintain fierce eye constant, tip your head down some, raise a brow then after approximately five seconds more of gazing, simply say 'yes' but like you're challenging him."

My eyes drifted over to her and I accidentally looked too done because Algernon looked off to the side, too. When he was looking away, I took a breath then tipped my head down a bit, raised my brow, and when Algernon turned back to look at me, our eyes locked. He actually appeared briefly surprised but then as the eye contact held, I could see the edge in his soften into something else.

"Yes."

Blinking at me for a moment, he shoved me away and started toward the door, pushing his glasses into place, "Terrible decision, really." He reached for the door handle and opened it for me, "Come along."

I had seen it for a moment, a fraction of an earthly rotation, the softness I knew existed in Algernon. I had witnessed it the night before, and now it was just a game of drawing it out from him when sober. As I followed him into the building, a slight smile took me.

It must have been tiring, holding up that mask all the time.

I stopped when I realized that we were in a barber shop. And it wasn't any barber shop, it was the manliest place I had ever stood in my entire life. Cutouts of magazines were plastered up the walls, grunge was the aesthetic, bold was the tone, just the obnoxious orange that recurred on the chairs and front desk and logic was enough to intimate me. I felt small in, the hairdressers themselves were of large stature, perfect hair and sprinkled with tattoos. Shrinking into Andrew's stupid shirt, I didn't know what to do with myself as I stuck close to Algernon. He tapped away on a tablet attached to the front desk and my eyes wandered until they landed on a cutout of a naked woman on the wall, then they jumped to the floor.

"Algernon," a man came walking up to us. Larger in stature. He had blue hair and easy smiling brown eyes as he pat Algernon on the back, "my favorite ghost guide, is it time for another cut already?"

"I'm actually here with someone else today," he pushed me forward despite how stiff I was, "this is my-" he paused, "uh, guest, and he, obviously, hasn't had his hair cut in forever. Can you do something with this? There's a face under all that."

Laughing, the guy bent down a little to look at me, "You bet I can. Does he have any idea what he wants?"

"Don't ask him," Algernon shoved me along as they continued to talk about me as if I wasn't there, "he'll ask for something edgy and trashy if you do. Make him look respectable, I'm sure it's possible."

Algernon said that there were only three kinds of people in his life.

I wondered which I was?

Being shoved in a barber's chair, I didn't have much of a choice. And I also didn't have much of an opinion on my hair so I didn't object. The last time I had gone out to get my hair cut, my mother had been harping at me the whole time. I couldn't even remember what for, but I'd never forget the public reprimanding for it. I probably deserved it, but still, people stared the whole time.

Algernon sat in the empty barber's chair next to mine, it wasn't very busy, as the barber put the sheet over me and clipped it behind my neck. "This is Maypon, he has been my barber since I moved here."

"That was forever ago, you were just a baby then," Maypon said as he started to run his fingers through my hair. "So, how short am I allowed to go?"

I was about to open my mouth but Algernon answered for me before I could even take a breath, "take it off on the sides, leave two thirds of the length on the top. His hair has a curl to it so if you do it right, it should just take a bit of product to make it hold nice volume."

Maypon made eye contact with me through the mirror, "That sound good to you kid?"

"Sure..."

Algernon definitely seemed to have put a lot of thought into this.

As Maypon got his scissors out, Algernon rested his head on his hand his elbow on the seat arm, "Your hair, it's so black I assumed it was dyed. Is it not?"

"Nope, never been dyed. I actually noticed that in the story about me, the dyed hair bit." Maypon started to spray my hair as he turned my head so I had to look forward and could only see Algernon through the reflection in the mirror, "Just now, you said you moved here? Where from?"

Algernon shifted his gaze to mine through the mirror, "Blazing Star. I ran away from home the day I turned eighteen."

"Why?"

He hummed quietly and I went stiff when the first lock of hair was cut off. My eyes rested on the scissors, they were black with a singular red gem on the joint.

"I'm perhaps too acquainted with the lack of tolerance that city possesses." spinning his chair around, he leaned his chin on the back of it, slowly coming to a stop as he spoke, "I was better off running to a city full of strangers alone and starting over on my own than stay there any longer. I had taken a ghost tour once on a trip here, and it never left me, hanging out in the back of my head. So the first thing I did when I got here was contact them and well, the rest is history I suppose."

I felt like there was a lot glossed over in that story.

"And so you lived happily ever after?"

The way he glanced at me as the chair stopped chilled my blood, "Yeah..."

Silence fell, the only sound filling it was the snipping of scissors.

He didn't know that I knew, he just knew that I knew he didn't want me to know.

What was I to do about this? I knew something he most definitely didn't want me to. I know I asked, but I did feel bad for knowing. It wasn't Andrew's information to give me, but I did ask more than once. So now I just had to sit there and pretend that wasn't already feeling the weight of Algernon's tragedy. My mind wandered, my eyes low and away from the mirror, as my imagination took that and ran with it. Algernon met someone, he fell in love, he trusted them, he took off his mask. He loved that person enough to move in with them, to marry them. He promised them forever and they promised the same. It was no wonder that he didn't want to let people in after he lied to him. If you can't trust the person you married, then who can you trust?

"So," Maypon's word was drawn out, perhaps trying to pull us out of the silence, "you're a guest of Algernon's?"

"That I am," my eyes wandered toward him, "he's letting me stay with him while I'm here."

"He doesn't usually put people up," he brought out an electric razor and turned it on, "you must be special."

Algernon snickered, but didn't say anything in reply.

That time when silence fell, it was heavier than the last.

"Alright," he spun the chair around, "what do you think?"

Staring at the stranger in the mirror, it took me a moment to realize that it was me. Suddenly I didn't look like a scraggly punk. I almost looked somewhat respectable. Glancing over to Algernon, I watched as his eyes rose from the floor to meet me. As if I had struck a nerve in him, he jumped and stared. Almost like a deer stuck in the headlights, his brain must have stalled.

"Well?" Maypon asked as he took the sheet off of me.

"You... you uh, you,"

"Your record is skipping," I laughed as I stood.

Algernon looked away, sharply fixing his glasses, "You read my mind."

"I figured this is what you meant," Maypon messed up the hair he had just styled as he started to the desk, "I know your type."

Algernon stopped dead in his tracks and I practically heard his heart lurch, "That's not why-"

Maypon just laughed, "Yes yes, he's just a guest, I forgot."

When I noticed that Algernon was taking out his wallet, I stepped forward, "My hair, I got it,"

"Oh yeah," he laughed, "you and what jo-"

He stopped when I pulled some bills out of my pocket and paid and tipped Maypon. Eying me the rest of the transaction, Algernon stayed quiet until he thanked Maypon and we left. Honore whistled as we stepped outside.

Looking me up and down, she circled around, "Well I'll be damned, you were secretly hot under all that hair."

"Did you..." Algernon stopped, making sure the door was closed before he continued, "rob a bank?"

"No," I looked to Algernon, ignoring Honore. "it was a gift from Honore."

He sighed, "Okay..." starting down the sidewalk, he refused to look at me, "I'll believe you." I got up to his side and he sort of glanced my way as we continued, "Now, onward to our next-"

His eyes grew, catching on something behind me and a moment later, he yanked me to the side. Crashing into the wall, he knocked the air out of himself as he held me close. A bicyclist cursed us out as they sped down the sidewalk, you know, next to the bicycle lane.

"Oh, oh, this is another good opportunity." Honore didn't even acknowledge that near disaster, she just smiled, "He's holding your hand, maintain that contact, rub the back of his hand with your thumb or something, then slowly let go and move along."

I glared at her for a moment before stepping out of Algernon's space, but didn't let go of his hand. "Are you alright?"

"Yeah, you just do not want to be hit by a bike. It hurts more than being hit by a car..." it must have been then that he realized I hadn't let go of his hand.

I wanted to roll my eyes at Honor's excitement as I tried to muster all the courage in the damn universe. But for some reason, each time that got a little less hard, like a resolve was forming, "I'm sure you'd know, Mr. Tour Guide," running my thumb over the back of his hand, I smiled at him, "Thank you, I didn't even hear them coming." Slowly I loosened my grip then lingered the touch of our fingers until his warmth was gone from my hand. Walking forward, I tried to keep my voice controlled even though my heart rate had spiked, "So, we were going somewhere else now?"

I walked quite a few steps before messy and hurried footsteps made their way to my side. "Yes, the mall around the corner. They have a store I feel like you'd like."

"Oh man," Honore laughed, "look at you, your face is blazing," she leaned over, "oh, and so is his! This plan is going wonderfully."

Methinks she was enjoying all that a little too much.

"So, Thaddeus," Algernon's words were a rare tone of interest, "tell me about your friends? You were grilling me earlier, now it's my turn."

"He's fishing for information," Honore said, skipping at my side, "this is a good sign."

"Well," I looked over to Honore, "I had one friend, and now she's a ghost, so I suppose that sums up my success rate nicely."

"There's no way she's the only one. You must have had friends from before."

"Not really," we approached a crosswalk and ended up in a small horde of stranger, "unless you count the other emo kids who all just sort of sat in a corner and grumbled about the abyss and shit. They weren't much for bonding, just competing in the pain Olympics. I played the drum set in band class, but I wasn't a cool drummer so I was just the *other* drummer guy. So yeah, no friends. As I'm sure you remember, I had a terrible attitude back then so it's safe to say that my absence from society wasn't really... a loss."

"Were things at home unsavory? You mentioned neglect earlier, yeah?"

"That's a rather," I looked over to him, my world slowing from the hum, "heavy question. Why do you care?"

"I've had years to wonder what was up with you," he opened the door to the mall, bowing slightly to me, "so please do pardon my curiosity."

Walking in, I could barely look at him. That was the silliest gesture I had even seen. "Well, not to get too dark on you, but there was a reason I wasn't allowed to stay home alone."

He followed me in, "Set something on fire one time,"

His impression of me was spot on.

But I didn't laugh.

I couldn't.

"Now it all sounds so, stupid, unfathomable really, but back then I was miserable. Mom was sleeping around, dad was too busy at work to see it. They were popular kids, cheerleader and football star, who never really grew up. I, obviously, wasn't planned and my mother doesn't know the meaning of the word responsibility so it wasn't too hard to convince myself they wouldn't miss me."

Algernon had been reaching for another door when he locked up. Hand frozen in extension, eyes wide, he was put on pause, or perhaps, petrified.

"They found me after I tried to overdose on some random pills. It obviously didn't go too well, I didn't put a lot of thought into it I suppose. But, don't get my mother wrong. She didn't drag me everywhere because she wanted me to be safe, no, one day she told me that my dying would just be too inconvenient for her so she wouldn't let me. That's when I lost the door to my room and any privacy or respect I once had the illusion of, anyway. And a therapist was out of the question because she didn't want to drive me there but she also didn't want to teach me how to drive, that would mean losing control of me. As much as I hated it there, at least in the hospital I was treated like a human. Sort of."

"Do you," he rested his hand on the handle but didn't look at me, "still feel that way? Like the world wouldn't miss you?"

"No," I laughed, "actually, well, maybe. But not in the same way," I opened the other door since he had frozen up, "the world would be better off without a punk like me," I smiled at him, "but I get a kick out of terrorizing the world so I don't care. It's stuck with me."

He stared at me so I just bowed a little, holding the door open.

"I am never letting you go home," he walked through the door and took my hand from the handle. Dragging me along with him, I stumbled, taken by surprise. "Fuck your family, they're not a family."

"What even is a family,"

A bitter laugh escaped him as he led me into a store, his grip on my hand strong, "Who knows."

When we stepped inside, I was met with black. Complete and utter edgy darkness, screamo played from the ceiling mysteriously, I was surrounded by lace and leather, by needless zippers and buckles. He laughed when I just stood there, looking around, unable to step further into the wonderful abyss.

"I thought you'd like this." letting go of my hand, it felt like he didn't want to, "Go have fun."

I pawed about, jumping from one rack to another. Personable blues had been my world for so long, I wanted to drown in the onyx. Algernon followed me around, hands in his pockets, a light bounce to his step, eyes never leaving me. I'd hold something up on occasion and he'd make fun of my trashy taste, smiling the whole time. I noticed when he nodded to employee and she smiled at him, but I pretended that I hadn't when her smile faded.

"Oh," he stopped walking then turned around, "I wonder if they still carry it?"

I followed him as he waked to a back corner of the store, "You don't dress like this, so why are you familiar with this store?"

"I used to spend a lot of time here, my- ah there it is," he pulled out a coat that while it was still emo, it was like, refined goth. It was formal, had a lot of buttons and held echos of revolutionary war aesthetics. "I never could convince him to get this one," holding it up to my chest, his knuckle accidentally brushed my jaw line briefly, sending a shiver through me that I tried to conceal, "You're way taller, you could actually pull it off." Taking me by the hand, he pulled me behind him up to a mirror in the other corner of the store, "Here," shoving it at me, he stepped back and crossed his arms.

Standing there, I took the coat off of the hook.

"Wait," his sudden word made me jump, "you can't try it on with Andrew's shit on, what was I thinking."

I didn't even move as he scurried around the store, picking up a plain black long sleeved shirt and black skinny jeans. Handing them to me, he shoved me toward a door I hadn't realized was a door until I was forced into it. It looked like a wall, a secret room of sorts.

"Try those on," and with that, Algernon and his smile closed the door.

A muffled conversation took place outside as I change out of Andrew's lame clothing and into the darkness from which I came. Sliding the coat on, the inner silk was soft and cool. I somewhat struggled to pull the front over itself, it was needlessly complex with its real buttons and fake buttons and overall design was too much but that's why I loved it. Buttoning the last on, I looked myself in the mirror. I sort of looked like a modern but also lowkey stuck to the past vampire. Opening the door wall of doom, I saw Algernon's back turned to me as he spoke with the employee as she leaned over the counter of the check-out.

"I wish I wasn't working so I could come see you. What costume are you wearing?"

Algernon shifted his weight from one leg to the other, "The same thing I always do."

"What," she slumped over onto her palm, "that's incredibly stupid. You're an attractive, young, fit dude, showing off your figure, and you're just going to bore everyone with the same thing as your other competitions?"

"I'm not showing off my figure, I'm showing off my form. And I don't really have anything else suitable."

"And yet you're always wearing some form of suit."

When he laughed, I laughed, too. Algernon startled then turned around and when his eyes met with me, he stopped. The girl at the counter whistled and I just stood there, under inspection awkwardly. Algernon said nothing his wide eyed just locked on me. His eyes rose to mine then it appeared that he had an idea. Walking back into the store, he messed around at a rotating podium display then came hurrying back. Walking right up to me, he made me step back into the wall door. Something must have tripped him, because instead of stopping, he crashed into me. The door wall opened behind me and made me go stumbling back. Algernon stumbled after me, reaching out to stop me from falling. Standing there as the door swung closed, we stared at each other.

Honore's head fazed through the door as it stopped moving, "Don't miss this opportunity. I leave this one up to you."

"I'm sorry," he stepped back from me, putting distance back as his eyes dropped, "I must have tripped on my own feet."

"What were you getting?"

His eyes fought to reach mine, "Well, you'd be surprised, the wonders these do for making someone look different."

Stepping closer to me, he slowly raised his hands then brought glasses up to my face. Sliding them on carefully, he brushed my bangs to the side and over the black frames. Looking between my eyes, a little too close, Algernon's high strung air softened.

"You clean up nicely."

A light smile took me, "You've managed to make a delinquent look respectable," stepping closer I made him step back into the door but it wasn't going to swing open that way, "What were you guys talking about?"

"Oh," the struggle to keep his tone even was real as he stood there, his back flat against the door, "I have a skating competition coming up soon. It's not a big deal, just something my rink puts on. I was thinking of dropping out."

"Because of what happens when you spin?"

He nodded a little, "I'm too scared."

"Well," I debated how straightforward I should be, Honore wasn't there to coach me this time and I only had the handful of romance movies I happen to see bits of in passing to go off of, "I think you should do it." Bringing my hand up, I pushed his glasses properly into place, the gap between us, small, "I'd love to watch. And if that does happen, then I'll be there with you. You're not alone anymore, Algernon." Dropping my hand down, I pressed it against the center of his chest lightly, "I'll fill that hole you feel right here, if you let me."

I felt his heart rate spike.

"Stay here, I'll be right back."

Leaving him speechless, I just continued to smile as I stepped around him, dragging my hand over his chest gently until I pulled the door open behind him and stepped out of the room, leaving him there. He said he didn't have anything to wear. I assumed it was formal, and my eyes had passed over something earlier. I had to stand up on my toes to reach it, but I claimed a sleek black coat. A blazer with two long tails, it was the fanciest formal thing I had ever touched. He already had a black dress shirt and pants on, so I started back toward the fitting room. But on the way I snagged black gloves and that's when I saw it. Taking the top hat from the head stand, I went back and the employee smiled at me the whole time. Opening the door, I handed the items to Algernon who appeared simply beside himself, a light dusting of red on his face.

"Your turn,"

When I closed the door with a smile, the lights flickered and the sound system started to jump. It flew through station after another, the static so loud it was jarring. My ears started to ring and at first I thought it was because of the volume, but then I heard it so loudly, I stumbled into the counter to brace myself.

No.

The lights went out entirely power to the whole mall outside was out too.

I can't do this again.

The static grew so loud, I feared it would bust the speakers.

I can't let him in.

The air hummed, like pressure was building.

I'm cursed.

The windows started to shake in their frames.

He'll be hurt too.

A window cracked.

But.

Everything stopped.

It's too late.

The static flipped channels again and left the calm air with the notes of a popular love song.

I'm in the freefall.

The door started to open.

I can only hope,

Algernon stood there, eyes low.

That he'll be there to catch me.

He forced his gaze up to mine.

And that he's strong enough that I won't crush him.

As the echoing voice faded from my mind, all that was left was him and that love song. Pushing myself up from the counter, I stepped toward him. That coat fit his frame perfectly, the darkness complementing his hair, the green of the tie highlighting the swirls of sage in his hazel eyes. Bringing my hand up to his arm, I ran it down the sleeve of the coat.

"I really like that fabric, it feels," my hand brushed against his as I took it back, "nice."

The lights turned back on.

Turning from him, I was proud of myself. The employee was beaming at me, as if her head was about to explode or something. Honore nodded my way as I went back into the fitting room to get Andrew's clothing.

"Can I buy this stuff and wear it out?" The employee nodded at me and I pulled some money out of the pocket of my leather coat in my hands.

"Get Algernon's too," Honore said, leaning over my shoulder.

My eye drifted to him as he collected his clothing and the employee caught my drift as we finished the transaction. I could just smile uncontrollably when Algernon realized what I had done.

He barked at me the whole way out of the store but it devolved into red-faced embarrassment as he begrudgingly thanked me.

"You've put me up at your house, it's the least I can do."

"It's really not a problem, I like the company..."

We walked along side in quiet but with every step, I could feel it grow. I wasn't sure what it was, but it was a weight. The kind that made itself known, but not the kind that could break you. The pings of a pinball machine caught my ear and I glanced over to see what looked like an arcade.

"That's a barcade, but minors can get in during the day." Algernon looked up to me, "Do you want to go in?"

"I used to love pinball, I haven't played in years."

He took my hand, stopping my heart as he pulled me in, "Then that's a yes."

The sort of nod he shot the bouncer and the smile he got in return spoke more than any exchange between them could have. Did Algernon just have every bouncer in the city in his pocket? There were lockers that appeared for staff use, but the bouncer let us store our folded clothing there too. When we stepped in, I was taken. Darkly lit, the walls were lined with blue and green light strips of different colors, giving the whole interior a Tron future-like atmosphere. Games sat around, everything from arcade games to pinball to newer games. A huge television display showed gaming tournament on mute and music played from the speakers. It was like we had stepped into a movie, the whole place just looked so perfect. As I followed him toward a coin machine, I admired the stools. They were black cubes, the edges lit up like they were straight out of a video game. I was ogling over a table decorated similarly when I realized that Algernon had returned with a handful of quarters.

"They do it old school here."

He shoved some at me, smirking in quite the same way I had earlier.

Following me as I scurried around the place, we talked back and forth about video games and the leaps that had been made in the last five years. Apparently that one game still didn't have a third installment and something suddenly made pixel skeletons attractive.

"And no matter what you do, do not join the literature club."

I stopped, my eyes catching on a machine that I recognized, not really paying mind to Algernon's previous statement nor the game it pertained to. "I used to be good at this," I put a coin in and Algernon hovered as I started. Entirely engulfed, I hadn't realized how close he was to me until I was close to breaking the current record on the display. I could feel his warmth, and he wasn't even touching me. The machine lit up and made sounds when I broke the record but I just kept going. I had been good at very few things in life other than being a punk, but this happen to be one of them.

I eventually lost, but only after annihilating the previous high score. Algernon dragged me to the counter to show the employee and we stood there and watched as he painstakingly slid every letter of Algernon's dumbly long name across the score board against the wall then added each and every number digit of my high score. We couldn't give him my name, unfortunately. I was on the run, after all.

With a glance between us and our fancy clothing, we were off, trying to beat any score that we could. Sometimes we played next to each other, sometimes the other would watch, and before I knew it, my mind was off of everything else. My world consisted of three things, the games, Algernon, and the smile he wore. There were no ghosts, no prophecy, no looming judgments days or growing holes. For a moment, I felt like the last five years didn't shadow my thoughts, that I hadn't run away, that my family wasn't broken. There in that place with him, I felt like someone my age should. I felt free to laugh, to smile and talk and play and banter. I was comfortable, and that was a feeling I had rarely ever felt before.

Algernon missed a shot in a game and groaned as his character flashed, re-spawning on the screen.

"Here," I put my hands on top of his, standing behind him with very little space between us as I looked over his shoulder to the screen. His hands were fine, fragile, elegant, the sort of hands that would weave the very strings that held the universe together. I ended up closer to him than I had anticipated as I was nearing the end of the level that mattered, my chest pressing into his back. His cologne took me, his warmth felt nice, and as I found myself staring at the winner screen, I also found myself not wanted to move.

I stepped back, slowly removing my hands from his.

"Hey, Thaddeus?"

"Yeah?"

He stood with his back to me for a moment before stepping around "What are you trying to accomplish? I've tried to figure it out, but you have me utterly confused."

"What do you mean?"

He started to sink into embarrassment, "I'm not sure if you're aware, but you've been giving signals you're probably not intending."

He stood with his back to the game, the winning screen flashing behind him, in the arcade shrouded by dim lights, the hum of music and the background clatter of game sound effects filled the beat. I was locked in my spot. I think I knew what signal he had caught, but I wasn't sure how it had been received. I was never great at subtlety, but any planning and tact I may have once possessed went out the window with Algernon in the room. He just caught me in a way I wasn't able to handle, and I loved being in his grip.

"Not intending?" I know Honore wanted me to drag this out, to make him drown in anticipation, but I couldn't bear it any longer, "I think I know exactly what I'm doing." I gently, slowly, pressed him into the game, my leg between his, ours eyes locked, "You asked me to do something, Algernon. No, actually, you begged." I hovered inches away from his face, "You begged me to make you feel something." I brought my hand up his side, trailing my way to his jaw, "I think I've been successful."

I wanted him to feel more than he ever had before.

There was a pressure between us, a tension, a friction.

An ache.

But this ache didn't hurt.

It was a need.

For what? I didn't know. I just knew that it was one of the most powerful things I had ever felt. I was trapped, hostage in his gravity and I could just feel it drawing me closer. I wanted nothing more than to collide with him, creating stardust in our impact.

"But," his voice shook with his every breath, though it wasn't out of fear, but from anticipation, perhaps even restraint, "you just met me."

Slowly, I took off his glasses, "I suppose. But for the last five years, there was one person who never left my mind. Someone I hated with every fiber of my heart. But that's a funny place for hatred to manifest, don't you think? Even back then," I folded his glasses, "this person made my heart jump. It had been the first time, I didn't even know what the feeling was. But," sliding the glasses slowly and carefully into his chest pocket, I brought my gaze back up to his, "now I realize what that was."

His gaze dropped to my lips then back up when I got a little closer, "I don't think you understand exactly what you're saying." He reached up, his hand fighting an undying tremor as he removed my glasses too and started to fold them, "I'm four years older than you, you have very little outside experience since you were locked up when you were just a kid. This is almost creepy," he dropped my glasses into my coat pocket, "what do you even really know about me?"

Without anything between us, I could see right into his eyes and deeply into his core. I could feel it, the hole in his chest, I could feel the gravity of it, the abyss that had taken him. I knew what I wanted to do, but I wasn't going to do it. He had to.

"I know that you care so much that you start to hate everything. I know that you've weathered a lot but still stand tall. I know it's a mask, this anger you wear, and that it's really covering up your loneliness. I know that you distance yourself from others in fear of hurting them, though you don't understand what hurts them exactly; you just know that it's you. You're willing to shoulder that anyway, to play the bad guy, but at the same time, you feel yourself being eaten away by the hole in your heart it causes." I brought my hand up to his chest again and I could feel his racing heart, "I also know that I want to fill that hole, to save you from it."

"But if that's your only motivation to... that's just the same as taking pity on me-"

"No," I smiled at him, "I am motivated to save you, because I care. I don't only care out of obligation to help you. I felt this way before any of this, before the prophecy. But like the words of it state, 'hearts intertwined'." I had to hold back a laugh as I spoke on, "It's fate, Algernon,"

The corner of his mouth twisted up, "You're ridiculous."

"I'm just dramatic." I got closer, "But I think you like it."

He laughed, gently pressing his forehead against mine, "Thaddeus Beau, the edgiest of the edge lords, what am I supposed to do with you?"

"Well," I brought my hand up to his chin, tilting his head up so that our eyes could meet again, "the ball is in your court, the next move is yours. I've put my intentions out there and if you want me to back off, I will. But if not," I was starting to succumb to the heat burning in my core, the adrenalin threatening to dump into my blood as my breath combusted in my collapsing lungs before I could speak, "if not, I'll make you feel again."

It was then that this got real. Really real. Way too real. I was inches away from him, basically saying something I never thought I would, under the influence of attraction and his gravity.

Searching my eyes for an answer, it appeared that he found it. With a light nod, he started to close the gap between us. My eyes closed when he got too close to focus on, every inch of me electrified. But then he stopped, stopping my heart with him.

He was so close to me, the smallest movement would join us.

His voice was a whisper, "May I?"

My chest tightened, my heart shuddering, trapped in a vacuum, I felt like I was going to implode.

"Yes."

His lips met mine and like a cloud breaking, adrenaline kicked into my being and tore me up in the most wonderful of ways. Stepping forward, I pressed him into the game more, bringing my arms up around him. The anticipation had shattered, the ache so overwhelming I couldn't even think. It became quickly obvious that I had never made out with anyone before, but I could just feel Algernon smiling into the kiss.

Surrendering to it, I lost myself to him and his embrace.

A roar of sounds took over the air as things grew heated. Like every game in the vicinity started hitting high scores, they dinged and played their tunes. Through my closed eyes, I could see blue and green lights flicker, I could hear the sounds of the arcade reach a roar, the music getting louder. The air was so electric, it felt like it was about to shock me. But nothing could exhilarate me the way he did when he deepened the kiss.

A sound escaped me and my hand found its way up to his head, lacing my fingers through his hair. When a sound escaped him, I swear my heart just fucking stopped. Emotions this strong shouldn't exist, something like this could end the world.

Time no longer existed.

He puled back, but it felt like it took everything in him to do so. When my eyes opened, I was stunned. Not only by the young man in front of me, by his hazy hazel eyes and red face, not only by his smirk or somewhat disheveled hair, but by our surroundings, too. As if trapped in a magnetic storm, a power surge ran through every machine and light. He didn't appear fazed, and I suppose neither was I. I was simply mystified by the anomaly.

"Are you still," his voice was soft, "cool with this?"

I turned back to look at him, "Are you kidding?"

With a slight shrug, his smirk returned to cover the light insecurity that had briefly taken him, "Just wanted to make sure that didn't feel wrong to you, since that was, obviously, your first."

Scoffing, I could just smile, "Yes well, this obviously wasn't your first and yet," I extended my arms some, gesturing to the arcade with a raised brow, "someone's excited."

He rolled his eyes at me when he laughed, taking my hand, he laced his fingers through mine then dragged me behind him. Snagging our clothing from the lockers, we ran out of the arcade. His grip was tight on my hand, and as my heart started to pick up again, my mind could only replay what had just happened. Racing through the mall, the lights above us went out, the music playing in stores as we passed grew louder, until we ran out the doors. As we ran down the sidewalk, every business we passed went dark. Yells escaped as we bolted by, making all the lights go out for a few moments. Each street light we ran under went out, every cross signal we passed flashed between the person and the hand, the traffic lights flashed like a slot machine. If his haunting was connected to his heart, then I must have been doing a good job at making him feel things.

The train passed us and we managed to run across the street and get inside the doors right before they closed. The moment they closed behind us, the lights started to flicker inside, the displays that read the stops started to malfunction. The train's bell rang out, faster than usual, and didn't stop when the train started. People were nearly thrown from their feet when the train sped off, far too fast. Standing in the last car, there were no other passengers near us. When the train jarred, I stumbled back into the wall and Algernon fell into me. Pinned there by the force of the train, his eyes locked on mine, it was only a matter of signals and moment before he kissed me again.

The rush that took me as he did made me feel more alive than I had in my entire life. Tangling my hands in his hair, pulling him closer into me, I never wanted this to stop. Once the anticipation had broken, we were left in its wake, arms around the other. It was probably a good thing no one else was in that last car with us.

"How are you so good at this," Algernon said after pulling away, panting as he leaned his forehead against mine, "you're so new to this that you're shaking."

As if my ego needed to hear that.

Stepping around him, I turned the tables and pressed him against the wall as the train screamed onward, "So are you." He looked away from me but I brought my finger up to the tip of his chin and returned his sights to mine, "you're right, I'm new, so I have an excuse. But you," I tipped his head to the side and gently kissed his neck, "you're adorable."

The shiver that took him made me smirk.

The train suddenly stopped and I went flying back. A hand grabbed my arm before I went tumbling to the floor. In that moment, I saw Algernon. One hand on a rail, the other on me, eyes simultaneously glaring and undressing me. The train's doors opened and as people picked themselves up from the ground, he pulled me out with him. Lights continued to go out as we passed and before I knew it, we were back at his apartment building.

I was surprised when he didn't let go of me, instead he dropped his hand and took mine as we walked in. The guard, the woman from before, eyed us, raised a brow, then laughed as the elevator audibly plummeted to meet us. Those moments, standing there in silence, his grip tight on mine, were so painfully long. When the doors opened, a breath escaped Algernon and he pulled me in with him. The moment those doors closed, I had him pressed into the wall again. Breaking the kiss, he leaned to the side and when he kissed my neck it shot something through me so potent my knees nearly gave out.

The elevator shot up, creaking and shaking the whole way, the lights inside flashing on and off, the numbers wrong as we passed each floor. I was barely able to pull away from him when the doors opened and his hand was in mine again, leading me along. He didn't have to unlock his door, it just flew open. Slamming shut behind us, it was a matter of muddled steps before he ended up in my arms again. Drawn to the other, it was like we had been waiting for something to feel this right our entire lives.

Stepping back, he accidentally backed up into the couch and tripped. Falling backward over the arm of it, he was left, staring up at me. Disheveled, red, panting, the image of Algernon laying there looking up at me was burned into my heart.

We were starting to reach territory entire unbeknownst to me. You couldn't get away with watching those sorts of movies in the hospital so I had never actually seen one. Getting down on the couch, I knelt over him, one hand on the cushion next to his head knees straddling one of his legs, the other hand found its way to the side of his face.

"Are you alright?"

"I haven't been this good in years." His eyes moved up to mine, drawing me in again, "You're surprisingly brazen."

"Believe it or not, this stuff has never really been on my mind before. So it must be making up for lost time, hitting all at once." I hovered right above him, barely able to focus on his eyes, "I want to make you feel everything," plunging into another kiss, this time I deepened it.

My hand on his face traced down his neck, making him shiver, until it stopped at the collar of his shirt. I was starting to try to do the top button when his hand met mine and pulled it away. I groaned into the kiss and I felt him smile. I guess one of us had to implement sensible pacing here. When his hands found their way to my back, taking the fabric into their grip as he pulled me down into him, I had to wonder how long he was going to manage that pacing though.

I was going to defeat the monster and save him, because I knew, as I lost myself to the roar of intimacy, that this was game over.

I was in love with Algernon.

And I wasn't going to live in a world without him.

7

REINFORCEMENTS

"What became of Thaddeus?"

Algernon stopped, looking over his shoulder at his tour guest, "Well, he did come back one day."

The whole tour stared, excitement lacing the air, "Really?"

Turning to face them fully, standing in the parking lot that changed our lives, Algernon tried to tame his smile but didn't do a very good job, "Yes, and I was right, he was haunted too, though we haven't been able to figure out what to do about that quite yet." turning, he went on, "I hated him every bit that I thought I would, but somehow, that punk got into my head, and with that," he stopped at the cross walk, "my heart."

"Wait, really?" One of the tour guests perked up, connecting the dots, "That's so cute."

"Yeah," Algernon's smile lit up the evening, "he's my boyfriend now."

"Is he hot?" I asked, standing next to him as we waited.

He rolled his eyes to me, smiling, "Winsome."

Staring at him as he started across the cross walk, I could hear his laugh. I'm sure he knew that I had no idea what that word meant. The tour behind me buzzed happily, whining about how cute that all was. Glancing back at the parking lot as we left, my eyes lingered on the spot. It had been a little over a week since the day I came barreling back into Algernon's world, and this was his first shift since. But just a hand full of days since the anticipation broke, and a series of nights of Algernon falling asleep against my chest, it felt like it had been so much longer. The days were counting down and we still hadn't stopped the haunting.

Honore dragged us to some witch shop, we played with charms and even brought back some sage to burn but the lights still flickered when Algernon entered a room. A plethora of internet searches turned up nothing, same with a trip to the library. Algernon refused to even come near a bible, and I doubted that held any answers anyway, but we were running out of time.

Honore spent a lot of time away, though I had no idea where she'd go.

As Algernon continued along his tour, I peeled off and started back to the historic hotel he worked out of. I had some questions that I couldn't ask in the company of his tour guests. Using the key he gave me, I slipped inside and hurried to the basement after snagging a flashlight.

"Hey, Mela," I called, my eyes adjusting to the darkness, "I did what you said to do, but it hasn't helped." Standing in silence, I let out my irritated breath that had been boiling in my core, "Mela, come talk to me godda-"

"Boo."

I flew away from the whisper behind me. Turning around, I saw Mela leaning up against the wall, laughing.

"Man, chill you. You look like you saw a ghost or somethin'."

I was obviously unimpressed a I turned to fully face him.

"So you really did it?" He pushed himself off of the wall, his tattoo images moving as if they were enchanted, his blue eyes churning with tones from the depth of the ocean, "That was fast, he must be really desperate to get laid."

I wanted to hit him but I knew it wouldn't work, "Not that it's any of your business, but he hasn't let me even take his shirt off yet."

"He probably feels weird," Mela circled me, scanning my every inch, "about being your first."

"How would you even know-"

"You scream virgin, kid." stopping in front of me, he crossed his arm in what felt like some form of challenge, "I bet he feels like he turned you, like some vampire."

"Well he didn't."

"Oh, I know that, and he knows that, but Algernon's exceptionally good at convincing himself to feel bad about things."

"You definitely talk about him like you know him, for someone who claims not to."

He shrugged, walking into the darker area of the basement, "Perhaps I lied, but I don't trust the others." he glanced back my way and I jumped, following him as we went on, "I think there's a traitor in the mix."

"A traitor?" I ducked under a low pole he simply fazed through.

"I have a theory," stopping, he turned to face me and extended his arms, "something is feeding off of the energy in this area and it's doing strange things to the people down here. But there's no way it's just here by happenstance. There must be someone pulling the strings. It's apart of the very air, the soil, like a parasite that has infected everything and is just waiting to engulf us all. I can feel it growing stronger."

I was almost afraid to ask, I didn't want to hear the answer filtered through the vibrato of his voice, but the silence scared me even more. "What do you think judgment day will be?"

"I think it's the day that Algernon dies, and whatever is haunting him is set free." He lowered his arms, pocketing his hands, "And you're the only one who can stop it."

"And I'm trying, but I don't know what else I can do."

"He must not trust himself to fall," leaning against the wall, he looked down, "I don't blame him, after what he did to Malus."

While I had been sleeping in the same bed he had, Algernon still hadn't mentioned anything about his dearly departed husband. And I felt bad, having him come up out of Algernon's company, but he wasn't telling me and I couldn't win this war without the right weapons, "Did you know Malus?"

"What has Algernon said about him?"

I leaned up against the wall next to him, "Nothing..."

A low hum escaped him, "Well, I'm not surprised. He probably doesn't want you to know that he killed his husband."

My shocked silence was my question.

"I knew both Algernon and Malus in life. They married young, were a match made somewhere but it definitely wasn't heaven. Malus was a poser, I honestly don't know what Algernon saw in him. They seemed pretty stable from the outside, but who knows what was going on in Algernon's world. Then after he met you and got his ass cursed, that's when things changed. Something about Algernon poisoned those around him, ever since then. He lost any friends he ever had, and then their relationship started to fall apart. It was hard to witness, something so perfect, disintegrate. Algernon was like a toxin, slowly ripping Malus apart by simply being around him. It was nothing Algernon actively did, I don't think, but the haunting must have messed with Malus' mind which ultimately ended in his end."

I brought my hand up to my eyes, clenching my jaw.

"I don't think he realized exactly what was going on when he fell into things with Andrew. It probably wasn't until Andrew started to lose himself too that Algernon connected the dots. That's when he shut everything out, stunting each beat of his heart. He's scared, I'm sure, he doesn't want to do the same to you. That, in itself, is a sign that he truly cares about you, which is good. But it's also a roadblock you're going to have to help him pass so that he can actually relax with you. Otherwise that key is going to stay in its own safe forever and we're going to run out of time. You have to give him a reason to stay."

The way Malus spoke about it, he made it sound like if Algernon died, the whole world would follow. That didn't really add any more weight to the situation because without Algernon, my world would end regardless. But it did make this bigger than me, bigger than us, bigger than trust.

"What do you suggest I do then..." dropping my hand from my face, my eyes lowered, "I know I'll never be anything compared to the person he married. But Malus forfeited any right to help Algernon when he left Algernon behind, so this is my job to do."

"To tell you the honest truth," he pushed himself up from the wall, "if I knew how to help him, I would have a long time ago. When I was alive, Algernon was just as much of a mystery as he is now. Malus did lose his chance, the piece of shit. Even his tattoos were trashy." he turned to look at me, "Don't tell Algernon about me, more than you already have. The last thing he needs on himself is the weight of more death. And don't tell the other ghosts about what we spoke of, either. I'm still not sure who the puppet of the demon is. We can't have them catching onto our goal to overwhelm it with love." He ran his hands through his hair, taking a deep breath as he turned away again, "What do you think of love?"

"I think it's a powerful emotion, perhaps too powerful. Strong enough to destroy the world, even." I pushed myself up from the wall, "And certainly powerful enough to kill someone."

"I agree." He started to fade away, his voice becoming more of an echo than anything else, "I want to beg you to save him from himself, but I know that in the end it has to be his choice. So all I can ask of you is to love him as much as you can and maybe he'll decide to drop that mask of his on the floor. He needs a reason to stay, and you have to become that reason. Without that, nothing will work."

"I won't give up."

When he faded away, I was left, standing in the darkness alone.

That was the most helpless feeling, knowing that no matter what I did, it wasn't up to me.

Footsteps clunked above me and I sighed. Stepping around a support beam, I hid in the darkness. Listening, I caught bits of the tour as Algernon instructed people about flashlights. It was beyond me, the amount of times he had to explain flashlights in his life. He came down into the basement and people soon followed. He went on about some history but then he sent people on their way into the abyss to investigate. He only did that when he was tired, he could speak for the entire hour down there if he wanted to.

Looking around the beam, I saw him standing back, watching people wander into the darkness. Stepping up behind him quietly, I grabbed him and pulled him around the beam with me. I manged to cut off his surprised yell with a kiss. Pulling back, I smiled at him and he quietly laughed.

"That's how you get maced."

I ran my fingers through his hair, "Are you alright? You're usually narrating right now,"

"Yeah," he let out a long breath as he leaned into me, "I'm just exhausted and I don't know why."

"I wish I could take credit for that, but," I laughed, messing up his hair as I took my hand from his hair, "you'll be done soon, I know you can do it."

"Thank you," he stepped forward and gently kissed me, "now, you're going to get me fired."

Walking around the pole and further into the basement, Algernon called out to his tour about some ghost thing and I just hung back, falling into my mind. Face in my hand, back against the beam, I didn't know what to do.

"Are you alright?"

I jumped, opening my eyes to see Huxley standing in front of me.

"Shouldn't you be playing with the tour?"

"Doug has this one," he shifted his weight, "something isn't right."

"Is that all you ever say?" I ran my hands over my face, messing up my glasses, "I know."

"It has gotten worse, exponentially so, in the last week. Doug isn't himself, I feel strange too. The energy in the air is so overbearing, I don't know how it could possibly get any worse without breaking."

"We still have a while before the end of the month, though, why is it getting so bad all of the sudden?"

"I don't know, but every night it gets worse. It swells and mellows throughout the day, but the evening is the worst. But just now, there was a spike and that's still lingering."

Screams came from the darkness and with them people ran back into the room I was in.

Algernon followed, obviously confused as he made brief eye contact with me before leaving the basement with his tour.

Huxley sighed, starting into the darkness, "Doug, what did you do? We have a rule, we don't scare nice people."

The shadows around started to twinge until they pulled together into his image on the wall. His eyes that were normally crimson, started to flicker white as I approached. That image made me stop, taking my breath away for I had seen that before.

"I don't know what's wrong with-" Doug's voice jarred, ripped and tore like an electronic scream, "it's not me, I don't-" the air became so cold, it sent a shiver through me.

People clapped upstairs.

Huxley reached out for Doug, "Is something hurting you?"

When he made contact, he yelled out.

Footsteps left above us, closing the door behind them.

A flash of white light took over the darkness, blinding me.

A thud came from upstairs.

Huxley stumbled back and away from Doug, his hand stained back. Doug glitched out, his shadow ripping until it tore apart and dissipated.

Staring forward, Huxley shook his hands and hissed, as if it stung, "I'll go chase him down and try to figure out what's going on. Keep trying to help Algernon, he needs it." And with that, Huxley disappeared too.

I was left staring there for a few moments longer before I started out of the basement. Was Doug the spy? He looked like the monster I had come into contact with years ago, the first time I was in that basement. Was that monster, the, monster? If something smaller was attached to Algernon, did that mean there was something bigger, badder, just trying to feed off of him until it kills him?

Exiting the basement, I climbed the stairs and rounded a corner.

My heart stopped.

Algernon was on his knees, the guests all gone. Running to him, I knelt at his side, putting my hand on his back.

"Are you alright?"

He fell into me and I wrapped my arms around him.

Thunder rolled outside.

"Algernon?"

He was weak, shaking, in my arms as a harsh breath escaped him, "You should stay away from me."

I tightened my grip, "What?"

"This happened before, right before," he pushed himself away and started to stand, though the struggle was visible in every movement, "I thought it could be different this time but it won't be," when his eyes locked on mine, I could see the tears budding in them, "I'm going to destroy you."

Standing too, I kept my arms out to steady him if he needed it, "No you won't,"

The bitter smirk that took him, I had never seen such an expression of self loathing before, "You underestimate me."

He took off from me, slamming drawers and putting away signs. I watched in pause as he fumed about, closing up for the night. The roll of thunder in the backdrop, I could feel the skeleton of the building quiver. What was this emotion painting Algernon? I couldn't pin it. What was going on?

He started for the door and I raced up behind him.

"Algernon, what's wrong-"

"I haven't been honest with you," I could see his persona cracking, his eyes shining, as we stood outside the door after he locked it. "you need to save yourself from me."

Thunder exploded, the bleaching light of lightning tore my vision apart for a moment. When it faded back, my ears ringing, my heart racing, I saw Algernon's back as he ran down the sidewalk away from me. I took off after him, yelling his name so loudly my voice cracked.

The cloud above broke.

Water came down in a sheet, the roar of rain deafening as I chased him. He stumbled, slipped, but he didn't stop, running so hard and fast I was terrified that he'd hurt himself. I could let him slip away from me, I was just starting to make progress.

He ran around corners, through alleys, showing no signs of stopping despite how fatigued I knew he was. Where was he leading me? Coughing, I did my best to stay in step with him, trying to close the gap, but I wasn't in the best cardio shape of my life so it was a challenge. With every step, I could feel myself falling behind. I couldn't lose him, I had to keep up. Nearly losing my footing, I stumbled and lost more ground but kept running.

It didn't matter how loudly I yelled his name, the rain down me out.

Rounding another corner, the city opened up into rolling hills and took what little breath I had left, away. I stopped for only a moment to take it in, the immense cemetery I had been faced with, before continuing to chase after Algernon into it. The grass was slippery as it was watered by the rain, making my steps sloppier as I tried to chase him up a hill.

I didn't like where this was going.

I slipped, tripping and ended up on the ground, covered in mud. I shook as I forced myself up and when I started running again, my racing heart lurched. Where was Algernon? Stepping around, I couldn't see him. Calling out, I couldn't hear my own voice over the thunder. Running forward I could feel helplessness settle into my bones but then I saw him around a tree. Running up to him, I stopped, panting so hard I couldn't speak.

My eyes dropped to the headstone we were standing next to.

Malus Amos

He had taken Algernon's last name.

"I killed him," Algernon yelled over the rain, the tears streaming down his face nearly indistinguishable from the downpour, "His name was Malus and he was my husband. I was married to him when you and I met, five years ago. And after that night, things changed. He spiraled into darkness. I don't know what I did, but I know it was my fault. The more I tried to love him, to help him, to save him, the worse he got and the sicker I felt. It got to the point where I couldn't even stand anymore, I felt so weak. I would have done anything to save him, but I didn't know I was the problem. Then one day, he killed himself in front of me. It was the only way he could escape me. Then Andrew, he was a functional adult before I met him, but being around me invoked something dark in him and I ran away before it could kill him. But it got close, I could feel it. I'm cursed Thaddeus, and the longer you stay here the worse it's going to get until you, until you too..." He devolved into tears, ripping his glasses off and bringing his hand to his face, "I killed my husband, I nearly killed Andrew, and I'm going to kill you."

He fell to his knees, crumpling under the sadness and the rain.

"It wasn't your fault," I got to my knees, too, but I didn't reach out, "it's the thing stuck to you, it's exasperating the negative things in your life to try to feed off of the darkness it creates. It's not you, it was never you, and you're not going to kill me."

"How can you still," he leaned away from me, his insecurity, frustration and anger all boiling up in the same moment, "how can you even say something like that? I killed my husband, Thaddeus. And I didn't tell you about him, that I had been married, that I drove him to suicide. You should get away while you can, how could you even-"

"I knew."

Lighting struck nearby, taking the sound away from the world with it.

As if everything slowed, the rain drops frozen in status, the thunder about to break, the air standing still, Algernon's hazel eyes stared at me.

"What?"

"Others told me. I knew about Malus, about how he died, about what happened to Andrew, about how you're scared to get close because you don't want to hurt me. I pressed you against that arcade game knowing all of this, and I didn't care." I got closer to him, "Algernon, I love you, and I promise, this time is going to be different."

His anger started to fade into the base of it all, crushing sadness, "How are you so sure?"

"Because this time we know what's causing this. This time, you're going to slay it. It wants you to suffer, it gains power from it. But you can kill it, you can make it wither away if you don't give it what it wants. If you let me in, let me help you feel, bring your heart back to life, then you'll be stronger than it. It wants a tragedy, but Algernon, you have to triumph."

His hair wet from the rain, his eyes glassy, his shoulders quivering, Algernon looked defeated, "But I'm scared. What if it doesn't work, what if it kills you? What if I let you in, just to lose you? I won't survive that, either."

"But what if," I brought my hand up to the side of his face, brushing his wet hair from his eyes, "it works? What if you defeat it and save everyone from judgment day? We woke something five years ago and it has been lying in wait. It wants to take everything you are, it wants to kill you. It doesn't want you to love, to be happy, to be strong. It has done everything it can to kill you, but it hasn't been working. And now I'm here, I'm sure it can see it in me. I am never giving up, so now it's intimidated. It's trying to take you down again because it can see that it's losing." I rested my forehead on his, closing my eyes as I pulled him closer, "Please, give yourself permission to fight. Andrew wants you to live, I want you to live, and I'm sure Malus would too if he were here." Binging my hand up to his chest, I set it flat against the wet fabric, "I would fight for you if I could, but I can't. You've been fighting for so long on your own, I don't know how you've done it. I can't fight for you, but," I hovered in front of his face, "I will fight with you. You just have to allow me."

Short of breath, dragged down by exhaustion and wet clothing, I sat there next to Algernon. The pressure in the air grew, as if lightning were to strike at any moment, as if the thunder was just waiting, as if the rain was holding back.

"Promise me that, no matter what, you won't die by your own accord."

I hovered there, able to see the fear in Algernon's eyes as clear as my own reflection in his tears.

"I promise."

A beat passed.

He kissed me.

Thunder shook the world, its vibrations in the air, as lighting struck a tree in the cemetery. The rain let loose, falling in a deluge, pelting everywhere except us. As if we were in our own space, a step out of rotation with everything else, the rain didn't touch us. Lightning struck again and again as he kissed me harder, pulling me into him with his shaking arms. I could feel the tears falling down his face, his shuddering heart in his chest, the need in his movements. He was falling apart under the pressure and he didn't want me to see.

He fell backward into the headstone, taking me with him. I was nearly in his lap when he broke the kiss, puling me into a hug. I wrapped my arms around him as he broke into pieces. I hoped I could hold his heart together as I felt the tremors take him. Algernon had been holding so much inside, I couldn't fathom the transcendent agony he must have been in all that time. He was able to repress it, that was the only way he had made it so long.

I sat there, surrounded by a barrage of lighting strikes around us, it was unlike anything I had ever seen before. Like with every pang of pain that took Algernon, the sky struck in solidarity. Trees burned around us, passionate reds like gems in the sea of personable blues the world had been tinted with.

The lightning grew closer with each strike, the thunder grew louder with every roll, and as Algernon's grip started to fade on me, all I could do was hold him closer. The paranormal and its powers invoked awe in me, and I was not audacious enough to think that I stood a chance against it.

"Thaddeus," his voice was so weak, I almost didn't realize it was his.

"Yes?"

"Thank you,"

Lightning struck us, but it didn't feel how I had expected it too. This lightning didn't hurt, it actually brought relief in its light. Algernon fell limp in my grip and I held onto him as we were surrounded in light.

"No," I smiled as my eyes glassed over. Tears escaped them as I closed them and hugged him, "thank you for fighting so hard for so long. Reinforcements are here, and we're going to win."

The light faded, the thunder subsided, the rain shopped, and I was left kneeling there. Algernon unconscious in my embrace, I held him tightly.

Birds chirped in the distance.

Taking him up onto my back, I struggled an embarrassing amount to actually get him in a way that I could carry him properly on my own. I was starting to walk away from the grave when I shiver took me. Staring forward for a moment, I hesitated, but then I turned around. Standing behind the grave was a white, cloud like, silhouette.

It nodded at me and made my heart stop.

Was that Malus?

I nodded in return and the silhouette dissipated into the air.

Every step out of there was careful, every movement calculated as to not jostle Algernon. It took me longer than I'd like to admit to find my way back to an area that I recognized. Street lights didn't flicker as we passed under, the underlying buzz in the air was gone, leaving a warmth in its wake. It was like for the first time, the area was at peace. Returning to the apartment building, the guard smiled at me sweetly when she saw that I was carrying Algernon.

The elevator was normal sounding as I pressed the call button.

"I was surprised when I saw him drag you back one day," Tasha said, leaning back in her swivel chair, "He made it a point to isolate himself for so long, I feared that was all that was left for him. I don't know how you did it, but you've made him smile again. He showed up here, all alone in this big ole city, with holes ripped in him so gaping, even I could see them. There have been others, his husband, that one nerd, but neither made him act so alive like you do."

The elevator door dinged, opening as she rolled back up to her desk.

"People don't think much of me, but I see them nearly every day. At the start of their adventure, as they return warily, and I learn a lot even if they don't intent to show it."

I stepped into the elevator, "Thank you for watching out for him even when he thought he was alone."

"He reminds me of a son I once had," she turned and smiled at me, "Now you take care of him and make sure he isn't ever alone again."

I nodded at her as the elevator door closed.

You would probably laugh if you saw how hard it was for me to open up his apartment door on my own while carrying him. Honore was inside and looked rather surprised when she saw me walk in, leaving puddles behind me.

"Do I want to know?"

"We were struck by lightning,"

She blinked at me, "What?"

I laid him down on the couch, "I think we made some progress," opening the closet, I got out a towel then came back to situate Algernon on the towel to spare the couch as much as I could. "We have a little under two weeks before judgment day. But I don't know where to go next. He's so scared of getting close," I brushed his wet bangs from his face, "but I don't think he can heal until I prove him wrong."

She joined me by the side of the couch where I was sitting, "Prove what wrong?"

"That he won't kill me." took his had in mine, "He's afraid that the thing haunting him will mess with me like it did the others, but I don't think that will happen. Since I'm haunted by something similar or at least altered by it, I think I'm immune to it."

"Well, you better not follow me." she smiled as she approached the window, "Dying isn't worth it, I promise."

I looked up to her back, "Are you alright?"

"Yeah," she turned and her smile maintained, "just dead, that's all."

I didn't necessary believe that but I also didn't feel like I had the right to pry. Instead, I occupied myself with taking my wet coat off and hanging it over a chair, "Where did you go today?"

"Today I visited your family home,"

I froze in the middle of my movement to reach for Algernon's coat, "Oh?"

"Yeah," she walked around the room, a jump to each step, "they don't seem all that concerned about you. Your mother told your grandmother that she was just waiting to hear for them to report that they found your body I the river."

When my next breath left me, it took some of me with it as I carefully removed Algernon's wet coat, "Sounds like my mother."

"She really doesn't see what she had," Honore leaned on the couch behind me, "it's a shame."

"She had a pain in the ass," I stood, ringing out my shirt, "I don't blame her for hating me."

"No, she had a punk who's trying to save the world," she followed me to the entry area and watched as I untied my shoes, "no thanks to her parenting skills. You grew into this person all on your own."

I couldn't conjure a reply as I returned to Algernon's side and stood there, faced with a dilemma.

She walked up to my side, "What?"

"Well..." I furrowed my brow, looking at Algernon, "he shouldn't spend all night in clothing that drenched, but at the same time..."

She snorted, "Oh, I see. Well what an interesting situation you have yourself here." She walked up to Algernon, that snarky smile already on her face, "On the one hand, if you leave him this way, he'll probably get sick. But on the other, what a creep you'd be if you undressed him."

"I wouldn't just be a creep," I sighed, falling against the wall and bringing my hand to my face, "doing that shit without consent is not okay..." my gaze found its way to him through my fingers over my face, "I guess I can try to wake him, but he's so tired, I feel bad."

"You'd feel worse if you undressed him,"

I groaned as I pushed myself up from the wall, she was right. Kneeling next to the couch, I wasn't sure how to go about this, "Algernon," I shook him some, "hey, you need to wake up so you can change,"

Honore hovered behind me, way too amused by this, "You may have to shake him harder than that,"

"But I..." my hands recoiled the idea of being even somewhat not gentle with him, "alright..."

Shaking him a little harder, I felt every fiber of me protest at the action. Algernon did wake, but not to any extremely coherent degree. I helped him sit up and he dragged his hands over his face.

"I'm sorry to have to wake you but, you should probably go change,"

He sighed, nodding.

Algernon with his guard down was too cute. I helped him stand and helped him to his room.

He opened his dresser and pulled out some pajamas, "I'm sorry, did I fall asleep on you again?"

"You could say that," I looked away, leaning in the door frame.

I was going out of my way to not look at him, but stay there in case he fell over or something, but then I heard him grumble some. Looking up, I could see him messing with the buttons on his shirt. I was about to ask if he needed help, but I knew for a fact that he didn't want me undressing him. He probably wouldn't have stopped me in this context, but he wasn't awake enough to consent to that. So instead I just felt awful as I clenched my jaw. He eventually got it and right when he was trying to hang the shirt up to dry, he lost his footing. My eyes jumped up without my permission and I caught him before he went falling into his dresser.

Without his dress shit, he was left with a white undershirt on. The shirt was thin, soaked, and because of that, see-through. I didn't try to stare, but my eyes had been caught by something. What at first glance appeared to be a tattoo, a black marking covered his left shoulder and stretched down his chest like veins, reaching for his heart. If I didn't know better, I would have simply thought it was a tattoo and left it at that. But that was the shoulder that the haunting resided over.

"What's that mark on your shoulder?" I asked as I helped him stand properly again.

"What marking?"

Algernon started to take off his undershirt and I turned completely around, looking at the ground. "Can you not see it? It looks almost like a black tattoo that reaches down toward your heart."

"I don't have any tattoos, I'm not you."

Not me? But I didn't have any tattoos either.

As he finished changing, my mind snagged on what he meant. I stayed silent as I picked up the pajamas I had bought at a store recently and went to the bathroom to change.

"Hey," Honore stopped me before I returned to the bedroom, "what do you think about love?"

"I think love is strong enough to kill"

She hummed a little, eyes drifting to the window as a slight smile took her "It may be, but I think it's also strong enough to resurrect."

I turned off the light then joined Algernon in the bed as I had the nights previous, though I had half a mind to stay on the couch that night as to not impose. I was just worried about him being cold, he was frigid when I made contact to help steady him. He got closer to me as I settled down and he fit right I my arms. Laying against my chest, I wondered if he could hear how slow my heart had become.

"You're so tense," he nuzzled into me, "are you okay?"

"Yeah..."

He hummed a little, "You've never been good at lying, Malus."

My heart broke in that moment.

I didn't reply.

Pulling him closer, I rested my arm on his shoulder. Relaxing, my hand slipped a little and ended up taking part of his shirt with it. That shirt he had on was much looser than the others he had worn at night. Lifting my hand to adjust it back, I accidentally made contact with his skin. That was the blackened shoulder, he was so cold. A pain shot into my hand, up through my arm, passed through my heart then went straight up to my head.

I don't think I had time to yell out, it just flipped me off like I was a light switch.

8

FOREVER

"Do you really think you can stop me?"

A voice I didn't know said, echoing around me.

My eyes opened and I was standing on a wide open plane, an abyss like room that went on forever in every direction. Looking up, I couldn't locale a light source but the whole place had a red hue, a sickly glow.

"Well, I don't know you or what you're trying to do. But yeah, I could probably stop you anyway."

"Audacious," every syllable of their word was drawn out, as if they were churning me over in their mind, "I like you."

I jumped because their voice was no longer an echo, but coming from behind me. Turning, I saw them, a black silhouette like Doug but somewhat different. The darkness that covered them was more fitted to their form, their glowing eyes were white, and on their head sat a white crown made out of what appeared to be smoke. Behind them was a throne that hadn't been there before as they stood on the steps in front of it. They looked like a king.

Staring to descend the stairs, they leisurely grew closer to me, "But you do know me, and you know what I'm trying to do." They stopped right in front of me, making the air cold, "I was banished by the King of the Netherside many years ago, but I locked some of myself in the core of this world to be forgotten about. It wasn't until someone knocked on my door, was I able to get out. But when you set me free, I was weak, I had to attach myself to something emotionally unstable. I was aiming for you but," they poked me with their long black fingertip, sending a shot of sheer agony through me, "I missed."

I stumbled back, hand clenched to my chest where they had touched, "You're what's haunting Algernon?"

"Indeed," their voice was so low it was almost distorted, "but I honestly couldn't have chosen a more repressed person if I tried." Turning, they walked back up toward the throne, "But you're fixing that problem for me, now aren't you? It's only a matter of time now," they sat down, crossing their legs regally and propped their chin up on their palm, "soon I'll be free."

The air there felt like it killed me a little more with each breath, "I know your weakness, and we're going to destroy you."

"Oh do you now? And what is that?"

"You feed off of negative emotions, so without them, you'll stave and die before you can kill Algernon." I smiled, keeping my ground as I glared at the shadow of a person sitting so leisurely on a throne as if they ruled the goddamn world, "I'll make him so happy, it kills you."

A beat passed.

They uncrossed their legs, leaning forward as their white eyes grew brighter, "Keep on thinking you know everything, see how far that gets you."

My shadow twinged underneath me then tore from my feet. Racing around, it circled me and trapped me before it froze. I stared at the figure for a moment before the shadow lunged on me. Being encased in darkness, I could feel every atom of me be dismantled. My yell was drown out by the shadows as they overtook me and the only thing I could feel above the sheer pain were the tears that streamed down my face.

Images flashed through my mind, a hospital room, pill bottles, scans, sterile chairs, a cup of water, personable blues, suffocating silence, my mother's car driving away, shattering the images and me along with them. I tasted blood as my world spun into the abyss.

"I'll see you again on judgment day."

A hand touched me and I flew up from where I had been laying, tears streaming down my face, terror consuming me. Eyes wide, the focused on the sunlight stained room around me and that's when I realized someone still had their and on my back. Turning to the side, I saw Algernon, hair somewhat amiss, eyes concerned, saying something to me that it took my mind a moment to catch.

"Are you alright?"

Nothing made a lot of sense as I wiped the tears from my eyes and nodded. The day before slowly came pulling into focus in my mind. "I am... are you?"

He looked away, sitting on the bed next to me, "Yes. I'm," he forced himself to look at me, "I'm sorry, I don't know what came over me yesterday. It feels like I'm on a yo-yo, one moment I'm composed and the next I'm a step away from detonation."

"You're fighting," I ran my had through my hair, getting my bangs out of my face, "there's bound to be ups and downs in a war, it's okay."

He gave me a small nod in reply, not really accepting or denying what I was saying, as he stood up from the bed. I watched as he looked to the calendar then jumped out of his fucking skin.

Startled, I stood, too, "What?"

"It's today,"

My blood stopped, "No... we still have two weeks-"

"Not that," he rushed to his wardrobe and pulled the fancy coat out we had gotten at the mall, "the skating competition." He rummaged through his drawers, "I thought I had another day..."

A breath of relief escaped me as I flopped over on the bed. Smiling into the sheets as I listened to him stress about, I looked forward to seeing him skate again. Getting ready for the day got a little easier with every one, I felt less like an alien and more at ease. I wasn't really sure what to call that feeling, but it was nice. Like every sound wasn't the end of the world, I could set something on the bathroom counter and not feel like the world was going to end. I could breathe for what felt like the first time in my life. As I left the bathroom, folded pajamas in hand, I entered the living room to see Algernon standing in the kitchen, ready for the day, holding two cups of tea. When he smiled at me, I finally put a word on how I was feeling.

It was like I was at home.

"Were you having a nightmare earlier?" Algernon asked, taking a drink of his tea after we finished eating.

"I barely remember it but," I looked to the carpet, trying to pull it from the back of my brain, "it didn't feel like a dream,"

"What do you mean by that?"

I sat back in the couch with my warm cup clasped in my hands, "It hurt too much to be just a dream." a flash of white shot through my head, making one of my hands sting as I hissed through clenched teeth. Then something popped back into my head, "Your left shoulder,"

He blinked at me.

I sat forward, "On your left shoulder, I could see it through your wet shirt last night, it looks like you have a tattoo."

"A tattoo?" he asked, setting his glass down and bringing his right hand up to his left shoulder covered by his white button down shirt, "But I don't have..."

"That's what you said," I set my cup down too, "And if you can't see it, but I can, that might mean that it's not of this world."

"Connected to the parasite?" When I nodded, he went on, "This shoulder has always ached since then, I figured I had just hurt myself but..." his eyes drifted back up to me, "How big is it?"

Getting up, I sat next to him on his couch. Lifting up my hand, I paused, "May I trace it out on you?" When he nodded, I carefully traced out the area I could recalled being affected by the black. Slowly, my fingertip trialled over his chest then stopped over his heart. Our eyes met and in that moment, I could see fear in his.

"That's where it hurts, what I meant by the hole." he brought his hand up over mine and I could feel his heartbeat, "right here." Closing his hand over mine, he held it for a moment before forcing a smile, "But it doesn't hurt terribly right now."

He let go of my hand, leaving it cold without his touch.

When he got up, I glared at his back, "Are you lying?"

"Well," He laughed, taking our cups to the kitchen, "it's hard to feel pain when you're numb."

I groaned, walking up behind him as he stood at the sink. Wrapping my arms around him, I leaned into him some, "I thought we had made progress yesterday,"

"I think we did," he washed one cup, "yesterday was just emotionally draining, that's all. It feels like I was hit by a truck or something."

"We were stuck by lightning."

He paused in washing the next cup, "What?"

I could just laugh.

The nerves became tangible as we got on the train, the lights violently flickering above us, the rails screaming as we moved forward.

I pressed him against the wall in the back of the empty train car, "Hey," I hovered inches away from him, "you're going to slay."

He rolled his eyes so hard I heard it.

I smiled.

"At least one of us thinks so," he rested his head on my shoulder, "Are you sure it doesn't bother you?"

"You're going to have to be more specific, but the answer is probably yes.

He sighed, long and drawn out, "That I was married,"

I wondered when that was going to come back, "Why would I mind?"

"Isn't it strange?

I hummed a little, bringing my hand up to the back of his head and pulled him closer into me, "Strange isn't the right word. I feel bad that you lost someone you loved so much, enough to want to spend forever with them. That's such an otherworldly idea to me, something I've never really thought about."

"What?"

"Forever."

The train sped up, nearly knocking me from my feet but he kept me steady. Pulling me into a hug, he tightened his grip but didn't say anything. I rested my face on his shoulder and I could feel the underlying tremor. I wondered if it was just nerves, or something more. He had been more physical with me that day. I couldn't help but ponder if it was from the nerves or if it was a step forward. I just had all the wires crossed. Walking into the mall with Algernon, I watched something happen that uncrossed some wires.

With every step, the tremor tamed, the mask rose, and by the time he interacted with someone from the rink, any hint of his nerves had vanished. It brought me comfort, knowing that he trusted me enough to show me the underneath, the storm before the rainbow. Staying a few steps behind, I observed his interactions. They were so cheery but simultaneously distant, it was an uncomfortable dissonance between friends and strangers.

We were there hours in advance so he could practice some, so I was prepared to sit by the rink and watch; but that changed when a pair of skates were shoved at me.

I held them and stared at him.

He smiled a little, setting his bag down on a bench, "See if they fit."

"I will fall and die."

"Then you'll be another pain in the ass ghost who haunts me."

"I'd love to be a pain in your ass..."

I thought I had mumbled that quietly enough as I turned that he couldn't hear me, but without missing a beat, he just casually replied, "It shouldn't be a pain if you do it right."

Gobsmacked.

Racing away from the locker area, I tried to contain my utter and absolute embarrassment as he laughed. Huffing, I sat down at a bench by the rink and burred my red face in my hands. Looking at the skates on the ground through my parted fingers, I sighed.

I couldn't help but smile.

Loving Algernon so fiercely was going to be the death of me, I swear.

After struggling to put the skates on, I sat there, terrified of standing up. Algernon eventually approached me and claimed my shoes, taking them back to his locker. When he came back, the look on his face said it all.

He knew I tied my skates incorrectly.

I knew I tied my skates incorrectly.

But was I going to admit it?

Hell no.

"So," he drawled, already mocking me, "are you ready to go out?"

"I was born ready," I tried to stand and balance was a thing of the past.

He crossed his arms, his smile lighter and brighter than it had been before today, "Sit down you dweeb."

I, begrudgingly, did as told and sat down. He knelt before me and untied my skates, "If you're not careful, tying your skates like this will lead to a broken ankle."

I studied him and his fancy clothing, his tie and coat tails, his button up and styled hair and glasses and smile, and I couldn't look away. Down to his very frame, he was elegant, refined, enchanting. When he was done, my skates were way tighter.

"Now," he stood, "that should be better."

I tried to stand again and still shook, but not as much as before. He steadied me, a laugh taking him as he took my hand.

That surprised me as I looked up to him from our hands, "Are you sure? People here actually know you, it's different than a poorly lit club."

"I'm sure," he started to pull me along with him, "now please be careful. I really don't want you to get hurt. Hold onto the bar and take it slow, alright? If you feel like you're going to fall, bend and put you hands on you knees and if you can help it, don't fall on your wrists. If you do fall, don't put your hand flat out on the ice to push yourself up, that's how you lose your fingers. Use a closed fist to push yourself up."

I tried to remember everything he had just thrown at me but it was hard to hear him over the sound of how perfect he was. I loved the feeling of his hand in mine, it made me smile. Stepping out on the ice, I immediately wondered what human thought 'hey see this dangerous slippery surface? I wonder what would happen if I tried to stand on it with a tiny blade and push myself about'. Algernon seemed wildly amused by me as I clung to the wall, terrified that one wrong move would send me crashing down. Skating literal circles about me, Algernon was just showing off of that point.

"You don't have to hang back on my behalf," I nearly slipped and clung to the wall even more, "go practice and shit,"

"If it wasn't the day of competition, I'd turn that down," he started to skate off with a wave, "you'll get the hang of it, don't die."

I would have waved back if I didn't have to hang onto the wall for dear life. Watching him, one could get too distracted and fall over.

I found that out the hard way.

Using my closed fist, I shakily pushed myself up from the ground, hoping that hadn't seen that. From what I could tell, he hadn't, so I tried to keep on. How did he manage this? Somehow we were both wearing somewhat similar skates, standing on the same ice, but one of us was struggling while the other soared. People lapped me and with every one, my pride died a little more.

"I hope you didn't hurt yourself in that fall earlier,"

I jumped, turning to look at Algernon who had silently skated up behind me, "I was hoping you hadn't noticed that,"

"I see everything," he guided at my side, eyes down on the ice, "so you're aright?"

"Only thing bruised is my ego,"

He laughed, but it wasn't as lively as he had been.

I tried to look his way but that was hard to do while also fighting to stay standing, "Are you alright?"

He nodded, slowly, as if I wasn't the only person he was trying to convince, "Just, nervous."

"I'm sure you'll do great in the competition, you look absolutely flawless out here."

A slight smile took him, "I'm not nervous about that," he looked up my way, "I'm going to win, the competition." He did some witchcraft that spun him around to face me as he skated backward as I skated forward, "I'm going to go use the restroom, don't die while I'm gone, okay?"

I was all sorts of taken aback by his tone shift and witchcraft so I just nodded and watched as he skated off and away from me. He got off the ice putting plastic hard covers on his skate blades and soon he was gone from my sight. Was he nervous about judgment day?

"Look at you go,"

That time the startle did make me lose my footing. Looking up at Honore as she smiled at me, I groaned. Shaking as I stood from the ice, I had half a mind to ignore her.

"You're quite a show, you know that?" She was able to just walk by my side on the ice, "You look all tough and edgy and tall but really you're just incompetent."

"And you're dead."

"That I am," she stretched, looking up toward the large sun dome several stories above us, "You and Algernon should get away for a few days. Enjoy each other for a bit before shit hits the fan. I think the atmosphere here is draining on the both of you. You're going to need to be on the top of your game if things go from bad to worse and you have to fight a demon or some shit."

"Go where? I don't know of anywhere since I'm not from the area,"

She shrugged, "Maybe Algernon will have somewhere he's always wanted to go."

I found myself wanting to tell Honore about what Mela said, that there may have been a compromised part among the paranormal company I kept, but I stopped myself. What if it was her? So instead we fell into silence filled by the scraping of skates.

"Are you alright?" I asked after a considerable amount of time had passed. She usually filled the gaps, teasing me, so the silence was strange.

"Yeah," that didn't sound very convincing, "just dead."

"If you could come back," I looked up to her from the ice, "would you?"

A beat dragged by, as if she hadn't really thought about that before, "No."

I nearly slipped, "Why is that?"

"I'm done, that's why I did what I did. I regret it, but at the same time, there wasn't a life for me there. I had watched so many people come and go through those doors, getting their freedom restored. I knew I'd never be one of them, my family was willing to pay anything to keep me there. But now that I have all the freedom in the world, and then some, I still feel stuck."

"You do seem to be trapped here," I had to grab the wall railing to save myself from falling, "you said you thought you knew what you needed to do? What was it?"

Her eyes studied me before she looked away, "Algernon has been gone for a concerning amount of time. I hope he's okay,"

My heart stopped when I looked around. She was right. Pounding picking back up in my chest, my mind didn't take to the sudden overwhelming panic and my thoughts flat lined for a moment. That mall was huge, I didn't know my way around, there was no way that I'd find him. Starting toward the exit of the rink, I tried to think of some plan of attack.

I slipped and hit the ice so hard my ears rang violently.

Paralyzed by pain, I couldn't move as my world blurred.

A hand extended my way, the first thing to come into focus. My eyes followed it up as the pain settled and I regained control over myself.

"I told you to not die,"

The sight of Algernon outweighed the pain with relief, "I never made any promises,"

"Actually," he helped me up, keeping me close as a light smile took him, "I believe you did."

A voice boomed over the speakers asking people to leave the rink so the ice could be resurfaced. I happily, and carefully, exited the rink and sat on a bench. Surprise took me when Algernon didn't sit next to me. Looking up to him, I saw him looking toward the locker area.

The nerves were palpable again.

"Do you need to go?"

He nodded.

I stood and pulled him into a hug, "You're going to win, remember?"

He laughed a little.

"Hey, Thaddeus, can I ask you something?"

I stepped back from the hug, concerned by his tone. Was he shaking?

"Algernon," a woman yelled from the locker area, behind a counter somewhere that I couldn't see, "we need you back here,"

Locked up, he stared at me for a couple moments before he said something hushed under his breath that I didn't catch and started back toward the lockers. I was left standing there, staring at where he had once been, wondering what unspoken question was now hanging in the air, invisible between us.

Taking a seat again, I looked out over the rink and thought about the first time I had watched him skate. He stole my breath and my and I don't think I ever got it back.

The competition started, and with every program that I watched, I was effectively unimpressed. While they each held heart, none held mine. It stated out at lower levels, with children that would definitely go far in the sport. Some of them were like four and worlds better than me. Others looked like they succumb to the nerves, the weight of all the surrounding eyes must have been overwhelming, I couldn't even imagine. As the levels started to climb and the skill grew, I wondered where Algernon fell. Adult one, two, three, four and five all came and went, and I was left wondering how many more there could possibly be. The advanced levels started and with them came an immense skill jump. Most of the skaters were girls, there were only three or four boys in the entire competition. I thought that was a shame.

"Algernon Amos," the name that had occupied my thoughts came over the speakers as the lights to the rink dimmed to an eery mood and I was left on the edge of my seat.

Music started to hum to life but no one was on the ice.

I started to get nervous.

The lights turned off and I stood.

The lights turned back on and standing in the center of the rink was Algernon.

He looked up to me, brow raised with a slight smile, and I knew what he was saying.

Watch me.

The music exploded.

I have never seen one person command a crowd like Algernon could. Whether it was on his tour or on the ice, he captivated us and held us hostage in his gravity. Like we were taken into another word, every set of eyes remotely near the rink were on him. His movements crisp, his execution perfect, his energy high, he must have known the effect he had. It was his super power, magnetism. We all fight to be seen, but he demanded it. He wasn't obnoxious, though, he was mythical. He ruled the world, though not by brute force, when he smiled he made us want to bow to him.

When he landed a jump, the surrounding people roared in cheers. Each successful move, every flashy trick, the applause grew. Building up to the climax, Algernon captivated us.

His last jump was difficult, something he rarely even landed in practice.

The crisp sound his skates made echoed as he nailed the landing.

I saw his smile of satisfaction when his eyes met with mine as he drew himself in for a spin that became so fast, I couldn't fathom how that was even possible. He was on the last move of his program, everything had been perfect. The sound of his spinning skates brought a smile to me. I hadn't been able to watch him execute a spin like that before, because the last time-

The lights flickered.

The music glitched.

The light turned off.

Everything was silent.

My world stopped.

Everything was suddenly painted in reds.

Familiar toxic air surrounding us, the shadows jarring about, Algernon and I were the only ones left in the world. But this time, Algernon didn't keep spinning, he stopped, power in every movement as he stood, center rink. His smile was daring as he looked to me, the darkness hissing inaudibly around us. Standing there, I realized something; I had a dream here.

"You're not going to defeat me," Algernon said as he glanced about as the approaching shadows that started to bleed across the ice like ink, "not this time."

I stood, barely able to breathe. His hazel eyes nearly glowed, not obstructed by anything because he wasn't wearing his glasses. As the shadows raced toward him, I raced toward the ice. I didn't know what his plan was, but I knew I didn't have one. I just knew that I had to back him up, I was the reinforcements after all.

You think you've won?

The same jarring growl I had heard in my dream roared around us, coming from everywhere and nowhere at the same time. I got onto the ice and struggled, but didn't fall. Shadows trialled me, slinking through the lines in the ice left behind by my skates.

"No," Algernon steadied me when I came, wobbling up to his side, "I know I've won."

A demented laugh ripped through the air, spiraling around us as the shadows raised from the ground. Surrounded by looming waves of black ink, they moved as if they were alive, as if they could breathe. Laying in wait, they hovered.

If you keep down this path, defeat is guaranteed.

"Why should we believe anything you have to say," I looked up and around but still couldn't find a host for the voice, "sky voice."

If I didn't know better, I would say that I heard it sigh.

I warned you.

The ink pounced on us, drowning out the reds and nullifying everything for a moment.

Inverted, the world was black, Algernon was outlined in white as if he had been rendered to lines, a piece of high contrast art. Nothing existed in that space, it was just him and I. Looking down to myself, I was outlined in the very same way.

His chuckle echoed softly as he looked around, "Well, this is new." his ability to shrug that all off was somewhat unsettling as he smiled at me, "let's add insult to injury, shall we? Would you turn around for a moment?"

I was so lost at that point that I didn't even ask and did as told.

"This thing just warned me to stop traveling down the path I'm on. And I suppose it's right, defeat is guaranteed if I don't stop. But it's not my defeat." I could hear him fiddling with something behind me, but I couldn't figure out what he was doing, "Though I find myself wanting to step further down this path, but unable to. Every time I try, I hit the same wall. So I have something to ask you, that's the only way I'll be able to move forward and defeat it." He took a breath, it was shaking. His skate scrapped oddly and a beat passed, "Turn around,"

The lights turned back on, blinding me.

As everything faded back, I was faced with quite a sight.

All eyes were on us, standing center rink as the last note of his program song reverberated around us.

"Thaddeus Beau," Algernon said, on one knee, a ring in a box in his extended hand, "will you marry me?"

Blinking at him, the gravity of what he had just said hadn't fully hit me.

I could feel the entire mall collectively holding their breath. Honore stood off to the side, hand to her mouth, but I could see that her eyes were smiling.

I know I just met him a matter of days ago,

The voice that wasn't mine echoed in my mind, trapping me in its tones.

But I have to know.

For the first time, the presence of the voice didn't cause me pain.

How far he's willing to go.

Looking down into his hazel eyes, my mind caught up.

I ran from the hospital without an end in sight, without a goal, without a plan. I knew just one thing, and it was that I had to find Algernon. I didn't know what I was to do after that, but even then I knew the only person in this world who would be able to connect with me was him. I had known that for a long time, since the very first time his hazel invaded my mind. I just didn't know what that feeling was until I was happily drowning in that hazel. And now there I was, still captivated by his color, submerged in it.

I still haven't said it... As the voice shook in my head, the tones became clearer, *I haven't told Thaddeus that I love him.*

My mind reeled, replying everything the voice had ever said. It yelled out in despair, begged to know why, it hurt and was angry and broken and erratic. It resembled a disease, it was so disturbed at times. But it wasn't sickness, it wasn't even a haunting. It was the heart of the young man before me, and it had taken me this long to realize it.

We were connected the day I shoved him into the vortex.

A slight smile took me, there was no way I was ever telling him about this.

The beat was weighing on him as he looked up at me, I could tell. This sort of power was something. Maybe that was what it felt like, to command the attention of an entire room like he did. I wanted to savor it for a moment longer, but I feared he'd be crushed under it.

Of course I knew my answer, I had no place in this world beyond his side; and I was happy there.

"Yes."

Excitement exploded around as Algernon slid the ring on my finger and that's when the embarrassment hit.

The lights flickered, a power surge so strong took the mall that everything, even the vending machines, turned off for a moment. With a flash of green, the lights returned and I was left, staring at Algernon. I had been cool, keeping my coy about me. But as he stood and faced me, I knew that had melted away. My eyes closed when he leaned forward and kissed me, wrapping his arms around me in front of the world. The lights flickered when I kissed him back, pulling him closer.

The ring on my finger felt warm.

Algernon got disqualified, but I don't think he minded. He dragged me off of the ice and it was clear that we were not staying long. Fighting through the swarming people with his personable smile and actor's wit as his weapons, Algernon freed us from the mall. His hand pulling mine behind him, my eyes were stuck on the ring. Black, simple, sleek, I wondered when he had obtained it. It almost glowed green, but it may have just been the light.

People laughed, calling out to us to have fun as Algernon dragged me out of the mall and toward a park across the street. As we ran between cars passing, the traffic light ran through the colors, the cross walk sign glitched, car alarms went off as we ran past parked ones on the side of the road. The park was a large square, existing within a city block across from the mall. Several paths all led to a plaza in the center, grass, trees, surrounded us, a small fountain sat far to our left, benches lined the path ways. It was a small calm in the middle of the city bustle.

Running around a large tree, Algernon shoved me into it with a huge smile. Pressing me into a kiss, his confidence startled me but I loved it. I pulled him closer, the sound of chirping birds comforting to hear in the city. Eyes closed, the temperature was pleasant, the world quiet, everything jut sat, suspended in that moment. Algernon was the only future I could ever want, the only place I'd ever want to be. He was the only person in the entire world who understood me, who cared, who wanted to know beyond my surface. And I was the only person in the world I could trust to not leave him, because I was the only thing I could fully control.

Stepping back from the kiss, his eyes searched mine. Brushing my hair back, he smiled and looked away, "I'm sorry, that came out of nowhere, I just needed to know-"

"How far I'd go?"

His eyes slowly moved back to mine.

I couldn't help but smile at him, "Are you pleased with my answer?"

"Yes, but," he leaned against the tree next to me, "you don't have to actually marry me. I just needed to know if you meant what you said yesterday." He leaned his head back and looked into the sky, "I couldn't allow myself to take it to heart until I knew."

"I want to," I took his hand, pulling him up from the tree, "where's the court house?"

"What?"

I looked back to him as I dragged him toward the path, "Yeah, so I can marry you."

"Thaddeus, we can't just-"

"Why not?" stopping, I tightened my grip on his hand, "Give me a reason."

When he just stared at me, my smile only grew.

Sighing, he looked away and tried to hide his smile, but I could see it, along with the red taking his face, "We'll need two witnesses."

I looked to Honore who was standing a bit away, looking at the fountain.

He laughed, "Living witnesses."

"Oh."

Taking the lead, he dragged me along his side, "We'll figure it out."

Falling into step with him, I could barely contain my smile. Every day had become an unpredictable adventure and I loved it.

Not all that long ago, I was stuck in routine, trapped in monotony and personable blues. Perhaps this was reckless, perhaps it was stupid and I was just too young and too dumb and too destructive. But as I followed him out of that park, I didn't care.

Two strangers charmed by Algernon, a registrar, boring paperwork, and a kiss later, tears streamed down my smiling face. Honore stood, smiling, looking at the ground, in the back of the room. As I pulled Algernon in my embrace, my eyes caught on her. She had been quiet.

I woke up that day, Algernon in my arms, and I was going to fall asleep that night, with a husband to my name.

Things were happening so fast, the world spinning into oblivion. It was dizzying, as Algernon dragged me onto a train, but I didn't mind. With bags in our hands, we watched his apartment building disappear into the distance. I wanted to forget about it, the impending doom. The possibility of failure, of defeat, of falling to the demon, of losing everything. I just wanted to focus on one thing and that was the young man pinned against the back wall of the train. His hazel and careful hands, his elegance and wit, his insecurities and fears, I wanted to be trapped by it all, forever.

I didn't know where he was taking me, and I didn't care.

We rode the train for a long time, most of it spent talking of somedays and happily ever afters. If we won, what would we do?

Where would we go? Who would we be? What dreams could we achieve? I had never had goals before, never even though happily ever after was a choice. But now there I was, sitting on a train, holding the hand of the young man I had just promised forever to, and suddenly it all came into focus.

The train stopped and we ended up on a bus, the buildings turned to trees, the sun setting on the day. Algernon leaning on my shoulder, he played with our intertwined fingers as our hands sat together on our legs between us.

"Is Honore still here?"

I looked up to her as she sat in the seat in front of us, "Yeah,"

She turned around to look at Algernon as he spoke on, "Where is she?"

I gestured to her seat and he made his best effort to look at someone he couldn't see, "Thank you for helping get Thaddeus to me," he sat up from my shoulder, "I doubt the dolt would have had the mind about him to do that on his own. I'm sorry that I can't see you, I truly wish that I could. And I really like your name, it's beautifully unique."

She smiled, leaning on the back of her seat, "Thanks, my mother gave it to me."

Algernon seemed confused when I laughed.

"Thank you for not kicking him out in the cold that night, he definitely deserved it."

I glared at her as Algernon shoved me a bit, "What is she saying?"

"She thanked you for not kicking me out that first night,"

"Aw, that's no fair, how dare you censor me." She draped over the back of her chair, eyes never leaving Algernon, "It seems I was right, there was a sweetheart under all that. I really like Algernon."

"She really likes you,"

Honore jumped and now she was glaring at me, obviously embarrassed as I chuckled.

"I wish I could have met her, I think I would have really liked her, too."

Her eyes sat on Algernon again, a small smile taking her.

"I doubt she's going anywhere, she'll haunt my ass for all eternity," I laughed, sitting back in my seat some, "maybe someday you'll be able to see her."

Honore turned around in her chair, and at the time, I didn't think too much of it.

My eyes caught on the window and I jumped forward, "Whoa," I just about crawled over Algernon, who had the window seat, as I looked up at the sky. It had been so long since I could see the stars, being trapped in the city. And even though they were still faint from light pollution, they took my breath away.

Two people laughed at me, making me embarrassed as I looked back at Algernon and Honore.

They'd never know, but as they smiled at me, they spoke in unison, "You're too cute."

Staring at them, a smile found me.

Yes, if things could just stay this way forever, that would be happily ever after.

The bus left us at a trail head in what appeared to be a forested area. It was so dark, though, I couldn't see much of anything else. But then I really couldn't see anything when Algernon put his free hand over my eyes.

"I feel like this is the part when you kill me."

Algernon laughed as he led me along, "Do you trust me?"

"I... suppose so."

"Oh man, I'm offended,"

"Is that right?"

He navigated me without a hitch and my shoes left the dirt and started onto wood. Was I on a deck? I wasn't sure as he led me a few more steps. Stopping, he took a pause before removing his hand.

"Set down your bag," he said as it sounded like he set his down on the wood.

I did as told and stood there, my eyes still closed.

"Okay..." I could hear his smile, "you can look now."

I had probably never been closer to a heart attack in my entire life. Standing on a bridge, well over a hundred feet up, a waterfall to my left, rolling forested hills to my right, Algernon above me, it was the most beautiful place I had ever been.

Stepping forward, he brought his hand up to the side of my face, eyes searching mine. He paused, as if he was about to kiss me then decided against it when his eyes lit up and he smiled, "Look up."

I knew the stars were beautiful, but I would have never fathomed that they could look like that. I had spent so much time in that cage of a room, it was freeing to stare up into oblivion.

Humbled by my insignificance in comparison to the overwhelming everything, I stood there, simply a speck. Algernon stepped into me, his hug gentle.

Funny, he was a speck, too, but to me, he was everything.

Aware of the ring on my finger, I brought my hand up to the back of his head and hugged him back, "Are you alright?"

He hummed quietly, "Never been better,"

The sound of the water cascading on filled my ears, but the absence of sound was even louder. I hadn't noticed just how deafening the city background chatter was until it was suddenly gone. I could feel the air, like the quiet was a tangible object insulating us alone in that moment in time. Nothing beyond us and that water existed. The stars as my witness, I closed my eyes and vowed to make Algernon the happiest person to ever live.

He shifted some, "What are you thinking about?"

"How my parents would flip shit if they knew I had a husband."

Stepping back from the hug, he shook his head with a smile, taking me by the hand, "Your parents are trash."

We picked up our bags.

"That's an insult to that wrapper on the ground over there," I smiled as Algernon led me over the bridge and onto another path, "So... are we just going to indefinitely wander into the abyss or..."

"No, my family has a cabin out here. They never use it and I haven't been here in nearly a decade, but I did swipe an extra key before I left home. Since I can't get too far away from town without feeling awful, I couldn't think of anywhere else to take you,"

My blood gelled, I had totally forgotten, "Are you feeling okay, we must be pretty far out to see the stars like this,"

"I am for now, but," he turned to look at me, "I don't want you to worry about that. We're on our honeymoon, after all,"

"Our, wait, what-"

A cabin appeared out of seemingly nowhere and actually managed to startle me as we stepped around the base of a huge tree. It was quaint, cute, but two stores despite its small appearance. I had never seen a log building like that before, and I had definitely never been in a cabin before either. Leading me up to the door, Algernon dug for his keys. I held onto our bags as he unlocked the honey wooden door and with a creak, he pushed it open.

"I'm going to go explore," Honore said as she started to wander into the trees, "this place is too pretty to not."

"Stay safe,"
She laughed, looking back at me, "I'm dead, Thaddeus,"

And with that, she disappeared into the night.

I followed him inside and was met with homey walls, pictures hanging, several couches near a dark fire place. A dining room was beyond that, a kitchen slightly further. A staircase sat forward and off to my left a ways. The floors were carpeted and felt nice under my socks after I took my shoes off.

While I liked Algernon's apartment, something about this felt nicer, safer, calmer.

Taking out his phone from his pocket, I watched as Algernon turned it completely off then sat it on the counter in the kitchen. Walking up to me, he followed my eyes that were locked on the dark fire place. With a quiet smile, he walked over to it and fiddled with it some, reaching around a storage shelf off to the side and producing a couple logs. I watched as magic happened and shit caught on fire and like that, the whole cabin came to life. Light reflected off of the pictures that sat about and that's when I noticed that Algernon wasn't in any of them. He must have noticed my staring at one family photo in particular. He took it in hand from the fireplace mantle.

"My mother, father, and siblings," he set it face down, "and I'm the one who took it," he looked around, "and all the rest. It was a clever way to both include and exclude me with the family tradition."

He sat down on the couch and I joined, slinging my arm over him. I pulled him close, "They are trash, too."

"Don't insult that poor wrapper again, how rude." He leaned his head on my shoulder.

Silence settled in.

Taking his hand in mine, my eyes rested on the dancing flames. Warmth, I liked warmth. Leaning my head atop his, I could smell his perfect shampoo. My eyes drifted closed, everything was so calm, I felt safe.

"Hey, Thaddeus," Algernon said after a while, and I may or may not have been dozing when he spoke.

"...Yeah?"

"I love you."

My breath hitched, my heart jumping, blood jolting. A smile took me, "I love you, too."

I was content just staying that way with him all night, but he moved and made me pick up my head. His eyes on mine, there was something burning behind them I couldn't tag. Reaching up, he mindfully removed my glasses then folded them and set them on the side table. Taking off his own, he set them next to mine then there was nothing left between us other than air and silence.

Getting closer, he was slow, careful, like he wanted to give me time and space to pull away. I glanced around to make sure that Honore wasn't in the room before I looked back to him and closed the space between us. This kiss was deceivingly soft at first, as if it could have just ended there, but as the light from the fire made it through my eye lids, the intensity swelled.

His hands tangled in my hair, and when he fell back across the couch, I followed on top of him. A leg between his, my hands on the couch at either side of his head, I was left to stare down at him. Hair disheveled, face reddened, eyes lively, it looked like he was begging me to mess him up more.

I was happy to oblige.

When I shifted to be able to deepen the kiss, I earned a sound from him that made my core jump with a spike of unfiltered passion. It was intoxicating and I wanted to make him do that again. I shifted again, earning another sound as I deepened the kiss, bringing my hand up and lacing it through his hair.

This ache didn't hurt.

But it was going to drive me mad.

Tightening my grip in his hair, I tried to withhold my frustrated groan. I knew his boundary, and I was going to respect it. He pulled me down onto him and I was worried my weight would crush him but he just smile into the kiss, wrapping his arms around me. With no space between us, I could feel everything, each breath, tremble, heart beat of his. I wondered if he could feel my heart racing, too.

Losing myself to him, I shivered pleasantly when he ran his hands down my back, grasping onto the fabric of my coat. His grip was tight on me, but I didn't ever want to go anywhere, so the tighter, the better. Breaking from the kiss, he panted a bit, eyes digging into mine with a lustful sheen to them.

"I love you," He pulled me back and moaned into the kiss.

I cannot even put into words all the things that made me feel.

It was just... just... damn.

My hands must have been shaking from the adrenalin as they sat, laced in his hair, because he brought one of his up to mine. Taking my hand in his, he broke the kiss then gently kissed my hand. Bringing my hand down, he laid it flat against his chest and I could feel the hum of his heart.

Have you ever loved someone so much you felt like you'd just die right there?

Plunging into another kiss, hands got rougher, movements got needier, the fire wasn't the only thing that was heated. Desperate, the couch groaned with each movement as I exercised great restraint and laced my hands back into his hair to keep them from wandering. My mind raced with his sensory until he did something that stopped everything.

Taking my hand in his, he brought it down again, but this time, he rested my fingers on the top button of his shirt. I pulled back from the kiss, eyes wide.

He smirked at me and gave a light nod.

I stared for a moment longer, just to make sure.

He nodded again, laughing a little.

I popped the top button, the rush of satisfaction from that so overwhelming it was nearly numbing. My coat got thrown away from me when he sat up, taking me up with him. Jumping into another kiss, he left me to fiddle with his buttons, blind and distracted. With each button that I undid, we got a step closer to Algernon realizing that I had absolutely no idea what the fuck I was doing. But the look he gave me as I removed his fancy shirt, leaving him in his undershirt, told me that he already knew.

And he was looking forward to watching me fail.

I knew I was never going to live this down, as I started to pull off his undershirt.

But as he pulled off mine, I didn't care.

I wanted to love him in every way.

His hands on my bare back sent a shock through me as I leaned down to kiss him again.

I surrendered to the heat.

Stars were on my mind, for I could see galaxies in Algernon's eyes.

We were nothing to the universe, but to each other, we were the universe.

And I would orbit the anomaly known as Algernon forever.

9

OBLITERATE

"Thaddeus,"

A soft voice pulled me back into the world and my eyes were met with early morning faded darkness. Waking, I saw Honore standing next to the bed.

"Good morning," she turned from the bed and toward the bedroom door, "I want you to come see something."

Carefully, I got up and out of the bed as to not wake Algernon. Slipping on my shoes, I took every precaution to be quiet until I was out of the house. Following Honore a small distance from the cabin, we approached a hill that dropped off to a cliff. She looked back at me and smiled as I stopped at her side. The sun was about to break the horizon, painting the sky in lights and lining the clouds in hope. The massive rolling hills covered with trees, the landscapes of Oregon never ceased to be breathtaking.

"It's lovely," she said, folding her hands behind her back, "it makes you realize what a gift being alive really is,"

A beat passed.

I wasn't totally awake, my mind partly down, another bit left in the night before, but some was there in that moment with her, "What's on your mind?"

"My family threw out my ashes today, they didn't mourn me much. The people at the hospital are, though," she looked over to me, "and they miss you." Stretching, her gaze found its way to the sky, "Are you content with how things went with Algernon?"

I jumped a little, "What do you mean?"

She dropped her arms back to her sides, "Well, I'd say you've effectively won him over."

A laugh took me, my near embarrassment draining, "Yeah, I am married to him now."

Even when saying it, it still felt unreal.

Another beat dragged by.

She started to laugh.

"You guys had fun last night,"

Stepping away, I could just feel my face light up.

"Oh Algernon," she moaned, looking to me with the most evil of smiles, "Algernoooon,"

Absolutely mortified, I was struck speechless.

"I knew I was right about Algernon's bunk, and you lasted way longer than I had expected-"

"I don't care that you're dead, I will push you of this cliff,"

It was nice to hear her laugh, no matter how embarrassed she made me. I stood there, face buried in my hands, paralyzed by the physical cringe that had taken me.

Her mocking tone faded, "I'm happy you found him,"

Slowly, I brought my blazing face from my hands to look at her, "I wouldn't have managed it without you."

The sun was but moments away from breaking the mountain crowned horizon.

"Hey, Thaddeus," she paused, "promise me something?"

I gave her a light nod, a bit taken by her sudden somber tone and saddened smile.

"Promise me you'll never lose him? You have someone who can look after and love you, I was worried that you'd be all alone after running away from the hospital."

"I promise."

She looked at the ground, her sad eyes glassing over as a shaking breath escaped her, "Mission accomplished."

When she looked up to the sky, I did too. The sun broke the horizon, bathing the world in its warm light. I had never watched a sunrise before.

"What mission?"

I got no reply.

Looking over, she was gone.

"Honore?" I stepped around, looking about, but she was not there. Looking back to the spot where she had been standing, I saw a flower that hadn't been there before. Kneeling down, I was suddenly taken by a wave of sadness. Hand up to my face, I was no match for the tears that came. But despite that, I still managed to smile.

"Thank you,"

Honore was a gillyflower.

I stayed there for a long while, the silence sobering.

"Hey," Algernon sat up from the bed when I returned, "are you alright?"

I nodded, getting back into the bed with him and pulling him close.

Time moved differently at that cabin. Playing house, making food, being taught how to use a laundry machine. He would send me to find beautiful places to picnic while he fiddled with paperwork, doing things I wasn't allowed to see. Algernon laughed more, the sunlight came through the right windows, the air was still. With the absence of distant sounds, the world felt so small. The days spent there were sweet, he taught me how to dance. If we could have just stayed there forever, the days filled with domestic magic and the nights tangled in the covers, I would have been happy.

But judgment day was upon us.

And so as we left that cabin, wedding ring on my finger, I vowed to return to this life. We had to go, we had a fight to win, but this was the sunset we were going to ride off into. My eyes rested on the gillyflower as we walked down the path.

I had a promise to keep.

Thaddeus Beau had busted through a door, leaving sirens blaring in his wake as he ran away one day. He never imagined that a short while later, he'd be standing back in the building where it all began, Algernon Amos before him, smiling. He would have accused you of lying if you had even dared to insinuate that perhaps he felt something more than hatred for the tour guide. And I can promise you, that if he ever knew that one day he'd have Algernon pinned to a wall, locked in an intimate kiss, he would have definitely tried to throw something at you.

But alas, there I was, Algernon in my arms, glasses crooked, deepening the kiss as we stood in the historic hotel we first met at. Pulling back took all of my will, but I knew his guests would be arriving soon and we both had jobs to do. It was his job to make people forget about the world for a couple hours, to become the center of their attention and hold them hostage in his charm. It was my job to confront what was threatening everything.

Doug was the traitor, and I was out for blood.

"I love you,"

He ran his fingers through my hair, pulling it all back as his eyes dug into mine. We sat in pause, as if he needed to make that moment last. "I love you too,"

Someone knocked on the door, making us job out of our skins. Thankfully we were standing behind the back wall, out of sight of the guests.

Sighing, he leaned back against the wall, "Duty calls,"

I fixed his glasses, "You'll do great," leaning forward, I kissed him softly, "you always do."

He fixed my glasses, "Thank you," he stepped out from my embrace, walking around the wall with a wave, I watched his back, "make sure you're done playing with the dead before my tour gets down there, alright?"

"Will do," I stood, watching him walk away and I didn't like it. That was the furthest away from me he had been in days, "Hey, Algernon?"

"Yeah?"

"Be careful,"

"I will be," he turned to smile at me as he reached for the front door handle to let in his guests, "I promise."

With his promise in my possession, I descended into the dark basement.

Footsteps above me, I felt every step of mine hit against the concrete floor. Vengeance burned in my blood, I was not leaving without a fight.

"Doug," I said as I stormed into the back room, the darkness totally surrounding me, "I need to talk to you." When I was met with silence, my grip tightened on the off flashlight in my fist, "I know you're here, come out."

The darkness swirled around me, sticking together and creating a human form before me, "Welcome back," Doug's jarring voice echoed, "what do you need?"

"I think you know what I want." I took a step toward him in the abyss, "Somehow the demon parasite knows my every move, there s a traitor among us."

"A traitor?" he blinked at m, his red pinhole eyes disappearing for a moment before returning and piercing my soul. "Who do you think it is?"

The audacity. I clenched my jaw, trying to contain the anger bubbling up, "The only one who can leave this building, who knows what is going on, and can control shadows is you."

"Me?" He jumped back away from me, "I'd never-"

"Are you trying to kill Algernon?" I approached, "Even after all this time, all his understanding and kindness for you when he wasn't even sure if you were there or not? You've watched him struggle and fall and become numb, just hoping one day he'd succumb so you could destroy him. Huxley trusts you, how could you," My thumb rested on the flashlight, "if you want to get to Algernon, you're going to have to get me first and can promise you, I will not lose."

Turning on the light, I shot it right through him, creating a hole in his center. He hissed and flew away from me, climbing to the wall at my left.

"I don't know what you're-" his voice turned into a yell, ripping itself apart as he jumped about the walls, the hole I created slowly closing.

Taking a step back, I watched as his eyes jolted between red and white, the temperature in the room violently dropping, the pressure growing.

His voice continued to distort to the point any semblance of humanity it once held was gone, "It's too late," shadows spun around me, "it's too late it's too late it's too late its too late. You have given him a reason to stay, so now he will be mine, forever,"

The flashlight was knocked from my hand and the last thing I saw right before it hit the ground and shattered was the struggle between red and white in Doug's eyes. The shadows closed in on me and I tasted the blood from my yell, but I heard nothing. For a moment, I did not exist. Suspended, I sat in wait, somewhere in a world all my own. My brain did not compute, I had no idea what weight Doug said held, what was going on, where I was, in that moment nothing existed.

I flew awake.

My vision was bleached by white walls, my lungs burned with sterile air, my hearing fuzzy.

"Are you alright?" A voice I knew broke the haze and when my eyes focused, I saw her sitting at my bedside.

"Honore?"

She nodded, looking back down to her book as she sat next to me in my hospital room, "You looked like you were having a bad dream."

Eyes locked on her, everything started to come spinning back to me.

"A dream?"

Metal music that had been blaring in the back of my mind started to taper out.

"Yeah, you tried new meds today and they put you to sleep."

The rough bed sheets made my skin crawl as my hands closed into fits at my sides, "But you're..."

"I'm what?" she closed her book, smiling at me, "I'm here, like I always have been, like I always will be," she stood, "just like you."

Black drained from my veins.

"Always..." my eyes drifted to the window, to that view of the parking lot, "but I left."

"In a dream, perhaps," she walked around my bedside to catch my gaze, "but we'll never leave. We're trapped here, and maybe it's better that way. They are here to help us, anyway." Sitting down on my bed, she sighed, "Tell me about your dream?"

I couldn't take my eyes from my window, from the outside, "I fell in love."

"Oh? With who?"

"Algernon."

"The tour guide?"

"Yeah," my eyes fell to the floor, "we broke out of here and found him. But it wasn't just that, I had to save him too, otherwise he was going to die."

"It's too late,"

I jumped, looking to her, "What?"

She stared at me, surprised, as she stood from my bed, "It's too late for you to be napping like that, try to stay awake so you don't mess up your sleep schedule more."

Blinking at her, my racing heart started to calm, "Oh..."

Starting out of my room, she didn't turn back to look at me as she left. Staying in the door, her back to me, her tone turned cold, "What a dumb dream. You, fall in love, save the day? You're nothing more than a bark, a tamed delinquent who lost it and will never leave this place. It's cruel, really, for your brain to put that all in your head. There's no way a delinquent could turn into the hero, it would take nothing short of an anomaly."

The lights flickered.

When they turned back on, she was gone.

"Anomaly," I echoed, staring at the door.

The music fell into silence and as the silence grew heavy, it turned into static.

All consuming static.

It was laced with sterile whites, personable blues, the hum of equipment, punctuated with the click of a door and the pop of a water bottle opening. It was the absence of everything, the great void of nothing, the want for something more but the lack there of. Looking around at my walls, my eyes darted from one drawing to the next. A young boy, a shadow, a pirate, Victorian dresses, silhouettes, echoes. Standing from my bed, I walked up to the furthest wall. Eye level with me was one of my drawings, staring back at me. Pinhole white eyes that broke through the scribbles, it was the scariest drawing of them all. Not for what you could see, but for what you couldn't.

It blinked at me.

I fell away from it, backing up into the foot of my bed.

The music flatlined.

The silence was crushing.

Those eyes struck terror into me, but why?

Stepping forward again I brought my hand up before me and reached out to the drawing. My fingertips made contact then images took over my mind in a powerful flash. A basement, a train, flickering lights and pinball, one after another they ruled me. A hand in mine, time spent intertwined, hazel and hair pulling, it took over my senses. Rain, thunder, elevator dings, everything swirled around me, as if I was stuck standing in the eye of a storm, just inches away from making contact with the clouds.

Everything felt so cold, my hand burned with it.

Eyes losing focus, my vision caught on but one thing as the rest of the world fell away.

My ring.

The silence was shattered by the spinning of skates on ice.

White took over my world, erasing me. It obliterated that room, the sterile air, the personable blues, and in the end, all that was left, was nothing. But in that nothingness, I found everything.

Algernon was not a dream, but this was.

A scream tore through my mind, ripping apart my world. The ground was hard underneath my back, the darkness heavy around me, everything was cold. A yell bounced, reverberating until it managed to echo through my brain and wake me fully. My eyes struggled to focus on Huxley in the darkness.

He was yelling but his words were jumbled in my ears.

Nothing made sense until suddenly, everything did.

"Algernon," his voice came screaming back into clarity as it cracked, "it's going after Algernon, you have to stop it,"

I was already running from the basement before my mind had gotten up off of the floor. Each wooden thud of my steps came quicker than the last, I didn't even feel the door as I shoved it open. Barreling down the sidewalk, I had no idea where he was, what stop of his tour they were at. I didn't even know what time it was, so the only thing I could do was retrace his steps. I could hear faint echos of his stories, see his expressions and eyes light up in my memory as I ran past stop after stop.

Past the firemen ghost, past the pirate and the people trapped in time. The music in clubs grew louder, fires sat scattered all around, people shouting and fighting it was like the entire area had fallen into chaos. Lights exploded as I ran past, car alarms blared like a clashing symphony in my wake, the anomaly was so strong in the air I could feel the energy buzzing in it.

Algernon was apart of these streets, just as much as those who lived on them. I could feel his every breath, his thoughts, his heartbeat. Rounding a corner, the parking lot came into focus and with it came his tour. Racing across the street, I didn't look at anything other than Algernon. He looked up to me, obviously confused as I yelled his name from across the lot. Shadows around us danced, jarred until they ripped from their host objects and started to crawl across the ground toward him. I had to be faster than shadows, I had to be faster than desperation and heartbreak and defeat.

The world flashed between two different planes, one where the tour guests stood around with their ghost hunting devices lighting all the way up, and the other where the sun bled red and Algernon was my only company. His eyes locked on mine, the hazel deposing into my blood. I had to keep that hazel alive, that hazel was my everything.

A man hobbled down the sidewalk behind Algernon, not unlike any other occasional transient who frequented the area. It was so usual that I almost paid him no mind, but then the shadows raced beyond Algernon and crashed into him. Algernon didn't seem to notice as he started to step my direction. Had the shadows gotten confused? I was nearing Algernon, but it felt like it was taking forever, as if the parking lot was stretching out under me, making my strides mean less as I sprinted with everything I had.

The world flickered violently between the two planes until it settled on the red one, the world that belonged to Algernon and I.

"You did it, what I thought was impossible," A voice boomed around us, leisurely footsteps echoing.

It didn't matter how fast I ran, I got no closer to Algernon as he stood, frozen, staring forward at me.

At first I didn't recognize the voice, of or it was distorted, but with each passing word, with each footstep that drew nearer, it started to clear, "You got him to fall in love again,"

That sounds like- Algernon's thought took over my mind for a moment, sending pain through my head as I brought my hand up to my hair.

Algernon's breath hitched when a knife was held to his throat from behind by someone I couldn't see. I yelled out, running so hard I felt like I was about to collapse but I couldn't stop. I had to break free of whatever was doing this to me, keeping this distance between us. I didn't know what I was to do, but I knew I had to do something.

A white circle appeared on the ground underneath them. It was then that I realized, they were standing over the vortex.

"You made it too easy, you walked right into my trap," stepping to the side, his voice devoid of static was Mela, knife in hand to Algernon's throat from behind. He smirked at my surprise, slowly tracing Algernon's throat with the tip of the dagger as if he was savoring every moment. Grip tightening on the blade, his eyes made contact with mine, a smile crawling across his face with such force it looked like it would rip his skin, the vibrato of his voice shook the entire world in and out of focus, "Beware the apple of emotion, for once it is in your eye, your demise rests in your devotion."

He tore the blade across Algernon's throat.

Red.

The world flicked back and forth, Mela switching out with the transient with a knife, until the real world came crashing back into line.

There was so much red.

My feet started to work again, shooting me forward.

The transient jumped away as Algernon started to fall forward.

Tour guests screamed, but I didn't hear them.

The only sound in my world was the clink of the knife as it hit the ground.

Iron.

I caught Algernon and dropped to my knees with him in my arms.

Blood felt like water.

His eyes locked on mine, his hand up to his throat, Algernon was trapped in stunned silence as the world ceased to rotate.

Hazel started to falter.

The transient ran.

I couldn't speak, my mind had turned off.

How could blood be so red?

There was too much red.

Hazel dulled.

A daze took Algernon as I held him in my arms, suffocated by all consuming trepidation.

Thaddeus...

He stopped breathing.

His hand fell from his neck and landed in the red pooling on the black pavement.

I may have yelled, I may have shouted and cried and cursed, but I don't remember. The only things I remember are how limp Algernon felt in my arms, how his blood on my hand quickly lost heat, how his eyes were still open. I remember the way the ambulance lights reflected in his eyes, the way the paramedics fought to pry me away from him, how cold he felt as he left my grip. But the thing that stuck with me the most, the sensation that would forever be searing into my soul, was the way my ring felt, burning into my skin, covered in his blood.

His blood was on my hands.

This was my doing.

This was my fault.

Mela was the traitor.

Mela suggested I bring Afternoon's heart back to life.

Mela lied.

And I followed his every instruction.

A blur of questions, of shiny silver blankets, of bumpers of ambulances and police badges and lights and sirens, became my world. Nothing made sense, everything was numb but also so potently painful at once. Everything blurred together until I heard a phrase that shattered everything.

"He's dead."

The paramedics stood from where they had been kneeling around Algernon, leaving him laying alone on the pavement of the parking lot. The last paramedic to raise from his knees gently ran his hand over Algernon's face, closing his eyes for him.

No.

It took three men to hold me back when I bolted forward.

It took even more to subdue me.

The strings on the electric guitar of my heart snapped and they took every bit of me with them.

A citywide manhunt followed, to no avail.

Andrew shattered in such a way that I didn't think possible. Clinging to me, his yells became one with me, resonating with the flat line ringing in my chest. So slow but so fast at the same time, every event lasted a life time and a fraction of a moment. They would never end, but ended too quickly.

Yes, he is my husband.

No I don't know of a will.

No I don't know how to contact his family.

These things escaped my mouth without the full weight of them setting in quite yet.

A memorial was planned.

The news was painted in the tragedy.

And I was left, dried blood on my hands, strangers around, standing in the parking lot that changed it all. I think it was then, it must have been then, that my mind clicked back into place and I realized what was going on. Algernon was dead. But then, I understood what that could mean.

What it had to mean.

People yelled out after me when I bolted, but no one chased me.

Andrew was left standing there, staring.

"Algernon," I yelled, barreling round a corner and toward his workplace, "where are you?"

He had to be there.

Busting through the doors, I raced toward the basement stairs, not bothering with a flashlight as I descended into the abyss.

"Algernon, Huxley, Doug," I choked on my own yell, pants taking me as I stood alone in the darkness, "come out, he has to be with you,"

No reply came.

"Mela was the traitor, he was working with the demon, he killed, he...." tears started to take me, "Algernon must be a ghost, he..."

The silence was crushing me and I couldn't take it. Tripping up the stars, I crashed through the front door when I ran out of the building and down the sidewalk. My voice cracked with every yell. The city was dead, the energy that used to lace the air with a toxic hum had drained. As if every bit of magic, of life, of excitement and tension had faded, the historic district felt like nothing more than dirty streets and sketchy clubs.

Algernon had to be somewhere, maybe he was just lost, confused. I had to find him, I had to help him, I was the only one who could see him. Algernon had to be a ghost.

My step caught on a curb and I wiped out. Laying on the sidewalk, I stared at the sky as my visor blurred under tears.

Algernon had to be a ghost, because if he isn't, that meant I wasn't enough of a reason for him to stay. And if I wasn't enough of a reason for him to stay, I couldn't be enough of a reason for me to stay, either.

"Where are you..."

I brought my hand up to my face.

I was alone for the first time in years, even the voice in my head had fallen silent, just as the person it once belonged to had. When Andrew found me, he found a broken instrument, he found something so harmed that it took all his strength to help me up. He spoke to me, but my ears no longer worked. He kept his harm around me, but I couldn't feel him. No one knew, no one understood what this meant. I failed, I didn't save Algernon, and now it was simply the quiet before the storm. The full moon was upon us that night, and with it, would come judgment day. And it was all my fault.

So many people showed up as the sunset tore through the sky.

Algernon had been so alone in this world, where were these people when he was alive? I couldn't help but feel the kind of rage that darkened you as a person as I stood at the front of the crowd of nicely dressed people, holding candles in the parking lot. No one approached me other than Andrew who stood at my side like a guard dog of sorts. I wondered why that was. Maybe he knew something I did not.

Another man approached us, nothing particularly noteworthy about his beige office worker appearance, but that was until I looked up to see his eyes. That blue, the way they shone in his skull like the bright lights of a club, I knew exactly who that was.

A woman sobbed, her cries precise, perfectly shrill, calculated and controlled to obtain the most attention just like her makeup and put together outfit. At her side stood a man in a business suit, silver hair and hazel eyes reminiscent of another. It didn't take much for me to connect the dots as they approached the front of the memorial and stood next to the makeshift tribute of items that sat on the ground where Algernon had died.

I hated that his body, the body that I had held so closely the night before, was locked alone in a freezer somewhere.

"My son," the woman said, her voice shaking in such a way that reminded me of my own fake mother, "today I lost my dear son."

I could feel Andrew tense.

"He was such a wonderful young man and follower of Christ," the man in the faded suit said, putting his hand on his wife's back as she continued to cry, "an angel has joined god in heaven."

I didn't mean to laugh.

I have never felt so many sets of eyes on me before. Looking around at a sea of strangers, my world darkened more with the setting sun. How much did I care? My eyes drifted to the picture of Algernon that sat on the pavement. I didn't have any reason to care anymore. He was the only person in this world that understood, the only one who knew my secret and believed me, the only thing with the power to turn this delinquent into something more.

"Heaven?" My eyes dragged up to the man, "Did you even know Algernon?"

"Of course I knew him, he was my son,"

I stepped from Andrew's side, and he didn't stop me, "You mean the son you drove out of your house? The son you told to die on the streets, the son you disowned and destroyed and forsook? You only claim love now for the pity," I looked out over the crowd, "And who the fuck are all of you? Where were you the last few years when his life was falling apart? I bet you don't even know his favorite color. You can't stand here and mourn someone you didn't cherish in life. There are only three people who should be here right now. The rest of you can fuck right off."

His mother's eyes rolled up to me, clear with poison, devoid of emotion, as she broke her pained act long enough to speak, "Who do you think you are?"

Standing before a crowed, noting left for me, I made a decision.

There was no going back now.

And maybe the world deserved to end anyway, if it was full of people like these.

My eyes rested on the memorial for a moment. Flowers, stuffed animals, candles, there was an assortment of basic items placed there by basic people. But there was one object that caught my eye, it was small, round, silver, like a coin but larger. It took me a moment, but I realized what it was. 24 hours sober. A light smile took me, Andrew had listened to me.

"Who am I?" I slowly turned to face her, "The fact that you don't know that just proves how little you knew about your son. My name is Thaddeus Amos and I am Algernon's husband."

Whispers broke out around.

I'm sure they knew who I am.

"Yes, that's right, the psychiatric hospital runaway," my eyes drifted to the news camera recording the memorial, "you guys ran a lovely segment on me," I started to approach the camera, looking straight into its lens, "send them after me if you'd like, they won't catch me. I'm not going back, I shouldn't have been there in the first place. I wasn't sick, mom, I wasn't sick or broken and you just left me there for the last five years. And you're about to see for yourselves, I'm sure, that I wasn't wrong." I walked back toward the vortex, the spot that started this all.

As I passed by a man who donned cammo, my eyes caught on something attached to his belt.

A smirk took me over.

Tears budded in my eyes.

The metal felt cool in my hand.

He didn't even notice.

Stopping on the vortex, one last long, deep breath took me.

"And when all hell breaks loose, I won't be here to save you."

Turning around, I brought the gun I had lifted up to my head.

Shock shook the crowd.

Andrew lunged forward.

Lady Spectra tried to hold him back.

If I wasn't enough of a reason for Algernon to stay, then I had no reason to stay.

I pulled the trigger.

You know, a lot can happen in twenty one years of life. You're born, and into what circumstances you have no control. Your family may have seemed normal at first, but as you grow up you start to see the cracks. You see the number of pills your mother takes grow, you notice when your father starts to go gray. Every time you think you've heard them yell the loudest they possible could, they yell louder. You learn the definition of the word "accident" very early on and from that moment, it is one with you.

You start to realize that your mother is never just "running late" to pick you up from school. You learn to hate everything because you feel like everything hates you. When you're an only child, your parents are your everything. You hear the way the other children talk of you, you start to believe their words, they shape you. You wonder why you're here, if no one would care if you weren't.

You fail.

Life gets even worse, you have no moments to yourself. They don't want to help, they don't care about what's wrong, they just want to control you. Because if you die, you win, you get away from them, and they can't have that now can they? So they suffocate you while simultaneously ignoring you. You are everything and nothing at the same time.

You put up walls so high that nothing can break them down, or that's what you think behind that front of dark clothing and evil glares. But then someone walks into your life and like that, even if you didn't know it at the time, everything changes.

I barely felt it.

I watched as my body fell to the ground before me, leaving me behind.

Andrew fell to his knees next to me.

My world froze, the crowd before me fading, leaving nothing more than the lot around me. A light brightened up the dulling surroundings and with the came a shadow obstructing it. Staring at a younger version of myself, I watched him grab Algernon by the tie, standing in the vortex.

The gun was gone from my hand, my footsteps made no sound, I didn't cast a shadow, "Get out of there!" I yelled, stepping out of the vortex, "If you don't, Algernon is going to die,"

They couldn't hear me.

I was left to stand there, watching my life flash before my eyes, the moment I regretted most, the moment that changed everything. It was the moment that my walls fell, the moment I felt hazel deposit into my blood, the moment I doomed Algernon, the moment I felt my heart beat for the first time. A black creature lunged for me but then it was blown back by a gust of wind and crashed into Algernon. White bleached my world.

Personable blues, fights with nurses, being restrained. Five years of the same thing, day after day after day after day, nothing changed but the weather. The van showed up less, Honore came in and out and in and out until they never let her leave again. The same food, the same pills, the same pop of a water bottle. Drawing after drawing, they occupied my mind until I couldn't think any more. There was one thing that never stopped haunting me, those eyes.

Those piercing white eyes.

Alarms, running, freedom, the screaming of an electric guitar, it all happened so fast, everything changing. But then, everything slowed down. Silver, hazel, cocky smiles and moment of weakness, the tour guide stood in my memory. I reached out for Algernon as I watched him give that tour again, but my hand went through. The memory turned into a swirl of glitter and smoke, spinning around me until it gave way to another memory. Pinball machines, laughs, heart racing, feverish emotions, devouring devotion and heated movements.

I watched as I pressed Algernon into the game, deepening the kiss. Lights flickered, music hummed, memories danced through my teary eyes.

Algernon.

An ice rink, a ring, a cabin, a top button popped.

Algernon was gone.

Red.

There was so much red.

A gunshot, silence, everything was still and I was left, standing alone in that parking lot.

I had woken that morning, Algernon asleep on my chest, and I ended that day, dead.

So why?

Why was I still here?

Stepping around, the silence was too much. The parking lot, the city, everything was empty. Running, I didn't ever tire as I went back to the historic hotel, wiping tears from my eyes with the sleeves of my nice jacket. I wasn't paying attention, couldn't see where I was going, when I ran into something.

But my heart stopped when I went right through.

Stumbling, I turned around to see that I was now standing in the historic hotel, having fazed through the front door. Looking down to myself, the tears stalled in the shock. I was a ghost? But I didn't have a reason to stay. Barreling into the basement, I ran into the darkness.

"Huxley!" My voice cracked so hard it hurt, "Where are you?"

I was surrounded by darkness, trapped in silence, crushed from the weight of it all, as I fell to my knees. Shadows approached me from all sides and I didn't fight as they engulfed me, taking everything I was away in their enveloping abysmal eternity.

Death.

Our hearts were intertwined, despite the fact that we were running out of time. The anomaly obliterated Algernon, what it had isolated. A king was no longer in wait, and he had sealed my fate. Algernon had been a key locked in his own safe, and no matter how much I loved him, I was too late. He had been the apple of my emotion, the only thing in my eye, and he met his demise because of that devotion. Where it started is where it did end, and it was an outcome that I did not intend.

Shadows in the night lay, and I wasn't prepared, for now it was judgment day.

10

DEVOTION

The ground was cold, hard, damp, so much so that I thought I was still in that basement; but then I heard a voice.

"Hey, are you alright?"

Slowly coming back to my wits, I ached as I shakily pushed myself up from the ground. Looking around, I was in what appeared the be a dungeon, locked behind a wall of bars, surrounded by three stone walls. It was dark, unbearably dark, so that's why I jumped so much when a faint pink light tore the shadows.

"Ah, good, I was getting worried," the little pink light said as they hovered, eye-level with me, "I'd say welcome back to the land of the living but that's not really the case anymore now is it?" the light flew around me in bouncy circles like a little fairy or something, "What is it with Algernon and liking dramatic boys?"

"You know Algernon?" I slowly stood, my gaze locked on the light as they bounced in agreement, "Where are we?"

"The dungeon."

I let a small breath escape me as I walked up to the bars, "Oh really..."

The light laughed, their male voice smooth and mellow but faintly familiar at the same time, "The dungeon of Mela's castle,"

"Mela," I clasped my hands over the cold bars as anger spiked through me.

The metal stung.

"We need to get you out of here, it's not too late to stop him. You didn't stand a chance when you were alive, but now you're on the same turf and you can keep him from destroying everything."

My grip loosened, my eyes locked on the abyss before me, "Why?"

"What?" The light flew over and hovered above my shoulder, "you realize what he's doing, right? He's using the power he has gathered for the last five years to create chaos flipside and fully escape from the vortex."

"No, I understand what's going on," I looked over to the light, the tears budding in my eyes becoming evident, "why would I want to save that world?"

"Why wouldn't you?"

I leaned my forehead against the bar, the thud echoing into eternity, "Because Algernon's not in it."

The light rammed into the side of my head, a little burst of pink sparkles and a faint ring of a bell followed impact, making me stumble to the side. Hand to my face, eyes on the little light, I felt attacked and somewhat embarrassed. It was like I had just been punched by cotton candy.

"What was that for?"

"You're so dramatic, do you even hear yourself?" They flew closer to me, "Algernon loved that part of town, you saw the way he talked about it. Why wouldn't you want to keep it alive? He's apart of it, always will be."

Their words fell on unwilling ears, "Why am I still here?" I allowed my gaze to drift back toward the darkness, "I killed myself to die, not to come back. I have no reason to still be here."

"That's obviously not the case," the light gently landed on my shoulder, they were much heavier than I had anticipated, "You have two choices here Thaddeus. You can either mope about here in the darkness, or you can escape with me."

"You've been trapped down here?" I looked over to the tiny light, "You can fly right through these bars though."

"This is true, but," the light lifted from my shoulder and floated through the bars, illuminating some of the darkness around them, "I hadn't any reason to, until now. Fate is funny like that."

"Fate," I let out a breath as I leaned my forehead against the bar once more, "if there is such a thing, it's out to get me."

"Or perhaps," the light approached, hovering directly before my eyes, "you don't know everything." They floated back some, "It's far easier to be a victim, but so much more rewarding to be a warrior. Both have been wronged, but one chooses to do something about it."

A moment passed, the ache in my chest becoming dull, dragging over my heart with every beat, the pain no longer shooting.

"I also can't open doors because I'm a light."

I sighed.

Lifting myself from the bars, images flashed in my mind. Lights flickering, club music shaking the ground, dirt and grime and alcohol, that part of town was a mess. But that's exactly why Algernon liked it, it was raw, real. It was a disaster, just like us. I should have known that disasters don't get happily ever after.

"Fine," squaring my shoulders, I looked forward, "if I'm stuck here, I might as well fuck shit up."

But just because I wasn't going to ride off into some sunset didn't mean that the rest of the world didn't deserve the chance. And perhaps the light was right, I didn't know everything.

"So, under Mela's castle you say? Who died and made him king?"

The light sat in pause before spiraling around me, leaving a little trail of pink sparkles behind them, "There's more than that going on here, but it's far too much to explain. What we need to do is to make it to the throne room. I think if I can get close, I can try to incapacitate him long enough for you to finish him."

The light flew right into the bars and with a flash of pink light, the bars disintegrated into sparkles and turned to glitter piles upon the floor. Following the light as they flew down a dark corridor, I was surprised by the power the little ball of light held.

"Finish him? Can one kill a ghost?"

"Kill? No. But banish? Yes." I nearly ran into a fucking door when the light suddenly stopped, "It's tricky business, banishment. Special objects hold that power, and they're hard to find. But I think you have one." They flew down to my left hand, their light reflecting off of the ring Algernon gave me, "This ring, and the vow it represents. It's a forever vow, yeah?"

Looking to my ring, my eyes lingered, "Yes, or, at least it was."

"Those can be potent when tangled with the paranormal. Since you both were heavily affected by other powers, I'm willing to bet that your vow holds more weight than the usual. I used to have one but I..."

"Willing to bet?" I asked as inspected the ring on my hand, not realizing that I had jut cut them off, "that's not beyond a reasonable doubt."

"Well this is where we find out," the light flew up to the wooden door, "I could never get further than this. I am but a remnant of what I once was, I hold very little power in this form. But you hold the power of eternity in your ring. You may be able to interact with this plane because of it. You must be here for a reason, we just don't know it yet."

"If what you just said makes sense to you, then that's good enough for me," I reached down toward the doorknob with my left hand and it stung upon contact. A green light started to emanate from my ring, surprising me as it burned into my skin. The light bounced at my side as the doorknob turned green. The green light grew until the doorknob started to crack, light erupting through the lines. Suddenly, the light flashed and with its fade went the handle, turning into a pile of green sparkles upon the floor. Staring down at it, a slight smile took me. That was kinda cool.

The light flew into the door and it creaked open.

"Fantastic." The light flew right up into my face and made me stumble back, "What we're about to enter is the equivalent of Mela's brain, and it may be hard for you to understand, but there's only one thing you need to know. Do not touch anything." they turned around and hovered for a moment, seemingly gazing into the dark abyss before us, "I can sense where he is, you just need to follow me," they took off, flying forward and I had to race to catch up, "Quickly, time is of the essence."

I didn't get tired, no matter how much I ran. The longer I was dead, the more alive I felt. Doing my best to stay near them, I followed the light through darkened rooms and winding halls. It was too dark to see much, but the occasional thing that was illuminated by the pink light led me to believe the castle we were in looked as if it cane straight out of a story book. One with a royal in a tower, an overbearing king presiding; the kind a dragon would guard. Simple designs, gold crests, royal blues, marble floors, the air held a lightness about it that felt out of place with the sinister undertones.

Like it had been poisoned.

We raced up stairs, I destroyed doors, nothing could stand in my way. One after another, they turned to dust in my grip and I was left to stare at the glitter at my shoes. What awaited us at the end of the search?

"We're getting close," they sped up, "a few rooms away,"

I could feel my heart start to rip a hole in my chest, was this the anticipation the knight felt as he ran toward the monster? I always thought the knight was brave, but what really was bravery? Was it rushing in, despite the risk? Was it the willingness to lose it all? Did in rest in the unapologetic and relentless pursuit of a goal?

A tour guide who wore a smile every day to put on a show pulled into focus in my mind.

Bravery was doing what was hard, and smiling the whole time.

My hand rested on the next doorknob, and as it started to crack with green light, my ring heating up, a smile found me.

Algernon's greatest anomaly wasn't the flickering lights. The true anomaly was turning me, the biggest punk ever, into a hero.

The door turned to dust and everything stopped.

A chill ruled the air, taking some of me with it. Faced with what felt like eternity, walls lined in glass orbs, onyx flooring, and no end in sight, it was staggering.

"Yes, this is exactly where we need to be." The light flew in without fear and I hesitantly followed.

My footsteps didn't make a sound on the dark floor.

The light went on about not touching stuff, about memories and souls and whatever but I wasn't paying any mind. I was too taken by the orbs lining the walls. Particles swam around inside them, small galaxies trapped in the glass. They were so drawing, like they called out, yearned, for me to reach and touch them. One in particular felt like it was screaming, like it needed to be seen, heard, remembered. It was off in the distance, so far out I could barely see it. But I could feel it pulling me toward it. Quickening my pace, my eyes sat locked on the distance. Running past the light, they said something to me that I didn't hear as I got closer to the orb.

I needed to get to it.

Nothing else existed in my mind in that moment, not the situation, not the fact that I was dead, not that Algernon was gone, not the impending doom, nothing more than that orb. I heard the faint yell of the light behind me as I extended my hand and it only processed once I had mad contact with the cool glass.

"Don't."

The moment I removed the orb, the whole room started to shake. Holding the small orb tightly, it fit perfectly into the palm of my hand as I looked around. Pocketing the orb, I was left to stand and stare as the others started to fall from the wall. My eyes locked on the little pink light as they raced toward me. The first orb hit the ground and black ink explode into the air, but moved as if the air was liquid. Slowly intoxicating the area with darkness, it was only a matter of moment before its whispers reached me, taking me away with them.

It felt like I fell for a long time, but it could have been but a moment

Coming to a stop, my eyes opened because it didn't feel like I had landed. The world I saw was not my own, but one faintly resembling it. Crowded club streets, dirty walls, vibrating air, flashing lights, I had been there before, but I hadn't, at the same time. Things looked warn, but less warn than I had come to know them. The same place, but perhaps, a different time.

It was then that I realized I couldn't move, as if I was being held hostage in the body of another.

Sitting at a metal chair, leisurely propping their edgy combat boots up on the metal railing of the outside bar, whoever I was inside was nonchalant in the most pretentious of ways. I hated them because they were cool, too cool, effortlessly so. Taking a drink of whatever it was they had, it didn't taste like nail polish remover but more like dirt with a bite. I wasn't sure what was more concerning to me, that they were willingly drinking that, or that I could taste it too.

Yelling erupted around a street corner and the person I was inhabiting paid it no mind a first, but then eventually after it started to escalate, they sighed and stood. Each step they took held a metallic click, commanding the beat of the universe in the moments between each one. They were the force of nature I always wanted to be, and I couldn't help but wonder who it was.

Turning the corner, a scene unfolded before us in the parking lot Algernon and I knew all too well. A group of transients surrounded a short young man with black hair, menacing and roughing him up. Every step my host took toward the situation felt powerful, unconcerned, playful almost. As if they were amused, had it under control, were simply playing a game. It was the kind of self-possession that gods coveted.

"Now what in the hell do you think you're doing?" That voice, the one that sliced the air with its pressure, I had heard it before. A deep rumble, a melodic addition to the world, it made the universe pause, held at the mercy of every vowel.

I knew that I knew it, but at the time, I couldn't remember who it belonged to.

The transients parted, startled by the presence that had approached. Scampering and ran off, they cursed as they vanished around corners. With them now gone, I saw him, the young man being terrorized. Hazel deposited into both of us, as the host and I stood, equally taken by the raw power we could feel harnessed with in those eyes looking back at us.

Approaching the young man, my host smiled, I could just feel it, as they extended their hand, "Hello, are you alright?"

The young man nodded, cautiously taking the extended hand.

His was shaking.

"They like to cause issues, but if you show them you are to be respected, then they'll usually leave you alone," they shook hands as the voice so dark it must have been forged from deep space continued on, "What is your name?"

"Algernon," his voice was so soft I barely recognized it. He was so much younger, fear evident in his posture, hesitation in his eyes, this was Algernon before the world made him jaded. "Yours?"

"Malus."

Everything ripped away from my vision, throwing me from that scene to different one. Discombobulating, it was as if I had been jarred from one orb to another. Now sitting in a coffee shop, Algernon in the same clothing as before, I was left to assume it was the same day. Staring at him through the eyes of another, I could feel the spark that had been ignited in the both of us. So this was Malus, the guy Algernon married? Malus was taken by Algernon at first sight as well?

"What are you doing, walking around this part of town alone like that?"

Algernon's eyes darted downward to the cup in his hands, his black hoodie youthfully charming on his frame, "I was practicing for an audition."

"An audition?" Malus took a drink, "For what, a convincing reaction to getting mugged?"

Malus was dry comedic indifference personified.

I could see the nerves taking Algernon over as he tried not to laugh, to keep the line of his mouth flat, as he spoke on, "No, for a tour guide job. It means a lot to me, but I'm not sure if I can do it. I have to memorize a couple hour monologue and preform it for the head of the company. But if I can pass that, I have the job."

Malus hummed, leaning back in his chair in that way you're told not to, as he sat in pause, "Do you have any friends who would be willing to walk around with you as you do that? It's not safe enough to just hang out around here alone. Especially when you're so..." he looked away from Algernon.

A strange beat passed.

"I just moved here, I don't know anyone."

"From where?" Malus dragged his eyes back toward Algernon, studying the sudden insecurity that had painted him.

"Blazing Star,"

"Why did you leave?" Malus took another drink, leaning forward in his chair with a click, "I've heard it's nice there."

"It's nice if you fit into their boxes, I suppose." The wayward look, the slight smirk, Algernon tried to hide them both as he took a drink and it obviously put Malus on pause.

"How old are you?"

Algernon sat his cup down, "Sixteen, you?"

"Seventeen,"

Malus filled the next beat as he took a longer drink than before, finishing off his cup.

"Well, let's hear it."

Algernon stared, confused, as Malus stood and stretched.

A light laugh taking him, Malus went on as he dropped his arms to his side, "The tour."

Algernon lit up, standing and nearly knocking his chair to the ground.

It was that easy to fluster him once upon a time? Malus had it easy.

Memories fell out of focus to then pulled back in and fall out again, a montage of the tour I had come to know in its beginning phases. Before me, before the vortex, when the story used to end with a vague warning about the parking lot. Before Algernon commanded the world's attention, before his smile grew into place, before he learned about the ghosts in the basement.

Before Malus broke his heart.

Laughter echoed through the blur of coffee shop visits, movies, boardgames and shopping. A familiar shop pulled into focus as Algernon held up needlessly edgy clothing up to Malus, just as he had done to me. The same worker stood there, ogling over them as they casually spoke about ice skating. Church bells, a small gathering, a kiss, cake, smiles, it was surprisingly wholesome. Pictures were printed, some framed, others put in an album that I had seen before. Tangled sheets, bottles of vodka, domestic mornings, I felt like I was intruding. Days at the rink, shows and competitions, nice dinners and dancing, I watched their love story flash before my eyes. Gaining momentum, it felt like it was unstoppable, strong, something that could only exist on the pages of a novel.

Then the air went cold.

Thrown into a scene, Malus sat on a couch in Algernon's apartment. Years must have passed, because when Algernon came stumbling through the door, he had started going gray. Malus stood and steadied Algernon, asking if he was alight. All Algernon could do was shake his head as Malus helped him to the couch.

"We don't have time," a little jingle of a bell took over my ears, faint pink in the back of my mind trying to pull me back. But I didn't want to go back, I wanted to watch what was going on, I wanted to know. So I fought it until the pink faded and all that was left was for me to continue to observe.

"Did something happen at work?"

"I don't know," Algernon sat back into the couch, hands over his face, fingers laced into his disheveled bangs, "there was this kid,"

My heart stopped.

"A kid?" Malus asked, carefully running his hand over Algernon's back.

"This asshole teenager, but that's not... there was a light or something, I don't know but I feel terrible and dizzy. There's a weight on my shoulder, it hurts. Everything hurts, my head and my heart and my body and everything it just..." he trembled, tightening his grip in his hair as a grimace took him "hurts,"

Darkness started to take the corners of my vision as the world spun into another montage. Long nights, agony, Algernon was being destroyed by something. Malus tried to comfort him but the pain started to spread, the toxin infected them both. I could feel it dragging him down, taking over his thoughts, dismantling his mind, and I was probably only feeling a fraction of it.

Vodka bottles piled up next to the dishes, blinds weren't opened, the light modern apartment turned into a cave. Fights, tears, glass breaking, running out, dropping to knees, sobbing, I watched things fall apart bit by it. Malus' confidence turned to self-hate, his mind turned from comedic to confused. And like that, the host I was inside was obliterated, everything I had sensed in him previously was erased and he was but a shell of what once was. Algernon lost weight, his smile was gone, he was always the one who left when things got bad; I wondered where we went. This was a horror movie, the unthinkable, two people falling out of love.

I could do nothing about it, and apparently neither could Malus.

Things slowed down, stopping on an evening where Malus spent a long while admiring his wedding ring.

He got up from the bed, taking me, his unwilling audience, with him into the rest of the dark apartment. The feel of the place I knew was so different, it felt like I had never been there before. Algernon was in the kitchen, leaning against a counter with a cup in his lightly shaking hand, eyes on the ground. He looked terrible. Malus approached and gently earned Algernon's attention with a forehead kiss.

"Come watch the sunset with me?"

Algernon gave a light nod and didn't pull away when Malus took his hand and started to lead him out of the apartment. Algernon's hand was so cold, I could even feel it. I didn't like where this was going, something didn't feel right as they ascended the stairs. If it were possible to watch the sunset on the roof, wouldn't Algernon have suggested that we do it at some point?

They walked out onto the roof, which had a small seating area and some rails to keep one from stumbling off. They were so high up, there's no way one would survive that. That's the thought that replayed over in my mind as they climbed up onto the security railing, totally defeating the damn purpose, and dangled their legs over the side of the fucking skyscraper.

"We've been together for a long time haven't we?"

Algernon didn't look away from the darkening skyline. "Indeed we have."

"I've been thinking a lot lately,"

"Is that right?"

This hurt to watch, everything about their interaction was forced, uncomfortable, cold. Like they both knew what was coming and it was just a matter of waiting for the other shoe to drop.

"A lot has changed in the last few months, and I think you need to see a doctor."

Algernon didn't look like he expected that as he quickly looked to Malus, "A doctor? Something happened in that parking lot, I didn't just suddenly develop an illness." Algernon sat back away from Malus some, his eyes studying his husband, "Do you think I'm delusional?"

"You're something, Algernon," the flair of Malus' tone startled Algernon and I both, "You're sick, something isn't right, and it's dragging us both down."

Algernon's shock drained to sadness, "Both?"

Malus looked away, for which I was thankful, because I didn't want to watch Algernon's heart break. "You're not the person I fell in love with. You've changed and I can't handle this anymore. I wanted to help you but I can't. Just being around you upsets me, I hate being in the same room. I can't even look into your eyes anymore without hating you. You feel too much and you care too much and you love too hard and I just can't stand being trapped here anymore." He looked to Algernon and what I saw through his eyes hurt more than any other agony I had known, "I never thought I could fall out of love with someone like you, congratulations on proving me wrong."

Malus was lying.

As tears streamed down Algernon's face, I could feel that Malus was lying.

Why would he say such horrible things, especially if he didn't mean them?

"You have every right to hate me, and you probably should. I could have gone about all this in a kinder way. In fact," he slid off his ring and clasped in it his fist, "please hate me, it'll make this easier. Hate me, hate everyone, and trust no one because they're just out to break your heart anyway." He stood up on the ledge and Algernon followed. "Can you promise me something, Algernon?"

Malus turned to look at the love of my life, heart broken and shocked, as he looked at us with those hazel eyes and nodded, "Promise me that you will never fall in love again. Please don't put someone else through this. Because if you do, I can promise," he took Algernon's hand in his and gave the ring back to him, "it will end the exact same way."

Taking his hands from Algernon's, he took a step away, eye contact remaining.

Algernon realized what had been placed in his hands. Startled, he was about to say something to Malus, perhaps something important, but it would remain unsaid for all eternity for a moment later, Malus stepped off of the roof.

In the fall, I realized why Malus lied.

As he tumbled, me his unwilling follower, he turned around in a way that left us facing the glass windows. It was then, moments before crashing into the ground, that everything crashed down around me. For the first time, I saw Malus' reflection. Staring back at me was someone I knew, someone who had hurt Algernon not once, but twice. I didn't know why I hadn't realized sooner. He gave me the false information, he sent me on the wrong trail. Mela and Malus were one and the same.

Everything went black.

He didn't die when he hit the ground, not really, and he had been planning his revenge all along.

As I came to, a pink light bouncing in my vision, a fire had been lit in me that would eat me up. But that was alright, I didn't have anything left anyway. The least I could do was take Malus down with me.

"I told you not to touch anything," the light few around me violently, "are you alright? What did you see?"

Sitting up, I let out a deep breath as I gathered my spinning thoughts, "Exactly what I needed to." Standing, I shook a little, "Malus, Mela, whatever his name really is, he's going to be banished for what he did to Algernon."

The little light slowed down and hovered in silence for a moment, "Did you see all the way to the end?"

"When he threw himself from the top of a skyscraper? Yeah." I started into the darkness again, racing toward a door I could see in the distance, "He has been sabotaging me the entire time, maybe even more than I know. He did this, so I'm going to end him."

The light started to follow me, but they stayed quiet.

All but crashing into the door, I took the handle in hand and with a tight grip, it lit up green and shattered. The door burned away before me, slowly revealing a throne room. This was it, the moment I was going to fuck shit up and go out like a blaze of glory. When I was going to save the place that Algernon loved, to honor the only person I'd ever love like that, and hopefully escape my own pain at the end of it all.

I was already dead, what more could I lose?

"Thaddeus, wait-"

I didn't listen to the light as I bolted into the throne room, a roar growing in my chest, "Malus,"

Standing in the front center of a vast throne room, I was momentarily taken by its beauty and intricacy. My eyes drawn away from my target as the light caught up with me, I was trapped in a breathless beat.

"Beware the apple of emotion, for once it is in your eye, your demise rests in your devotion," Malus' darkly melodic voice resonated with the aching heartstrings in my chest, "Devotion is dangerous, Thaddeus. Play with it, and you risk losing it all."

My eyes dropped from the ceiling down to the throne before me, but that's when I saw that I stood before not just one, but two thrones.

Hazel.

Eyes locked, I stood, paralyzed.

There, at the throne that sat at Malus' right side, was Algernon.

"Thank you for all your help kiddo," Malus, looking like a demon in dress, crown above his head, started down the steps that kept the thrones above me on the floor, a bounce in every one of his movements, "without you, I wouldn't have my king back by my side."

"Your king-" my eyes jumped back to Algernon, "But that can't be Algernon, I watched him die."

Malus stopped right before me, a smirk nearly tearing his skin, "We're all dead here,"

"No," Algernon's voice sent ice through my veins, "Thaddeus can't be... you didn't follow me, did you?"

I stumbled back away from Mauls. My fire was confused, staggered, on pause, in my chest for this wasn't anywhere near what I had expected. I was going to come in here, deck Malus, then fuck him up with my ring. I didn't think, I could have never guessed that...

"Thaddeus, you need to get out of here," Algernon's yell echoed through the vaulted ceilings, "he's gong to use his power to try to escape and when he does, this will all be destroyed too. I'm being held here, but you need to escape,"

"I'm not leaving you here-" my sentence was cut short when Malus dissipated then reappeared directly in front of me.

Latching his fist around my throat, he pulled me across the room closer to Algernon then slammed me into one of the metal walls. "I wish I knew how to thank you, you followed my orders wonderfully."

"I trusted you," I was barely able to talk under the weight of his grip.

"It's not my fault that you're dumb." He tightened his hand then gestured back to Algernon with his other. It was then that I realized Algernon's ankle was chained to his throne. "I can't believe you actually trusted me, though. Did you really think the power of love could fix anything? I needed you to wake him up from his emotional nuclear winter so I could gather the remaining power I needed from him. He's been hardcore repressing for so long, I though I'd never escape."

"...the reason we're here right now is because I got Algernon to feel?"

Malus nodded with the satisfaction of a king.

"It's my fault."

"Yes it is," Malus threw me to the floor and started back toward his throne, "I was trying to make him miserable but that wasn't working, he was too comfortable in it. I needed something that could catch him off guard, then look who shows up out of the blue, as if it were fated." It must have been then that Malus noticed the little pink light all but hiding behind me, "Oh, looks like you found some trash down in the dungeon." He sat in his throne, leisurely crossing his legs donning edgy boots, "But, alas, as much as I wish to escape, it seems that I'm still short some energy. Havoc is already taking place Flipside in preparation for my grand entrance, but it appears that I need just a little bit more from my host. Unfortunately, the mere sight of me turns him numb, so that's why I've kept you around."

"How could you kill the person you promised forever to?" I struggled to stand up, "You didn't just kill him, you destroyed everything that he was."

"I did my best but it obviously wasn't good enough," Malus stood and walked up to Algernon, grabbing him by the jaw, "what can I do to destroy you?"

Anger spiked through every atom as I bolted toward him. The light yelled at me to stop but I barely heard them over the red that was taking me over like a hot ball of poison, spreading through my entirety. How dare he touch Algernon. Malus turned slightly to glance at me over his shoulder. I only saw it for a moment, the smirk that had taken him, before I was frozen where I stood. Unable to move, I had no idea what had taken me over. As if an outside force had wormed its way into my muscles, I was ossified.

"Maybe I can't destroy Algernon but..." he started to descend the stairs and approach me, "perhaps you can."

"Malus," Algernon raced forward until the chain stopped him, "leave Thaddeus alone. I don't know what happened to you or what you think you're going to do, but this is absurd."

"Absurd?" He stopped, slowly looking back toward Algernon, "What's absurd is this ring on his hand. You married him? You said you'd love me forever,"

"You jumped off of a roof," Algernon's voice cracked, "you're the one who broke our vow, not me."

With a roll of his eyes, Malus looked back to me but continued to speak to Algernon, "I only did that because you drove me to it. You're toxic."

My mind, while panicked, did manage to pull something out of this story that didn't make sense, "How could you have been the thing trying to harm Algernon this whole time when it was the same thing that ruined you?"

Malus was not thrilled with my question.

Something didn't add up.

"You talk too much," raising his hand, shadows jumped up from the floor with his movement. They hovered there, his nebulous eyes studying me, "He's a downgrade in every way. I thought you had standards, Algernon."

He directed his hand toward me and with it came a wave of shadows. Engulfing me, they drown out the light, leaving me surrounded in nothingness.

"Just give up Thaddeus," Malus' voice echoed around me, "I've already won, enviably it'll go my way. If you fight, you're just prolonging the suffering of the greater." He appeared out of nowhere right before me in an endless black room, as if we were standing in an abyss. "So kiddo, what makes you tick?" he brought up his finger to my forehead and when it made contact, my blood spiked cold, everything inside of me stopped.

My mind went blank.

Everything came back into focus and I suddenly didn't remember where I was or what I was doing, I was just standing in the bathroom of my house, pill bottle in hand. Staring down at the label with teary eyes, it took a moment for me to snap back.

Oh yeah, that's what I was doing.

The world would be better off without me.

Young, I knew that I knew best, of course, because that was the illusion of youth.

My grip tightened on the pill bottle, as I closed my eyes, tears falling from them.

"Do it."

A voice so deep it rumbled in my chest startled me and I jumped back when I looked up. Standing in the mirror next to my reflection was a young man, a goth god perhaps. He was not in the room next to me, simply standing in the mirror as his deep blue eyes studied me.

"What?"

"Do it," he looked down to the bottle, "You want to leave, don't you? Why not get it over with? I'm sure everything would be better off without you. If you're not willing to fight and be a useful member of the world, then what's the point, right?"

I was trapped in awe of the shadow before me, I had never seen someone who looked exactly like what I wanted to become. Something about him repeating my thoughts to me made them feel justified, concrete.

"Are you a demon?" I asked, opening the bottle after a slight struggle with the child-poof lid.

"Indeed I am," he walked around to my other side, "after you die, you can join me."

"I can be a demon too?"

"And a powerful one at that," the metal chains on his pants clicked when he bent over some to be eye level with my reflection, "All you have to do is shake my hand. I need your help, I'm trapped somewhere and I need to get out. I'm sure you understand that feeling. But I don't have enough power to do it alone."

A godly demon needed my help? That thrill of significance deposited into my heart, being pumped through my whole being, as I stared at him, "What do you want to do when you escape?"

"Rule the world, of course."

I didn't even feel the smile that took me, I was enthralled in the moment.

Extending his hand, I stared at his reflection and wondered how I was to shake hands with a mirror. The lights flickered and when they turned back on, he had replaced my reflection in the mirror, hand still extended.

"Are you ready to become more than you ever thought you could?"

Reaching my hand toward the mirror, a pink light flickered in the back of my mind, as if was calling me to wake from a dream. It made me pause for a moment, a light jingle taking over my ears. But it wasn't strong enough and as it faded from my attention, the only thing that mattered was becoming more than an insignificant dot on this planet of endless people. I yearned to be more, so much more, than what anyone expected of me, of what my parents said about me, of what I thought about myself. I wanted to be more, I had to be more.

My hand went through the mirror and I took his.

The satisfaction lasted but a moment for it was then that it felt as if a million needles launched into my heart.

He smiled so wide it nearly ripped his skin and he no longer looked godly, but demonic.

For only a moment, a thought floated in my mind.

I had fallen into his trap, again.

Malus was otherworldly in the most dubious of ways.

Eyes opening, I was standing in the throne room. A darkness crawled into the corner of my vision and the longer it was there, the less I noticed it. Something had a grip on me, a dark emotion, a cloudy mind, it was like I was still me but I wasn't at the same time. Algernon stared back at me, frozen as he stood next to his throne.

The sight of him dripped black ink into my blood and with every step I took closer to him, what had a grip on me grew stronger, fueling my thoughts, warping my feelings, until I couldn't tell where I ended and it began. As if every negative feeling I had toward Algernon, every minute annoyance or slight disagreement I held, all grew and was steeped in resentment.

I had no idea how it happened, but suddenly, I hated Algernon.

"Could you possibly get any more dramatic?" I stopped right in front of him, making him back up until the length of chain had been pulled entirely tight. Bringing my hand up, I forcefully placed it on his chest, "A hole right here, one that could just eat you right up? You must know how needlessly edgy that all is. You'd rather wallow in the drama of self pity and isolation. You think you're so cool, but no one is buying it. What you need is to get the fuck over yourself and grow up. It's no wonder your last husband killed himself, you could drive anyone to jump off a skyscraper."

I shoved Algernon to the floor when I saw tears start to bud in his eyes.

But for some reason, I didn't care.

As if his voice had been taken from him, Algernon was speechless as I yanked him up from the ground and shoved him into the back of the throne. The pink orb flew at me but with a swat of my hand, I hit them across the room. They fell to the ground, their light flickering as they stopped moving.

"How long did you think I'd humor you?" My attention rolled back to Algernon as a rumble grew in my ribs, a dark growl that I didn't know I was capable of, "I just stuck around hoping one of these days you get over yourself and stop taking yourself so seriously. But you just care so much about your oh so terrible life that you don't care that you drove Malus to death, and turned Andrew into an alcoholic. I took a gun to my head at your memorial and ended it right there. I no longer have a future because I fell for your show too. I was so young, Algernon, how dare you. I should have let you to rot in your own bullshit."

There Algernon stood, pinned to the throne, eyes wide and locked on mine, looking at me with the purest terror I have ever seen. Something about that sight gave me satisfaction.

"What, not sure what to do now that someone is standing up to you and not just folding under your charm?"

After those words left my mouth, my eyes were snagged by something. My left fist was closed over Algernon's shirt and on my ring finger sat my engagement ring. It was glowing green, heating up, as if it was rejecting me. Hissing through my teeth as it stung more, I ripped it from my finger and crushed it in my fist. It turned into a cloud of green glitter before fading away. Algernon's eyes sat on the fading sparkles for a moment before slowly returning to mine.

"I thought you loved me."

The quiver of his voice, the weakness in every word, it was music to me as I savored the crushing moment that passed between us.

"No one could ever love you, Algernon."

His breath hitched and the pain was viscerally palpable.

Wait.

What the fuck was I saying?

As if woken from a daze, I was suddenly aware of the force overpowering me, bending me to its will, making me say and do things I never would. Malus had infected me, used me to hurt Algernon in a way only the one person he let in could.

I felt a tingle in my hand as the light in his eyes started to dim, tears falling from them, his color draining. I had made Algernon feel something and now Malus had what he wanted: power. The blood dropped from my head, making me dizzy as my knees buckled. Falling back from Algernon, he was left, petrified, as my shadow ripped away from me.

"Perfect," The deep rumble of Malus' voice started to distort, "you are a great puppet Thaddeus, my words sound so good rolling off of your tongue."

The pressure in the room was so crushing even I felt it. Algernon's hand flew to his face as he stumbled to the floor.

"Without that ring, there's nothing you can do to stop me." The shadow grew into a monster, long, tall, dark, white pinhole light eyes, death personified.

The little pink orb came racing toward us, "Don't let him leave"

A bright white light exploded bleaching my vision. When it faded out, there was a vortex beaming up from the center of the throne room.

"With this power, I'll be able to reopen the gate to below and allow my friends to take back the Earth." Shadow Malus started to move toward the beam as I struggled to get up.

The pressure was bad, so bad, I couldn't even breathe. Algernon fought against it too and the pink light started to fly around me in a panic.

"Stop him, do anything,"

When I lost balance and fell into the side of the throne, my hand brushed against my blazer pocket. Eyes jumping to the shadow as it grew closer to the vortex, my hand grasped the orb in my pocket. If it could transport me somewhere, then maybe it could transport him too. In one last test of strength, I bolted toward the shadow, orb in hand, vengeance powering every muscle under the pressure. Algernon looked up to me, unable to move further than the length of his chain. I wasn't sure if he truly knew those words weren't mine, but I didn't have time to tell him.

Catching up with the shadow, I wound back my arm, my grip tight on the orb, and with everything I had left in me, I threw it at him. I lost my footing and went down as it crashed into his back shattering. A moment later, everything went black.

Falling, I felt like I was falling. Opening my eyes, I was on the ground. Looking up, I saw the sky; but that didn't make sense. Sitting up from the concrete, I looked to one side and saw Algernon laying there, the chain broken but still attached to his leg. He woke and jumped up, eyes on me. But then they drifted to the side, and that's when they went wide. Turning around, I saw Malus' mangled, bloodied body laying there. Looking up again I realized, we were in the shadow of Algernon's skyscraper.

I thought we had watched it all, his memories up until the end. So why were we here again?

His body didn't move, but a moment later, his ghost sat right up from it. Algernon and I both startled, but it appeared that he couldn't see us. Malus fell away from his body, obviously panicked, looking it over. He didn't say anything, but I could see a million thoughts race through his mind as he was taken by confusion, but then; then he was hit by something, a realization so strong it took the air down with it.

"Algernon,"

As he ran toward the building, I knew what he was feeling. It's what we all feel right after: regret. Algernon and I stood, chasing after him. Malus couldn't reach out and touch the door, though he tried. After failing a few times, he went to slam his side into it a fazed through though. We followed him through the food, fazing beyond it as well, to see him standing there, shock painting him. It only lasted a moment before he went racing toward the elevator that was opening from another tenant leaving. We barely made it inside with him. As Malus tried to interact with the number pad, Algernon looked at me.

"What is this?"

"I think it's a memory. I accidentally ended up in them earlier, so I know about what happened between you an Malus. But I thought they ended when he died. I took one of the things holding his memories earlier, and that's what I tried to stop him with just now. I was hoping to capture him inside it too, but I don't know if I did."

Malus tried to slam his hand into the number pad but when it went through, the whole elevator hummed and shot upward, nearly knocking all of us from our feet. The door violently opened on Algernon's floor and we followed Malus as he ran toward the door.

It was then that Algernon stopped running.

I stopped too, turning to look at him as Malus continued to run.

"Don't follow him."

"Why not?" I wanted to keep running, but I didn't want to do it without Algernon.

"I don't want you to see what I did,"

"Algernon, please. It's a memory, it can't be changed."

With a heavy sigh, Algernon took off running again and I rushed with him. We caught up to Mauls just as he ran fazing through the door and when we followed, what I heard was Earth shattering. Malus yell Algernon's name, looking at him as he stood on a chair next to a noose hanging from a pipe on the ceiling.

"Algernon, don't do it," Malus couldn't make contact with Algernon, he just kept fazing through, "Algernon, I'm sorry, I'm sorry, don't follow me, Algernon, please, I love you." He tried to interact with the chair but he couldn't get it to move, couldn't get Algernon away from the noose as he stood there with it in his hands, contemplating.

"You are right Malus," the younger Algernon from the past said to nobody, "I am a plague, I'll destroy everyone around me. You shouldn't have had to be the one who died, I should have been decent and exterminated myself."

I stood, horrified, staring at the scene unfolding before me.

"No, it wasn't you, I don't know what possessed me. Algernon, you can't die. You have so much promise, you can't..."

Malus stepped away as Algernon started to put the noose over his head. Stumbling back into the end table with a home phone line sitting on it, Malus tried to reach for it. A shock of electricity later, he jumped back and the phone fell off of the receiver. It started to ring, then when the other end picked up, we were met with the 911 emergency operator. Algernon didn't even seem to notice the phone or the woman asking about his emergency, he just continued to speak on to nobody.

"Once I die, maybe whatever is haunting me will die too. The world would be better off without me, I'm not adding anything but fairy tales to it. If the ghosts were there, they would have reached out to me by now. There is nothing, I'm nothing, we're all nothing."

The operator seemed concerned, asking where his location was.

Algernon fell quiet, looking at the ground, noose tightened around his neck, a storm swirling in his eyes. I looked over to the Algernon of the present who was standing by my side, looking at the ground as well.

"Don't follow me," Malus' cracking voice cracked my heart, despite knowing what I did about him. There had to be more to this story, because as I watched him fall to pieces, begging Algernon to live, I knew he loved him. "Please, Algernon, don't do this. You'll regret it, please,"

As Algernon started to bring his hands down from the tightened noose, I saw a dreary resolve formulate in his eyes. I knew that look, I had seen it within my own eyes in a mirror one dark night years ago. I wanted to stop him, but I knew somehow, someone must have; so all I did was stand there and watch as tragedy unfolded.

Algernon stepped off of the chair. A short drop later he started to choke and struggle as Malus yelled his name. The door flung open and running through it came the security guard, Tasha, that I had watched Algernon converse with before. She yelled for Algernon and when she entered the room we were in, I could hear her heart break with her gasp. Running to Algernon's side, she pulled out a knife and cut the rope. Holding him in her arms, she told him all the things a mother would: it's going to be alright, you're going to be okay, help is on the way, I love you.

Please don't die.

For a moment, I think I knew what family, actual family, looked like.

Malus of the past went stumbling back, obviously distraught, as paramedic sirens blared outside. They were so loud, we could hear them all the way up there. As Malus ran from the apartment and we followed, I glanced back at Algernon of the past and wondered what he was thinking. Did he have any idea that that was just the beginning of the end?

Exiting the apartment building, I had no idea where Malus was going and when I looked over to my Algernon, he didn't really seem to either. Winding around corners, running through people like the ghosts that we were, it was all startling. It was still unreal, the idea that I was now dead because I felt so very not dead. We started into a part of town I knew well, but Algernon knew it better. Clubs pulsated, coming to life as the night grew darker. As we passed the bouncers I had come to know, I wondered if they'd remember me now that I was gone.

I was gone.

My pace started to drag as my mind drifted.

I was dead.

After a convoluted chase, Malus lost speed, stumbling to a stop.

We all knew this parking lot well.

This was where Algernon made my heart jump for the first time.

This was where we got cursed.

This was where Malus murdered Algernon.

And this was where I killed myself.

But yet again we were here, why?

Malus started to race around the look, looking about, "Where are you? You vortex thing?" His yells didn't echo, even though they were loud enough to, "Show yourself you cowardly piece of shit. You cursed my husband, you ruined our lives. At least come out and fight me." He stopped, just staring forward in utter desolation, "I have nothing else to lose."

A white light flashed so brightly it bleached my vision. When it faded out, there it was, right where it had been the day I met it: the vortex.

Slowly turning around, Malus saw the vortex behind him, beaming up into the sky from the ground. After a moment, he started to approach it. The white cracked into black, a dark figure stating to form in the light.

"Nothing left to lose?" A deep voice so low it was distorted ripped the air.

"You've taken everything away from me," Malus stopped a few steps away from the vortex and the shadow growing inside, "You did something to my husband, you made us both sick. To what end? What did you want?"

"Do you want your husband to be free of me?" The dark figure extended their hand, "If you give yourself to me, I will finish what I started and in doing so, Algernon will be free."

"Malus," My Algernon said from my side, taking a step forward, "don't..."

"You promise?" Malus extended his hand but hesitated.

The shadow nodded.

When their hands made contact, the shadow overtook Malus, drowning out his scream. As he was engulfed in darkness, I couldn't do a thing but be shocked and watch. Soon his entire being was taken by it and when his yelling subsided, all that was left was a faint pink glow in his chest. The shadow that was one Malus reached into his own chest, his dark hand disappearing inside of him. A few moments later, he ripped a small pink light from his core.

His voice was twisted with darkness as he inspected the small pink light, "Thank you for the vessel, I'm one step closer to returning to my glory. Humans are so precious, they put up bold fronts but truly, their souls are nothing more than a bit of light." crushing the light in his fist, the shadow started to fade and Malus was left standing in the vortex. But as he vanished into it, I now knew, that wasn't really Malus.

Everything started to fall out of focus as I looked over to the light floating next to me.

The vortex was our enemy from the start.

Waking up was strange, it was slow then all at once. Flying up, I found myself on the ground in the throne room, Algernon at my side, the small pink light floating above us. The vortex sat in the middle of the room, but the demon was nowhere to be seen. The walls were crumbling, this inner world was starting to fall apart.

"So it seems I've been outed," the light floated away from us and toward the vortex before coming to a stop, "maybe I should have told you."

A heavy sigh came from my side, making me look over to see Algernon sitting up, holding his face in his hand.

"Perhaps," Algernon stood, "if you had said something earlier I would have been more inclined to deck that fucker when I had the chance."

I stood too, "Why didn't you tell us?"

"It's... embarrassing." The light flew around in distressed circles, "You know how I used to look I'm sure. I was the perfect aesthetic of punk and classy goth. Now I'm like, a fucking pink light."

Algernon groaned through clenched teeth, visibly picking his words carefully, "You've been trapped here since that day?"

"I have," the light slowed down, "you've gotten older."

Algernon looked away and I could see the conflict evident in the deepest swirls of his eyes, "Time does that."

"So you don't know about anything that has happened?" I approached the light, giving Algernon space, "You're really Malus and that thing is parading around in your, uh... ghost body?"

"All I know is that he took me over then locked me away. He'd visit and taunt me sometimes, knowing I couldn't get out, and tell me some things about his plans but I never could do anything about it. I'm not strong enough on my own to take myself back from him."

"What could help?" I asked, looking at the vortex as it showered the room in light.

"The ring but, he destroyed it."

"Ring?" Algernon asked, obviously startling Malus the light.

"Yes, the engagement ring Thaddeus was wearing. Because it was made with a special vow, it has some sort of powers. He'd mumble about it being a problematic weakness."

"So if somehow we were able to make an opening, would you be able to get in there and take yourself back?" Algernon's cogs were turning, I could see them.

"It's no exact science of course, but I think so."

Algernon gave a light nod, thinking as he looked down.

"If you guys have the start of a plan, we should go after him. Who knows what he's doing out there." I started to reach toward the vortex as the others joined me, "How are we going to find him, the city is so big."

Algernon extended his hand out toward Malus the light and spoke softly, "We don't want to lose you, you're our secret weapon."

After a pause, the light flew into Algernon's hand and he carefully closed his fingers over the light.

Taking Algernon's other hand, I looked over to him, "We have things to talk about,"

His pause held the weight of a universe in its silence, "We do,"

"But," I looked back toward the light, "let's fuck up a demon first."

Algernon nodded and together we stepped into the vortex.

It stung like it did the first time, I could feel my existence being taken apart bit by bit and I could only hope that I'd be put back together correctly on the other side.

My mind swam with possibilities, with fights and fears and failures. I didn't know what to expect, but I did know one thing. The demon found it to be an advantageous weakness of ours, devotion. But as my grip tightened in Algernon's hand, I knew it was going to be what saved us; if anything could at this point.

11

VORTEX

Being thrown, I wasn't able to catch my footing before I fell to the hard asphalt of a parking lot. My skin crawled, the air was cold and electrified. Sitting up, aching and shaking, my eyes were met with the vortex as I knew it, a beam reaching into the sky from the lot. Clouds, rumbling, it was dark, as I looked around. Algernon sat up not far away from me, opening his hand and saying something quietly to Malus' soul, the little light he held carefully. I watched as he nodded then started to fiddle with his crooked glasses.

Standing, I was suddenly crushed by the size of the city. How were we going to find him? My eyes searched the sky then they caught on something. A huge storm cloud, a reverse tornado of types. Lighting struck from within it, the rolling of thunder followed, bouncing off of the skyscrapers surrounding.

"Where should we look?" Algernon came to my side.

I pointed up at the storm.

He stared at it for a moment.

"Giant doom cloud," he looked down to me, "seems like a reasonable place to start."

We were about to take off running when a shill voice stopped us.

"I warned you,"

Stopping, we turned to see that same rainbow vomit stain of a profit person who approached Algernon and I once upon a time in a store. They ran to us, their matted dreads bouncing behind them as their entire appearance managed to still be glaring in the darkest of days.

"Can you see us?" Algernon asked, turning to fully face them as he messed with his glasses.

"Of course I can," they stopped, "you're dead. You caused a lot of issues for those good people at the memorial, Thaddeus. I hope you know that."

Algernon looked at me.

I looked away.

After a long sigh, they looked around, "Where's the girl?"

My heart dropped as I looked away and that's when Algernon probably realized I had stopped talking about Honore a while ago because he appeared saddened. "She moved on,"

They nodded, "Good for her," a pause passed as they looked over and saw the vortex. It took a moment to click, then they jumped away, "It's open?"

"That it is..." I tried to drag my mind back into the present and away from a flower on a grassy hill with a view of the world, "the demon stuck in it has escaped. He's possessing a... friend, and we're going to go stop him."

"Or we're going to try," Malus' little pink soul flew from Algernon's hands, "He's trying to open some door to a place called Netherside. He said something about reclaiming Earth, coming out of hiding. I'm not too sure, but it's not good."

"The storm over there, it must be where things began." They started to inspect the vortex, "So it's where this will all end. If you head there and are able to expel the demon from the host, I'll work on closing this so he'll have nowhere else to go and he'll probably dissipate."

"Thank you," I started to turn away from them, "Hey, do you have a name?"

They looked up to me, put on pause, "Arlene."

"Good luck Arlene," Algernon said as Malus' light went back into his hands, "I'm sorry we didn't understand your warning. We did try, I promise."

"I didn't really understand it either," they waved us off with a laugh, "paranormal shit is just like that,"

That wasn't the most comforting thing to hear in the universe. With it, though, we went running off down the sidewalk. We were running across a road when a car cane rushing by and went right through me. I nearly fell from my feet, but then I remembered again.

I'm dead.

I'm really dead.

Algernon called out to me and I came running, but every step felt heavier than the last. Looking down, I did not have a shadow, I didn't make sound when I made contact with the ground. I felt as if I didn't belong, like an unwelcome guest in this world. That if I close my eyes hard enough, they'd never open again. Was this how Honore felt?

Windows were broken, people ran around yelling. Blood stained the sidewalks, car alarms blared. It was like we had fallen into another world, one plagued by horror. We ran by an alley, and as we passed, my eyes caught on a severed human arm.

My heart stopped.

I couldn't feel anything as I just kept running.

What was going on?

As we grew closer, I realized what building we were approaching. Algernon's apartment building stood darkly in the sky, crowned by a storm. This was where it all started? With the remnants of a plan, shaking spite the only thing to our names, we fazed through the front doors. But soon, we were faced with another issue: the elevator.

Standing outside the metal doors, Algernon and I stared at them for a moment.

"How did you do this last time, Malus?" I asked as Algernon opened his hand some for the little light to see out.

"I have no idea, ghost shit is nonsense."

"That it is..." I paused then looked to Algernon, "Wait, are stairs a thing?"

Lighting up, he started running again. As we raced down the lobby hall, we passed Tasha. She paused in her step then turned around entirely. Staring back, it took her a moment but then she called out.

"Algernon?"

Algernon stopped, the air going still for a moment in the middle of the chaos. Staring back at her, he took a few steps her direction as she started running toward us, "Tasha, you can see me?"

Tasha stopped, looking around desperately, "I think I just saw you, just for a moment." her heart visibly breaking, sadness only ruled her expression for a moment before her glassy eyes were met with a smile, "Sweetheart, if you're here, just know that I'm proud of you. You fought through so much, you rebuilt in the wake of tragedy, and I watched you every step of the way. You helped me through rough times without even knowing it, you saved me. I hope you're not stuck here, if anyone deserves to find peace, it's you."

"Tasha," Algernon stared at her, and in that pause, I saw warmth flash over his features, "thank you for always being here. I wish you could hear me, I never really thanked you like I should have. You saved me too..." Stepping forward, he tried to carefully wrap his arms around her but not faze through her at the same time.

A quick breath took Tasha with a shiver. Looking down, she smiled a little as tears started to take her, "Do what you need to do kiddo, I'll see you on the other side." she laughed a little, bringing her hand up to her face as Algernon stepped back. "The world may be ending as we know it though, so maybe I'll see you sooner than previously anticipated."

Algernon took one last long look at Tasha before looking away, "I won't let that happen,"

And with that, we were running back toward the stairs at the end of the lobby hall. Fazing through the door, we were met with towering staircases, many of which we had to ascend. I instinctively cringed at the thought, but then I remembered something.

I'm dead.

Following Algernon up each flight of stairs, I now knew what it felt like to be able to run without restraint, without getting winded, without pain, and though I was dead, I felt alive. But with each flight of stairs more, I knew we were growing closer to something that was now scarier than death. What happened to a ghost, if they were to die again? I had passed the first unknown and found what was on the other side, but again I was faced with a greater unknown, a death beyond death.

A demon awaited us, and if he won we wouldn't be the only ones facing a death beyond death.

Reaching the top door, Algernon stopped.

"Thaddeus," he turned to look at me, "do you trust me?"

"Of course I do," I put my hand on his shoulder, "but with that said, what are you planning to do?"

"I think I can catch him off guard long enough to make an opening, but it may not work."

My dead heart started to slow, "I can't watch you die again."

His eyes searched mine, the pang of sadness that took him visible as he looked away, "I know, I'm sorry. But he is trying to destroy my home, my late husband, and everyone I care about. I'm already dead, Tasha isn't." He faced me entirely, "I'm not planing on losing, but Thaddeus, please, you're just going to have to trust me."

It took every fiber of my being but, "Okay," I stepped forward, my heart jumping as I kissed him. A beat passed before I carefully pulled back, hovering inches away, "I love you."

"I love you too."

A moment of pause, eyes locked, we looked into each other, before we fazed through the door.

Stepping from the stairwell to a storm, the winds blew through us but somehow I could still feel them. Darkness, lightning, the walls were cracking, the poles on top of the building being torn out. As if we had stepped into the center of a black hole, the gravity was compelling, the vacuum compounding, light being ripped apart as it struggled to pull through. A layer between everything, a dimension of its own, that's what this looked like the beginnings of.

A gate lingered in the sky, woven out of dark clouds, as it hovered above us. The center was yet to form, all that sat inside was the distant glows of red. We could feel the heat in emanated from all the way down there where we stood. It was clear, whatever that gate led to would be the end of us all, living or dead.

"You finally made it," Malus' possessed form emerged from the brewing clouds around us, leisurely approaching with each soundless step, "I thought you had given up. Which you should, really, there's no stopping me now."

The look Algernon wore, it held echo of the shrewd tour guide I met back then. It was the face of an actor analyzing a scene, reading a room, formulating a plan. It was dangerous, powerful, what sat at his core. The clouds parted some as he took his first step forward and with each that followed, the rumble of thunder grew.

"You have taken everything away from me." Algernon's voice held every ounce of agony in the undertones from the last five years, "First, you derailed my mind, then you poisoned my relationship. You destroyed my spirit and darkened my life. You obliterated my husband then tried to take me down with him. You annihilated my ability to connect with people, you dismantled Andrew. You took happiness, you took anger, you took sadness and excitement and peace and love, you left me with nothing but numbness. You turned me into a record on repeat, a rerun tragedy. Then, after all of that, you took my life. I've done nothing but defend and try to reach out to things like you, to the paranormal, and I was met with radio silence the entire time. But I never stopped because I knew what it felt like to be overlooked, that's why I chose to be the center of attention just to bring attention to you too." His pace quickened, his tone rose, "I gave you the benefit of the doubt for years and you gave me profound nothingness. This is my home, my place in this world. And I would rather be banished to the void than let you take this away from me too."

Algernon darted forward.

The demon stumbled back but he wasn't quick enough.

The clouds froze, all movement and sound around us ceased.

Algernon's hand lodged in the demon's chest, a pink light grew. The demon yelled as he fell away, a pink hole growing in his core, eating away at his insides as he stumbled back. When

Algernon pulled back his hand, I saw a ring on his finger that was the source of the light.

The smirk he wore was wild, "That was in honor of my first husband," Algernon lunged at the demon again while he was discombobulated and landed another punch that sent off another chain reaction, as if the clouds around us caught fire at the corers and started to burn away like paper.

The air smelled like melting plastic.

This time when Algernon pulled back, the pink lingered in the demon's chest and a moment later, pink exploded, sending Algernon and I flying back. Crashing into the wall, my eyes lost focus for a moment. When it veered back, I saw the demon falling around, his shadow glitching, hands to his head, as the pink spread throughout. Looking over to Algernon, I saw that he no longer had the little light that was Malus and that's when I figured out his plan. The pink overtook the demon and the ground started to rumble, the sky flashing all sorts of colors as the air dropped.

In a suspended moment of silence, everything was still.

Black exploded and tainted the surroundings, twitching as if it were alive. Malus fell to his knees, coughing violently. Without a bit of hesitation, Algernon sprinted toward him. It took me a moment to catch up to him. On his knees next to Malus, hand on his back, I couldn't help but feel a twinge of jealousy as I watched Algernon dote. But I knew that was unfounded, they had been married first, they had loved longer.

I had no right to feel that way.

"Did it work?" Algernon watched as Malus sat up, looking like a goth god even in his most worn of states.

The way Malus looked at Algernon, that's what did it, what created a crack in my heart. He loved Algernon so much, I could just see it.

"It did," Malus jumped onto Algernon, hugging his so excitedly that he almost knocked them both from their knees. Algernon helped him up but Malus nearly fell over. Laughing, he draped an arm over Algernon's shoulders, "I've been that little light thing for so fucking long I forgot what having legs felt like."

I glanced out toward the city as the clouds around us started to dissipate but the gate remained.

My heart stopped.

The vortex still stretched into the sky, it hadn't been closed. The ground rumbled and another light shot up into the sky, followed by another and another. Beams screamed into the clouds, ripping apart the sky. Vortexes surrounded the skyscraper from all sides, and they were just growing closer.

The black around us started to twitch.

"Very clever," the demon's distorted voice came from everywhere but nowhere at once.

The sun turned red.

"But before you attack an enemy Algernon, you should make sure your side is secured, that there are no cracks."

A line of fire caught on the ground and started to race toward me. I took a few steps back and that's when my eyes caught on Algernon's. The terror in them told me what was about to happen. The last time he got inside my head, I didn't defeat him. The last time, he chose to let me go. We saw what he had done to Malus, and as the fire circled around me, there was no telling what he'd do to me.

Algernon yelled something, running from Malus' side as the fire around me grew into a wall. He may have made it to me in time, but Mauls grabbed him, pulling him back.

The last thing I saw before my world was taken by the flames was Algernon not fighting to get away from Malus.

The crack grew.

"Problematic, isn't it Thaddeus?"

When the flames rose, they cut off the rest of the world. Silence took the air, the roar of the flames dulling. The fire flashed black and before me, the shadows materialized into a solid figure. The black silhouette, the person I saw when Algernon's world jumped dimensions, was a matter of feet in front of me, staring me down with their pinhole white light eyes.

This was what scared me out of the basement back then, the noxious pressure following Algernon, the parasite that yearned to be a king, the poison that had infected the entire night club district, the shadow that locked the area in a limbo, a world of its own. I was facing the vortex, the demon who lived inside, and no one was coming to save me.

"It was easy, when Malus was the bad guy, but now you can't hate him. Your cause was a just one, fueled by devotion, but now, what do you have now? You are faced with an eternity of ghostly time, which could be considered a happy fate, if it were just Algernon and you. But could you really stand an eternity of standing by, watching them be together? Even if Algernon chose you, would you even believe he didn't love Malus?"

Staring at the demon before me, my mind snagged on itself. Were the feelings he was dredging up inside me warranted? Or were they the product of a society that valued monogamy, could I be happy with both, or neither, or what, I just didn't even know. Romance wasn't everything, but Algernon was certainly important to me. He was trying to unravel me with this love triangle bullshit and as much as I hated to admit it, it was working. As much as I knew better, as much as I understood why it shouldn't, the idea of Algernon leaving me hurt. I knew he had loved Malus first, that if Malus hadn't died, they'd still be married. That if we had met then, Algernon would have never acted on me.

My happiness was built on Malus' headstone and that was horrible.

I wanted Algernon to be happy, but I wanted Malus to be dead, and that was even worse.

I was awful.

The fire ripping around me carried my darkest emotions, my taboos and my forbidden thoughts, out into the open. I knew he was a demon, I knew that this is what he did. But knowing that didn't make it any less effective.

"Why are you doing all this?" I asked, dragging my eyes away from the fire and onto the demon's white pinhole lights.

"All of it? I dream of escape, of acceptance and power. You know, you and I aren't all that different. Back then when you stepped on the vortex, I was actually aiming for you. I sensed a certain, understanding. We know what it feels like to be ostracized as if it is apart of us, we are both outcast from a land, both running from ourselves. I was like you once, and the longer you stay here, the longer you are trapped with these dark emotions, the closer you get to flipping the script, to becoming what you hate. You think you are a protagonist right now, but could a hero really feel what you are? You felt it in the dungeon, the want to forsake it all, the destroy everything. That's still within your power. Make a deal with me. You will get the power you wish for, I will have a vessel, and together we could be something great."

Feeling the heat from the flames rise, I was starting to become aware of their ever movement, "Do you really assume I'm that stupid?"

"Stupid? No, of course not. That's an insult to my judgment." The demon started to walk circles around me, the fire dancing behind him as he passed, "It would be stupid to say no. What do you have waiting for you? An eternity of uncertainty, of romantic tensions and nothingness. Think forward, imagine a hundred years from now. No matter how much you may love Algernon, in a hundred years, every feeling you have will be gone. You will deteriorate, you will fester and turn into me. I needed Algernon's emotions for power because I have none of my own, not anymore." He stopped, swiping his hand into the fire and made a heart in the air between us with it. "So you can either expel me here and hope I don't find a new host in time, slowly becoming what you once thought yourself above." he swatted the heat, causing it to dissipate, "Or you can accept me here and we can destroy everything that has wronged us. We can set my people free, to be apart of this world once again and we can sit on top of it all. Wouldn't you like to see your family suffer, to see the faces of everyone who thought you were nothing? You've spent your whole life being nothing, don't you want to be something?"

He was enchanting, his words wove magic behind my eyes, tales of drawing dreams and unmatched audacity. He was darkness, he was power and robustly regal. He was everything I wanted to be, everything I wished I could become. Algernon was the happily ever after that was too good to be true, Malus was the reality I wished I didn't know, and I? I was the no-good kid with no future. I was locked away, I was forgotten, I was an imposter hero. I had been tamed once, drown in personable blue and pills, but now that I had my colors back, what did I want to be?

He was right.

One of two things were going to happen, if I kept my hand at my side.

I would either spend eternity watching Algernon be happy, unable to be happy for him and hating myself. Or leave it all and spend forever slowly turning into the monster that stood before me.

"Why wait it out and go through all the pain it takes to become numb," the demon extended his hand, "when you can make a deal with me and become something great in a blink of an eye?"

When he saw my hesitation, my reservation, my pause, he probably knew he was getting close to breaking me.

"And if you say no, I bet I could get Algernon to say yes. It's you or him, Thaddeus."

"I don't suppose you'd just go back into the vortex and leave us all alone, would you?"

He laughed, and somewhere deep in the rumble, I actually heard something a little human in there, "Even if I wanted to, I couldn't. The realm inside is imploding, there won't be anywhere to go back to soon. Once it's closed, what's on the other side will be destroyed. It's a shame really, it was a nice castle. Not as nice as my last one, but it was okay."

The flicker of a third option lit in my mind.

A slight smile took me.

I had made my decision.

There was only one way that this could end, one choice that would hurt the least.

He may have been able to sway me, to sell me on the ideas of power and dramatics. But I fell in love with a tour guide and knew how to see through an act. I knew that nothing but suffering was behind that bravado, that maybe there was something of substance to it once upon a time but now, his promises were empty. That he didn't mean it, he was just going to use me like he used Malus and I'd be damned if I ever let him do it again.

But he was right, I would become him, if I expelled him.

I loved Algernon, and I wanted him to be happy. But I was not audacious enough to believe myself impervious to the fickle faults of the human heart, that I wouldn't someday come to resent him and Malus out of my own selfish devotion. But I didn't want that to happen, so to me that was the part of me that was a redeemable human being. Perhaps I wasn't on par with a demon for feeling these things, not yet anyway.

And I wasn't about to give myself the chance to be.

As I took the demon's hand, my heart slowed.

I hoped that Algernon would be able to get over me.

It probably wouldn't be to hard, he now had Malus after all.

He only loved me because Malus was dead, so the same must be true the other direction too.

"Deal," I was resigned to my fate, the choice I had made, and I could only hope that the demon hadn't seen right through me too.

"Fantastic," with the rumble of their voice, the black fire imploded on me, burning my every inch for but a moment until it became apart of me, "Enjoy the power, I'll give you the wheel."

Like the door opened on a space ship, the air left the sky and we were left in a vacuum. A fractured moment, a fraction of eternity, we were trapped in it.

Algernon and Malus stared at me, thrown against the far wall next to the door as if the power of my deal had thrown them away. I stood, boldly before them, smile on my face, but inside I was still.

"You didn't..." Malus ran up to me, leaving Algernon on the floor behind, "You betrayed us."

"The only allegiance I have to you is in my respect for Algernon," I pushed him away from me and he went violently tumbling, "Don't pretend like you understand,"

Power coursed through me, and for the first time, I felt like I could actually do something.

"Thaddeus," Algernon came running right up to me, very little space between us, "did you make a deal with him?"

I could see my reflection in his glasses, my eyes were black, "That I did,"

He was breathless, being visibly crushed by the paranormal pressure, "Why?"

For a moment, just a moment, I wanted to go back. I wanted to undo what I had done, to try to make eternity work out, but I knew that was simply nativity. Slowly leaning forward, I initiated a kiss. His eyes fell closed as he kissed me back and I followed, wrapping my arms around him.

Maybe he noticed how badly I was shaking.

It took everything that I was to keep this power caged, to not fall to it. Now that it was in my blood, it felt like a drug, and I wanted nothing more than to act on the immense need to conquer. My mind raced with murder, my heart spiked with adrenaline, I could understand how this breed of toxin could contort a person's soul.

Whispering for it was all I could mange as I felt myself be liquefied from the inside, I tried to keep my tone even as I pulled Algernon into a hug, "Because someone has to stop it."

Throwing him away from me, I could see the confusion, the concern, the heartbreak, all splash over him in waves. Taking a few steps backward, I could feel the demon inside start to revolt. He had probably caught on.

"He thinks I am his host, but he is my hostage. The vortex is going to implode once it's closed, everything inside will be banished beyond. That's the only way to stop him, but he won't go back willingly. Now that he has infected me, I'm going to go back inside it. That way, he'll never be able to escape again."

Algernon and Malus picked themselves up and ran toward me again, Algernon faster than Malus as he yelled, "But that means you'll be banished too."

It was difficult, but I managed a smile as I stood on the edge of the skyscraper, an open vortex directly behind me way down on the ground. "I know. It's better this way," my words were cut off by a cough, the demon was trying to take control but I wasn't going to let him, "This way, you two can have the forever you promised each other. You won't have to worry about me getting in the way," I looked up to Algernon, tears budding in my eyes, "and I don't have to watch."

That was the moment, the one that would be seared into my soul.

The moment I knew that I had really, truly, hurt Algernon.

I was one of the few capable of it, one of the only ones he had given enough of himself to to be able to forge it into a weapon and shove it right back into his heart.

Love was dangerous, playing with knives.

One of us was bound to get cut eventually.

I took a step back, one closer to stepping off of that roof and becoming nothing.

Uniquely situated, I was the only one suitable to sacrifice. The demon was right, I was worth very little. But that just made me the perfect one to take him down. Malus standing at Algernon's side, his eyes wide, they were locked on me.

"I would rather die a death beyond death," I took another step back, fighting with every muscle in my body, "than watch myself fall out of love with you, than watch time turn my devotion to resentment, than to be in your way, than make things harder for you, than to lose myself." I fought to take another step back, "Please be happy Algernon, you've spent so long in misery, you deserve an eternity of happiness."

"Yes," Malus said, starting to walk toward me, "you're right, he does." Malus stopped before me, looking right into my eyes, "I get it now, thank you Thaddeus." he extended his left hand my way, "I spent so long trapped in that basement, thinking about everything, wondering why it all happened this way. But I get it now, you helped it make sense. Thank you for taking care of Algernon, but before you step off, can you promise me something?" he took my left hand and a slight smile lit up on his face, "you'll never stop?"

He shook my hand.

What?

Suddenly my arm stung, a little pink light emanating from our hands. I realized what was causing it, the ring Malus now wore. I could feel it, ripping the demon out from inside of me, "He has already lost one husband over this ledge, don't make him lose another one." he stepped forward, trapping me in a hug as he whispered, "I was locked away, kept here so long, so when you were prepared to give everything up for Algernon, you wouldn't have to. When you were trapped in the fire, he tried to get through it, no matter how much I tried to stop him. I wanted you to burn, but after seeing the way Algernon looks at you, I know I'm the one who deserves to."

Pink exploded, making my ears ring.

I was yanked away from the ledge, thrown inwardly and in the confusion, I fell into someone else's arms.

Standing there as the pink faded, Malus was one step away from the ledge, looking over at us in visible pain as his eyes went black, "We were faced with the same choice, Thaddeus. But you picked the right one."

I could see the tears as they rolled down his face.

"If you see a girl named Honore on the other side," my voice cracked, "would you say hello to her for me?"

He nodded.

The ground rumbled, shaking the building.

"I love you Algernon," Malus said, starting to take his last step back, "don't forget me,"

Algernon struggled to maintain composure as the ground rumbled again, "I couldn't even if I wanted to... trust me."

Malus laughed, wiping his face as he wore a smile.

Taking one step back, our eyes locked for a moment before he plummeted out of sight.

Algernon did not reach out for him.

Running up to the ledge, I looked down to see nothing but a humanoid shaped dot before it crashed into the vortex below. The light turned pink, shooting into the sky. One after another, the vortexes around turned pink, the lights growing, engulfing everything around them. As we watched, we stood in silence. Unsure if it worked, unsure if this was the end, having no idea what to expect after having passed the first unknown, we took each others hand and held on tight. Turning to look at him, Algernon's hair was messy, his clothing dishevel, his glasses crooked, his eyes watery. He turned to look at me too and probably saw a similar disaster at his side. Leaning forward, I took the back of his head in my free hand ad I pulled him into a kiss. Closing my eyes, I could still see the pink light as it engulfed the world.

As it took us too, everything felt warm for a moment.

Soon, all that was left was pink.

Everything was pink.

And as everything faded into that color, there was a small sound chiming in the background of my mind: a little bell.

12

TOUR GUIDE

"What was the first thing you noticed about me?"

Algernon walked next to me, looking up at the sunset sky, "The color of your eyes. They're a fascinating shade, chartreuse." We rounded a corner in the night club district, "What did you notice about me?"

"Your dumb hipster glasses."

He laughed, adjusting his glasses.

It had been a while since it all fell apart, since judgment day brought with it havoc and unexplained chaos. Physiologists were all over it, but there was no explanation for the mass hysteria, for the spell that had taken over the night club district and all who inhabited it.

An anomaly, they called it.

We knew the truth, though no one would ever believe us.

Approaching Refuge as the sun disappeared, welcoming the stars, I smiled at its rainbow flags and loud music. Algernon nodded at the bouncers before walking through the door that was being held open. I followed him toward the bar toward the seats we had sat in the very first time I came here with him. Sitting down, I looked around at all the dancing bodies, the flashing lights and smiles. I liked it there, it really did live up to its name.

Lady Spectra came up to us, sliding two glasses our way. "I hope you boys have been having a good night so far,"

Algernon looked down at the glass, a slight smile on his face, "The good nights outnumber the bad ones these days."

Lady Spectra leaned up against the bar, her color scheme of of reds and oranges tonight as her makeup glittered and her dress shone, "Things have been quiet since everything got bad. I really thought it was the end of times or something."

Someone sat down next to Algernon.

Looking up from my drink, I saw Andrew, painted in the flashing lights of the club, a small smile on his face, "It was something, it was like everyone got possessed. Like four people were killed in a two hour span down here."

Lady Spectra tuned to face him, a small laugh on her breath, "Don't do drugs kids," she started back into the bar, "What can I get for you, Mr. Sober?"

"Just water please," Andrew leaned back in his chair, looking up to the ceiling covered in mirrors, "I'm not drinking anymore but I still like the atmosphere here,"

"And the memories," Lady spectra started doing something with a glass.

Andrew let out a deep breath, "Yeah..."

Algernon's gaze lingered on Andrew for a bit, "It has been a few months now, huh? Congratulations, you're winning the fight against your demons."

Andrew didn't reply, just stared up.

Lady Spectra slid the water Andrew's way, "Did you check out the rumors I told you about?"

Andrew took a drink, "I did, I sat at the rink for hours then after a while a bunch of the hokey bros just couldn't seem to stop tripping on the ice. It was actually pretty funny. Then eventually it just stopped and they were fine."

Lady Spectra laughed, starting to work on another drink that had been called back to her, "Maybe the rink is haunted."

Andrew took a longer drink before setting his glass down, "Yeah, maybe."

Algernon jumped when his eyes landed on the clock behind the bar, "I'm going to be late for the tour," he stood, looking back to Lady Spectra, "Thank you, we'll be back next week."

The bar stools spun as we went running from them.

Andrew waved, eyes down.

Running across the street, we went in the back way to the tour office. The lights were off as we quietly descended into the dark basement, taking one rickety step at a time. There were faint voices in the deeper rooms of the basement, muffled by the brick walls. They grew in clarity as we approached and I could make out what Robert was saying.

"Now that I've told you about all of them, there is one more ghost I want to introduce. His name is Algernon and he was the best tour guide I've ever met. He gave this very tour for many years, and he probably would have never stopped. But earlier this year while he was on a tour in the mystery lot, he was senselessly murdered by a passing person; you may have heard about it on the news."

There were scattered gasps, some whispers, as Algernon and I approached the room, finding a group of about ten huddled back there, holding out their EMF detectors in a circles, green lights lit in the darkness.

Robert sighed, "He always said he'd come back and haunt me."

A girl, owner of a slight tremble, spoke barely above a whisper, "Is he here?"

Algernon stepped into the center of the group, making all of the EMFs light up a bit. Gently, he reached forward and rested his finger tip on her EMF in specific, sending the lights up into the red.

The room fell into a soft silence as the lights grew brighter.

I could hear the smile on Robert's face, "Hello Algernon,"

"Hello Robert," Algernon set off his EMF detector, making the group gasp again.

"Are you alone?"

After Roberts asked that, Algernon dropped his hand and all of the lights went down to just a single green light being lit.

"Are you with Thaddeus?"

When I stepped up next to Algernon, all of the lights went up into the red.

"Thaddeus is Algernon's husband, they died the same day. Thaddeus took his life at Algernon's memorial,"

I could see the wayward look Algernon sent my way, but I chose to ignore it.

While Algernon was thankful for my eternal company, he was equally displeased with my being deceased.

"Hey, guys," Algernon called out, "this looks like a good group, come out and play with us,"

"Okay!" Huxley's voice echoed around us as the shadows gathered together.

Doug and Huxley faded into the room with us, smiling at Algernon. The lights spiked up, shocking the group and Algernon just looked around, smiling.

"Are you guys ready to put on a show?"

Huxley nodded, beaming, "Always,"

The lights danced, going up and down in a circle, in a memorizing and pointed pattern. The room went cold, Doug fazed through the ceiling and started pushing around chairs upstairs, causing groaning sounds from above. Huxley kicked around rocks here and there, I knocked on the wall, and Algernon stood in the middle of it all. As the energies reached a crescendo, tensions high, wonder exploding among the gusts, Algernon walked up to one of the girls and looked at her glasses. Carefully, he leaned forward and ever so slightly, fixed them for her. She jumped, hand flying to her face. He stepped to the side and adjusted a hat someone was wearing, messing with the tie of the next. He bushed one girl's hair behind her ear and fixed the necklace on another. One person at a time, he caused them to jump, startled by his soft, cold paranormal touch. Finally he stood, facing Robert with a huge smile on his face. Reaching forward, he pulled Robert's name tag off and held it there, in the middle of the circle for a moment, before dropping it.

Everyone jumped, a couple people yelled a bit, but the most important thing was: they were all smiling.

I saw it, as the EMF lights flickered back down, Robert was crying.

Though, he was smiling, too.

"Though he's dead, he still the best tour guide I have ever met. He always puts on a great show," Robert said as he brought his sleeve up to his face, "and he's the reason I changed my mind about ghosts. I used to believe they were bad, scary even. I refused to admit that I believed because if I admitted that, I admitted that I was afraid. But Algernon has taught me that ghosts are good and that they aren't out to get you. It's hard to dehumanize a ghost when you knew them in life."

As I watched Algernon stand there, smiling, I knew this is where he belonged. And I knew that I belonged right there, watching him. But with that thought came one I often chased off. It was the image of a flower, sitting on a hill. Honore moved to a greater beyond when her unfinished business was done. But what was ours?

I wanted to look forward to forever, but was it forever, really?

When Algernon laughed after spooking someone a bit, my mind was pulled back into the present. I could figured that all out later. For now I was okay not knowing everything.

The moral to this story?

Never fall in love with a tour guide, they may put you in a story and tell thousands of people about how bad you were when you were sixteen and thought you knew everything.

Because trust me, you don't know everything.

Made in the USA
San Bernardino, CA
17 February 2020